DISCOVERING HOME

A SWEET CONTEMPORARY GAY ROMANCE

BLAKE ALLWOOD

BLAKE ALLWOOD PUBLISHING

Blake Allwood
Visit my website at BlakeAllwood.com

Printed in the United States of America
Box Elder, SD

First Printing: Apr 2023

Blake Allwood Publishing

Ebook ISBN: 978-1-956727-42-5
Paperback ISBN: 978-1-956727-43-2
Library of Congress Control Number: 2023906218

CONTENT WARNINGS

Religious controversy
Religious intolerance
Mental illness
Homophobia
Loss of a family member
Disappointment
Family drama
Abandonment of adult child
Ostracized family
Employer/employee relationship
Legal disputes

Join Blake's email list to get advance notice of new books and receive his occasional newsletter:

www.blakeallwood.com

MM Romance
By Blake Allwood

Transitions Series
Aiden Inspired
Suzie Empowered (MF Romance)
Bobby Transformed

Chance Series
Love By Chance
Another Chance With Love
Taking A Chance For Love

Romantic Series
Romantic Renovations (1)
Romantic Rescue (2)
Romantic Recon (3)

Melody Series
Melody of the Heart
Melody of the Snow

Road to Rocktoberfest Anthology
Changing His Tune - 2022

Coming Home Series (2023)
A Long Way Home
Family Home
Discovering Home
Finding Home
Bound For Home
…and many more

Novellas
Tenacious
Moon's Place

Romantic Fantasy
By Adam J. Ridley

Big Bend Series
Love's Legacy (1)
Love's Heirloom (2)
Love's Bequest (3)

The Witch Brothers Series
Emerald Earth (1)
Diamond Air (2)
Ruby Fire (3)
Sapphire Water (4)

Acknowledgments

Special thanks to the following amazing people who helped me get this book finished and into your hands:

Jo Bird: Editor
Renee Mizar: Editor
Ann Attwood: Proofreader

And of course, a big thank you to my husband who puts up with my endless stories and handles the formatting and final publishing of all my books.

ONE

MATT

I WALKED TOWARD THE old rundown log cabin and shook my head at the rusting nineteen-sixties trailer that stuck out along the back of it. Despite my grandpa being wealthy, we'd lived there for several years after my parents had died.

I used to tell my grandpa that when I grew up, I'd fix up the log cabin and live here on the farm.

He just laughed at me. The cabin wasn't likely restorable, but it was a nice dream.

Even all these years later, I still loved this land, though not necessarily its location. It sat halfway between Mayville, where I went to school, and Crawford City, our bitter rivals.

Ironically, for a time, our mill had been the only one used by Mayville and Crawford City alike. But that was before the Civil War, back when the silenced mill was hopping with activity and the rotting log cabin was newly built.

The old mill still stood proud next to the stream, looking more or less how I remembered it as a kid. The water wheel, which had rotated for more than a century and a half, had stopped turning since I'd left. I could still hear the rhythmic sound of churning water in my memories, though.

As I roamed around the property, I parked myself on the mill's plank bench—another thing that'd been here for generations—and basked in the beauty of the old place. I had missed it, missed home.

After I went to college, my widowed grandpa met and married Elizabeth Carey from Crawford City. Elizabeth, who went by Beth, was first cousin to the beloved Crawford City Cross sisters and was wealthy in her own right. Ms. Beth owned a nice brick ranch house in Crawford City, just a short distance from her cousins' Victorian mansion. That was where my grandpa lived now.

I didn't visit often. That might have made me an awful grandson, but I had my reasons.

"I need you, son..." my grandfather had said while I sat next to him in the hospital. "You know I wouldn't ask if I didn't..."

"I know, Grandpa, I'll be there. You can count on me until you're better," I'd reassured him.

Of course, I'd told him that. My grandpa was my family, the last of my family. Sure, I had a few relatives left on my mom's side, but we'd never been close. Not like me and Grandpa. I'd honestly do anything he needed me to do, even though I didn't really want him to know that.

The week he got out of the hospital, I'd come back to stay with him and Ms. Beth. That was when he'd told me he was turning the old farm into a winery.

"Grandpa, you don't drink," I said, laughing.

"Well, I don't, much. Before you say anything, the good book says, don't drink *much*, not don't drink at all. Besides, my sweet Beth likes her wine, so I've been playing with the idea off and on for a while."

He paused like he was waiting for me to contradict him, and when I didn't, he continued. "Anyway, I need you to tend to those vines until I get the use of my body again," he'd told me.

I shook my head as the old religious teetotaler completely shifted his ways in front of me.

Although the stroke hadn't been bad, it had partially paralyzed his left leg, and his left arm was pretty weak as well. Still, the day he returned home, he began pushing for me to take him to the mill property.

"I want to show you how to do it," he insisted.

Ms. Beth nodded her agreement, saying the doctor had told him, as long as he took it easy, it was fine.

I sighed and agreed to his demands.

He talked about the vines and how to care for them, the amount of water they needed, when to let them get dry, and how to use manure from the local chicken farm to provide nitrogen. I had no idea about most of it, and since we'd never farmed the land we lived on, I hadn't learned about farming.

"Grandpa, you're gonna have to write all this down. I'm not a farmer. I'm an artist."

He nodded. "And a good one too. Don't you forget that, son."

That made me smile. Grandpa had always encouraged my artistic abilities. What he hadn't been able to deal with was my sexuality, and it wasn't ever something we talked about directly. I largely attributed that to the intolerant church he attended, and donated huge amounts of money to. But he'd embraced my choice of occupation with no effort.

After graduating, he'd put me on an allowance, saying, "Anyone with a gift like yours needs to focus on that and leave the corporate bullcrap to those less fortunate." He'd meant those who didn't have artistic abilities, not financial. Despite the wealth my grandpa had acquired, he didn't think money made him better than anyone else.

The only reason Grandpa had money was because he never spent any. When his father sold the government a huge portion of the land our family owned to make a reservoir, my great-grandfather had invested the money, which then turned into more money, and so on and so forth.

I'd used Grandpa's allowance to pay for a warehouse in Lebanon with a small apartment attached. "Live close to the bone," he'd admonished me all my life, even as a young adult. I had done so and now I appreciated the values he'd taught me, because living on a tight budget allowed me to live the life I loved. It allowed me to paint and not to have to hawk my wares, like every other artist I knew.

"Wow," I said as we walked into the young vineyard, Grandpa hanging onto my arm for balance. "This is like you see on TV!" Beautiful rows of grapes grew along a hillside that'd always been leased out to a local cattle owner. I'd never thought much about this part of the property, since the mill and cabin had always been my favorite.

I had to admit, however, I might be changing my mind. There was something magical about the vineyard. My fingers began to itch for my brushes. I could almost imagine what the area looked like in the late evening as the sun set over the forest that bordered the vineyard to the west.

I must've stared at the property for a full fifteen minutes, imagining how the scene would unfold on canvas. I'd all but decided I'd want to paint it in watercolor. I could see the muted tones melting into one another when I heard my grandpa clear his throat, snapping me out of my reverie.

When I looked over at him, he chuckled. "You were imagining it as some of your art, huh?"

I smiled. "You caught me. It's just so pretty, Grandpa. You've done something wonderful here."

He nodded over to an old nineteen-twenties barn that had been leased out to the same cattle rancher. I'd actually never been inside the building, but when we walked in, I stopped dead in my tracks.

The old barn had been converted into a usable space, with concrete floors and boarded walls. It even had electricity and, apparently, running water.

You couldn't tell all that from the outside, which looked sort of run-down and rustic like it always had.

"When did you do this?" I asked as we walked back out.

"It was finished a couple months ago," he said, sounding a little discouraged. "I have all the wine-making equipment in here, but now I'm too feeble to do much with it. I'm hoping you'll take over, though."

I just stared at the building as Grandpa stood silently beside me, letting me consider his proposition. I had no intention of coming back to this hateful part of the world. Visiting once in a while was doable, especially whenever Grandpa and Ms. Beth needed my help, but live here? Lebanon was about as rural as I wanted to get, and to be honest, if I'd had more money, I'd probably have moved to Nashville.

Not that I got out much, and forget dating... most of the time, I just wanted to stay home and paint or cuddle up with a book. I wasn't much for socializing. I guessed that made me a recluse, but whenever the subject came up, I'd tell people I was a serial introvert.

"Grandpa, thank you, and I'll help as long as you need me, but I can't see myself living here, and I sure as hell can't see myself getting this place up and running. I'm an artist, not a farmer, or whatever they call people who run vineyards."

Grandpa chuckled. "Son, I know this will all be uncharted territory for you. But someone has to oversee what's going on, and you and my sweet Beth are the two people I trust most in this world. As for the grape growing, I already put feelers out for someone to come run the vineyard, and I've hired a man who's coming from California to help. He knows his stuff, and has already been here to tour the place."

I nodded. "Sounds like you already got it all set up," I said, feeling better about the whole thing. "At least I won't have to learn how to make wine and actually run a vineyard."

"Well, see, there's a problem. He won't arrive until after harvest, because he's still under contract with his current employer, but he's provided instructions on what to do. We'll have to pick, sort, and destem the grapes, then do some crushing and get them into the processing units to begin fermenting."

"And you want me to do all that?" I asked.

"I want you to supervise. But yeah, you'd need to do some of it," he said. "The new guy will be here to manage most of the fermentation process."

My grandpa hardly ever asked for my help, and he clearly needed it now. He'd raised me after my parents died, paid for my education, and had been sending me a nice allowance every few months since I'd graduated. I could and would do this for him, despite all of my personal reservations.

Two

Logan

I NEVER THOUGHT MY life as a viticulturist would lead me back to Tennessee. Not that I'd found much success in the wine-making industry elsewhere.

I'd been to Oregon and California, working at vineyards in both places, and had quickly been sent packing as soon as they heard my Southern drawl. It didn't matter that I offered valid suggestions to improve their processes. Overcoming the general assumptions that people who sounded like me were either dumb or couldn't possibly know anything about growing grapes and making wine had proved a tough nut to crack.

I'd studied hard in college to learn the trade, receiving the highest grades among my peers, and even developing more than one award-winning batch of wine before I'd graduated. That had opened the door to being hired at those West Coast farms, but none kept me around long enough to make an impact. Ironically, they'd all embraced my progressive ideas on paper, then didn't take me seriously when I'd tried implementing them. That'd been the story of my career, so far.

I was on the verge of giving up when a small California vineyard hired me. It was tucked into one of the mountains above Napa. I thought I'd finally found something lasting, and we were doing well in our second season, when the fires broke out and burned everything, including the winery buildings, all the equipment, and the entire vineyard.

Seeing the complete disintegration of all we'd worked toward, and knowing there was literally nothing left to salvage, was heartbreaking. Understandably, the distraught owner had no immediate plans to rebuild and were even thinking of leaving the wine-making business altogether. Truth be told, looking at the vast wasteland that had days ago been a thriving landscape, I felt the same way.

I'd briefly considered staying in California since my contract was now void thanks to the fires, but I was tired of fighting. Fighting for a job, fighting to be heard beyond my Southern accent, and fighting Mother Nature. While still in Napa, trying to figure out what came next, I called my parents in Nashville. I mentioned to my father that I was looking to move home and that I'd need to get a job, maybe as a sommelier or something.

My father grew up east of Nashville, in a small town called Crawford City, and he kept in touch with relatives and old friends who still lived around there. He told me if I was really considering coming home, he knew someone in the area who'd been developing a vineyard and needed help running it.

A Tennessee vineyard, I could just see how well that'd turn out. I'd worked in Napa Valley, California's most celebrated wine region, and around Salem, Oregon, located in the heart of Oregon's Wine Country. I'd tasted the best of the best, and however brief my stints at a given winery, I'd been a part of the process in making great products.

Tennessee was well-known for its whiskey, and artisan breweries producing IPAs and craft beers had become commonplace as well. But I couldn't imagine a Tennessee wine. Not that I was in any position to judge. A job was a job, and it'd be good being close to home.

So, despite my reservations, I called the owner and after a lengthy chat, tentatively accepted the position. I did so with the stipulations that I'd need to see the vineyard before fully committing and, assuming we were a good match, I wouldn't be able to start right away. I needed time to settle things in Napa, move back to Tennessee, and give my parents a long overdue visit before diving headlong into a new job. The owner agreed, and we set a meeting date.

When that day came, I flew to Nashville and then drove to an old farm outside Crawford City. I was greeted by a tall man well into his seventies or early eighties and built like a typical farmer—strong and lean, and his sun-damaged skin lined with age.

He shook my hand, introduced himself as Josiah Brinks, the owner, and without much small talk led me to the bottom of a hill and pointed upward. I was astonished to see beautiful rows of vines, all perfectly aligned on the hillside that maximized the sunlight. Maybe there was hope here.

He told me he had good equipment, and led me to a barn that looked like it could collapse at any moment. My preconceived notions about making Tennessee wine flared back up until I walked in. The interior had been completely renovated. Once again, I was pleasantly surprised.

Without any further discussion, Mr. Brinks led me to the back of the barn. He opened a cabinet, pulled out an unlabeled bottle, and uncorked it.

"Try this," he said, and poured a generous half glass of wine for me.

I sighed inwardly, determined not to make a bad impression on the man, but I was dreading tasting what I thought would be a sickly sweet concoction.

Instead, I took a drink and was blown away. Sure, it was far from perfect, there were definitely some undertones that weren't right, and the wine hadn't aged nearly enough, but I could taste its potential.

Enjoying the man's no-nonsense approach to idle chatter, I said, "I'd like to see the vines up close."

He smiled, the first one I'd seen on his face since I'd arrived, and I took it as a sign we'd gotten off on the right foot. We walked up the hill, and the scene before me was exactly what I'd hoped to see. The vines were healthy and vibrant. They were all still young, none of them more than a few years old, but full of potential. I didn't hesitate to begin asking questions.

"What's the pH balance of the soil?"

He told me and I shook my head. "There's not enough nitrogen. You'll need to pick it up significantly. That's why some of the flavors in the wine you just gave me tasted off. But it's not a problem. Do you have access to composted poultry manure?"

Mr. Brinks thought for a moment, then said, "I think so, yeah."

"Then you need to put that around the vines. Now, never put green manure around them, that's too much nitrogen and it'll kill your vines. I'd say it needs to be composted at least a year."

He nodded as we kept walking, then briefly mentioned that he had to irrigate for half the summer. I wasn't surprised since the wine wasn't too sweet, and the punch of flavor indicated the old farmer knew how to keep the water levels right.

When we reached the top of the hill, I stood alongside Mr. Brinks and looked out at the acres of opportunity spread before us.

As was usually the case, I could almost taste the wine we could create under my direction. It wouldn't be top shelf or win awards, but it'd be good table wine that would sell.

I got lost in thought, then mostly to myself, said, "Now, if the conditions permit, we could probably stress the vines in July, maybe even August. If we did that, we might be able to coerce them into giving us an award winner."

When I turned to the man, I found him grinning at me like a Cheshire cat.

"Um, sorry. I'm a bit of a wine geek and your vines have a lot of potential. I should be answering your questions."

The old man shook his head, and said, "No, son, you should be doing exactly what you've been doing. Ask the question you wanted to ask."

I chuckled. The guy seemed to have my number. "I wanted to know what your rainfall was last July and August."

"What rainfall?" he countered with a frustrated expression. "I had to irrigate heavily both months. We get great rainfall all winter and even in the fall, but late summer isn't good."

When I smiled, he looked baffled. "Ever heard the saying, 'stressed vines make the best wine'?" He shook his head. "I was just thinking, if you could reduce irrigation during the hottest months, I think your wines would be outstanding. I mean, you've already got a special wine, but it's table wine. Not something that'll rival the western vineyards, but I really think you could, with a little help."

"With your help?" Mr. Brinks asked.

I stared at him for a moment. "Maybe. I'm giving up on California. I've worked out there for nearly eight years, and I keep hitting roadblock after roadblock. I never thought I'd get a chance at growing quality wine here at home."

We walked companionably back to the renovated barn, and as we reached my rental car, the man outstretched his hand for me to shake. "When you were looking at my vines, you wore the same expression as my grandson when he's painting. It's clear to me you already want to nurture this vineyard to its full potential, and that's the kind of obsession and care I want in a manager. The job's yours if you still want it."

Grasping Mr. Brinks's hand in a firm shake, I confirmed he was my new boss and I'd start work following the harvest. I hadn't felt excited or optimistic about wine-making since graduating college. I just hoped I was up for the challenge.

THREE

MATT

GRANDPA HAD MADE GOOD strides in the weeks after I came to stay with him and Ms. Beth... until the morning he didn't wake up. He died from a second stroke, caused by a blockage the doctor had missed. Condolences poured in from all around the county and beyond, which Ms. Beth accepted with grace, but if one more person told me, "At least he wasn't in pain," I'd throttle them. I wasn't ready for my grandpa to be dead. He was the last of my immediate family and had always been my hero.

As was his wish, we buried Grandpa on the farm in our family graveyard. No embalming, as *that was unnatural*, or so he had dictated. That meant he'd been buried within days of his death.

The hateful Pastor Atwell prayed over the grave and sneered at me during the entire service.

The next day, my grandpa's attorney, a man I didn't know, visited Ms. Beth's home and presented us with the will. I learned that Grandpa had signed a prenuptial agreement when they'd gotten married. So, she'd been left out of his will.

I nodded. I wasn't surprised about the prenup since my grandpa was a smart man when it came to money. He'd protected my inheritance, just as he expected me to manage it responsibly now, and Ms. Beth was already well provided for with her own money.

"There's one stipulation, however," the attorney said, unable to look me in the eye. "You'll have to go to church every Sunday for one full year."

I shrugged. "Yeah, I expected he'd probably make me do something like that. I really don't mind. There's a church I've gone to a couple times in Nashville that I like..."

"No, you misunderstand, Mr. Brinks. Your grandfather stipulated that you attend *his* church every Sunday for a year."

My face grew hot as anger coursed through me. "I have to go to the hateful church in Mayville?" I asked, practically shouting before regaining my composure.

The attorney nodded and I swallowed the lump in my throat. "But they don't welcome gay people. The pastor hates me, and my grandpa knew that," I said, feeling confused and a little betrayed. "Can I contest it?"

It was the attorney's turn to shrug. "You can, but you'll lose. Your grandfather was clear, you either go to that church every Sunday or you lose the inheritance."

I nodded but not in agreement. I'd vowed long ago to never go to that hateful church and subject myself to its homophobic pastor's preaching ever again. I was already dreading my grandpa's memorial service at the church on Sunday. No way in hell would I survive a full year of being ripped to shreds just for being me. Not that my grandpa had given me much choice. I couldn't lose my inheritance, our family's property, the old mill. It was as much a part of me as painting, and I couldn't envision my life without that connection to the land.

Maybe I was wrong, maybe the church had changed since my childhood. Heck, considering it'd been years since gay people could legally marry, perhaps some gay weddings had even taken place there. Given Pastor Atwell still ruled the roost, I knew the chances it'd changed in any positive way were slim, but I had to hope.

On Sunday, I accompanied Ms. Beth into the imposing building I'd purposefully avoided since I was old enough to do so. The megachurch still had the same carpet and the pews still lined up along the aisle, forcing the congregation, even if they'd rather pull every tooth from their heads, to see the horrible man at the pulpit.

After the hymns were sung and the church choir performed the same old song they had since I was a child, Pastor Atwell stood up. I'd tried preparing myself for the vile words he'd likely direct at me and was ready for it, or at least I thought I was.

"We are here today, celebrating the life of our brother, Josiah Lee Brinks. A spiritual and faithful man. In his wisdom he has brought us a lost sheep, his grandson, who will be here with us for the next year. That is, if he wishes to inherit the bountiful offerings his grandfather has bestowed."

The miserable old coot chuckled, then he paused a moment, gesturing toward me and causing the entire congregation, at the very least five thousand strong, to turn in their seats and look at me. *God*, I silently prayed, *if I kill him, will I be sent to hell, or will I be forgiven considering the bastard is the seed of Satan?*

I waved appreciatively to the crowd, knowing they had at least three cameras pointed directly at me. If I hadn't been reminding myself all morning that I was there for Grandpa, to celebrate his life and honor his wishes, I'd have given the pastor and his cameras my middle finger and stormed out of the place. Given my prayer a few moments ago, God would've understood.

When we'd arrived at the church, Ms. Beth and I had been escorted up to the front. The first three rows were reserved for our family, because my grandpa, and his father before him, had been among the church's biggest benefactors. Not that we needed that much space. With Grandpa gone, Ms. Beth and I were the only ones left to represent the Brinks family, so we sat in the front row, alone.

After having all eyes on me for what felt like several minutes, Pastor Atwell drew the attention back to himself. To his credit, assuming he deserved any, he'd allowed the spotlight to be on someone besides himself for a moment. In this church, even during a memorial service to honor a lifelong congregant, he usually re-mained the star of the show.

"Today, brothers and sisters, we will look at sin."

Well, of course, we will. That's what you do when you're giving a memorial service, you talk about sin. It was all I could do not to roll my eyes, and I felt Ms. Beth subtly pat my leg in sympathy. At least I had her support. Pastor Atwell and his hate speech disguised as sermons was the main reason she'd kept attending her old church in Crawford City after marrying Grandpa.

"At how sin is infiltrating the lives of our beloved children," Pastor Atwell continued. "Child molesters, sex-crazed lunatics, all are teaming up to pass on their agendas. They will not stop until they corrupt the very foundation of our country. Perverting it to their evil ways."

With a flourish, he opened his King James Bible, which I noticed fell open to a particular place perfectly, as if the asshat had stretched the book over and over until it did that on command.

"Romans 1: 26-27," he said, then began reading. "'*For this cause God gave them up unto vile affections: for even their women did change the natural use into that which is against nature: And likewise also the men, leaving the natural use of the woman, burned in their lust one toward another; men with men working that which is unseemly, and receiving in themselves that recompence of their error which was meet.*'"

The old coot glanced at me then, a look of pure elation on his flushed face. He gave me a barely perceptible wink before he continued, and I grit my teeth. "God has made it clear that homosexuality is a sin. Even in the New Testament, Paul makes this very clear to us. Why do those who promote this abomination think it is okay? Why do they come into these hallowed halls to spread their perversions of nature's laws? Let them come before us now and be saved, let the blood of our Savior cleanse them!"

Without any direct prompting, the entire congregation turned toward me again. I looked at my watch, six minutes after eleven. *Grandpa*, I said silently to myself, *I'm not going to make it. Looks like your winery will be sold off and the money can be given to devil worshipers for all I care.*

I patted Ms. Beth's knee to get her attention, shook my head when she made eye contact, then stood up and smoothed my suit down before making my way down the aisle. I heard several people gasp as I did so. I was sure they'd expected me to just sit and take the man's bigotry for the next however many hours. Sorry folks, I've got more self-respect than that.

Before I got very far, though, Pastor Atwell's voice boomed through the sound system. "Matthew Brinks, you walk out that door, and you turn your back on God and all that is holy and good."

I kept walking, my jaw clenched, but head held high. Inside, I was fuming and this close to taking the self-righteous pastor down a notch in front of his entire congregation, something I'd wanted to do for years. But today shouldn't be about me, it should be about Grandpa. I didn't want his memorial service turning into more of a public spectacle than it already had, thanks to Pastor Atwell. Better to just leave.

"If a man lies with a man as with a woman," I heard the idiot excitedly paraphrase from Leviticus, "...they have both committed an abomination. They must surely be put to death; their blood is upon them. You are an abomination; you represent all that is unholy and disgusting. Leave... be gone, Satan!" The son of a bitch literally yelled the last bit into the mic.

Just then, I saw my teenage cousin on my mom's side, who I'd caught kissing her girlfriend one night about a year ago behind the old mill. She'd begged me to keep her secret and, of course, I had. I locked eyes with her and decided right then and there, I was going to give old Pastor Atwell a dose of humility. Trying to appease my grandpa no longer mattered. The hateful dogma had to stop.

My heart was beating fast already, but now it all seemed to force all my blood to my face. I balled my fists next to my side as I steeled my resolve and turned around.

A hush fell over the congregation as I backtracked, walking up to the deacon who held the mic for testimony. He handed it to me and, after taking a deep breath, I said, "Pastor, you seem to be very keen on Leviticus and you're correct, that is what that scripture conveys. You're also correct about the verses from Romans you read before. But it's so easy to point the finger, isn't it?" I looked out over the crowd spanning the enormous auditorium. "It's so easy to pass judgment when you stand upon a great stage, thinking you are somehow better than the thousands gathered to hear your message." I made a big sweeping motion, indicating the entire audience.

"The funny thing is, Leviticus is pretty tough on lots of people, isn't it? Just a few verses before the one you so hatefully tossed at me, Pastor Atwell, is Leviticus 20:10. *'And the man that committeth adultery with another man's wife, even he that committeth adultery with his neighbor's wife, the adulterer and the adulteress shall surely be put to death.'*" I paused for effect, and sent a silent prayer of thanks for my evening Bible study sessions with Grandpa growing up. Being able to recite verses on cue was coming in handy now.

"Oops," I said and couldn't hold back a smirk. "That's inconvenient now, isn't it?" I let the question hang in the air to build anticipation, using Pastor Atwell's own tactic against him, before I continued, "You stand there and dare to direct your sermon at me when this is supposed to be a time to celebrate the life of my grandfather, a man who embodied the teachings of Christ more than any other person I've known. You stand up there at your great pulpit and personally attack me like a common schoolyard bully on the day I have come to grieve for the man who raised me." I waited until some of the people around me began to stir uncomfortably in their seats. They all knew his behavior was unacceptable. Attempting to publicly shame me at my grandfather's memorial service, of all times, was indeed shameful.

I stared hard at the pulpit until Pastor Atwell met my gaze. Fire blazed in his eyes, hot enough to drill a hole through me, but I didn't give him time enough to seize the attention. "However, since you've decided we are going to discuss sin today, let's start with you." I pointed at him. "Would you agree, sir, that you yourself are guilty of one of the deadliest of sins?"

I was privy to more information than I should've been. Being one of the congregation's biggest donors, my grandpa had served on most of the church's committees since I was a kid, so over the years I'd heard my share of gossip and potentially embarrassing truths.

"If I recall correctly, this congregation was asked to forgive you, to give you a second chance, when you broke Leviticus's law against adultery. Yet, when you were given the same gift that Christ gave to the woman at the well, *go and sin no more*, you chose to do otherwise. Instead of honoring your commitment to be a man of God, you repaid the congregation by committed the very same sin, not once but three more times. Oh, and these weren't single women, were they, pastor? Each and every one of them was married, were they not?"

"Deacon, take that microphone away from that... that abomination," the pastor shouted, but everyone, including the old deacon, was too caught up to move.

"You dare stand at your pulpit and judge me and others like me, when Matthew seven tells us clearly, *'Judge not, that ye be not judged'*?"

I'd dreamed of giving Pastor Atwell his comeuppance my entire life, but never on the day I was supposed to say goodbye to my grandfather. However, as I stood in front of thousands, not to mention the untold numbers watching the livestream, I was resolved to be heard once and for all.

I sighed deeply as a wave of grief passed. I let the skills I'd learned during my drama classes take hold and lead me through the rest of what I still needed to say.

"'*And why beholdest thou the mote that is thy brother's eye, but considerest not the beam that is in thine own eye? Or how wilt thou say to thy brother, Let me pull out the mote out of thine eye; and behold, a beam is in thine own eye?*' That's a direct quote, folks. One I know because the man whose life we are supposed to be here to honor studied the Bible with me. He celebrated the holy scriptures and taught them to me, not out of obligation, but out of pure admiration." I turned my attention from the pulpit back to the audience. "As instructed by the teaching of my grandfather, I would never presume to judge anyone, for aren't we all sinners? Even the pastor here has sinned, but far be it for me or anyone else to judge him, even though he has indeed judged me." I looked back up at the pastor, who was wilting in front of me.

I lowered my head then and sighed into the microphone. "I didn't ask to be here. In fact, I'd have rather avoided the hypocrisy that I've been all too aware of most of my life, but I was put on the spot by the person I loved and trusted most..." I paused to gather my thoughts since even my imagined speech as a kid hadn't carried me this far. "Let me be clear, sir, to you and to everyone watching this morning's sermon. God put us on this earth and loves us. He loves us with everything that he is, and I know this because I have read the Bible from start to finish multiple times. I am a man of God and do not hide my sins or my faults, although I do not believe it is either sin nor fault that I am who I am. However, as God is my witness, there is no amount of money, no amount of land, and no title great enough that I would hand you my self-respect and cower down to your hatred." I was about to leave then, but stopped, glancing once again at my cousin before directing my words to the man at the pulpit. "You say that when a man loves another man, or a woman loves another woman, they are to be put to death. To that, sir, I say, may he who is without sin, cast the first stone."

I turned, handed the mic back to the astonished deacon, and walked out the door, effectively turning my back on my heritage. It wasn't what my grand-pa would've wanted, and my words probably would've stunned him as much as everyone else in the crowd, but deep down, I also knew he'd have been proud of me for standing up for myself and all who'd been on the receiving end of Pastor Atwell's vitriol. That was the man Grandpa raised me to be.

I walked for about a mile before Ms. Beth pulled her Lincoln over and gestured for me to get in. I did so without argument.

We didn't talk as she drove the twenty minutes it took to get from Mayville to Crawford City. After she pulled the boat of a car into the garage, she turned to me. "You were right, son. That man is a horrible person and had no right to say what he did, much less say it on the day we mourn for your grandpa."

I couldn't hold back the tears that began to flow. "I was supposed to be able to say goodbye," I said, and the pain of losing yet another parent washed over me.

"I know, son, and we'll have a real service soon, okay? I'll call my pastor and she'll do what's right."

I didn't know what else to say, so I nodded and let my step-grandmother comfort me. Grandpa had always called her his "sweet Beth," and she really was just that.

"I'll get out of your hair and let you get on with your life," I said, and was about to ask that she let me know when the service would be when she interrupted me.

"That's nonsense," she said. "You'll stay here, and we'll mourn your grandpa together, properly. Then, if you want to, you can go home. But for now, I want you to go through your grandpa's things and take what you want to keep."

I shook my head. "No, I gave up my inheritance today. I won't set foot in that hateful place again. I just can't."

She frowned, but nodded. "Sweetheart, I told your grandpa to remove that stipulation. But he thought that since the will specified the church would continue receiving his monthly donation so long as you attended, that horrible pastor would keep his mouth shut. He thought you'd help bring the church along."

"Seriously?" I asked, overcome with frustration. "They will never see my side. They hate me because of who I am, not because of what I've ever done or not done. He thought they'd change?"

She nodded. "He really did."

"So, what happens now?" I asked. "Does the church get all of Grandpa's money?"

She laughed out loud at that. "You didn't know your grandpa if you thought that. No, son, I stand to inherit it all. If you decided not to accept the terms, the entire estate would be turned over to me. Of course, in that case, the church will get nothing either."

I nodded, wiping away my tears. "I'm happy you're getting it. You were his wife, after all. It probably should've always been yours. And if you care what I think, you'll never give those bigots another penny of my grandpa's money, especially after they disrespected his name at his memorial service."

"Oh, rest assured, I'll never give them anything," she said, and patted my knee. "Now, let's head on inside. The ladies from my church have been working on putting a potluck together and we'll be inundated with food in just a few moments."

She was right, and things felt better as the Crawford City folks stuffed me to the gills, a Southern tradition of how best to deal with grief. Become so full, you forget you're sad.

I ended up staying at Ms. Beth's all week, going through Grandpa's things and packing up family pho-to albums, mementos, and other heirlooms. Knowing Grandpa's widow would want to get as much of it squared away as possible, I then drove up to Lebanon and unloaded the boxes at my apartment.

I knew that'd only be temporary storage, though, since I wouldn't be able to afford the place any longer. I'd not sold much of my art, so I wasn't well enough known for my art to cover all my expenses. I'd always relied on Grandpa's allowance to pay the rent. Because he'd sent money every three months, I could afford paying for the two months required to give notice, but that was it.

I sat down at my computer and wrote an email to the building owner, letting her know I was giving notice. I thanked her for being such an amazing landlord, and mentioned I'd send her the remaining amount owed by the end of the following week.

I then sent emails to the galleries I showed at in Nashville, Knoxville, Chattanooga, and the one I'd been lucky enough to show at a couple times in Atlanta to inform them I was closing my studio indefinitely and had inventory I could send.

I'd always been picky about what I sold, wanting only to showcase my best work, or at least the best I didn't keep for myself. I wouldn't have room to store or display anything now, though. No matter how much it felt like I was tearing my heart and soul to shreds by doing so, I had to let it all go. I fully expected boxing up each treasured piece to ship would be its own gut-wrenching experience, but I'd save that pain for another day.

As promised, I drove back to Crawford City the next day to stay the weekend with Ms. Beth. With the help of her congregation, she'd managed to arrange a proper memorial service for my grandpa. I'd attended church with Ms. Beth a couple times, and thought the people there were good as gold, more like a proper church should be, and the polar opposite of the sanctimonious Pastor Atwell and his flock.

I needed the chance to properly say goodbye to my grandpa, and I knew Ms. Beth needed that too.

Four

Logan

I SHOWED UP AT the Tennessee vineyard a month earlier than planned. In the aftermath of the Napa fire, my old boss had offered my help to people as a means of finishing out my contract, but it'd been turned down. The other vineyard owners said they already had plenty of help to get by, so I had no reason to stay in California any longer.

I pulled up to the renovated barn on a late Saturday afternoon, found the keys where the old man had shown me they were kept, and let myself into the small apartment on the east side of the building.

Fortunately for me, the owner had furnished the apartment, or I'd have been sleeping on the floor. It took me little time to unpack my belongings, few as they were, and the groceries I'd picked up on the way.

On Sunday, I planned to reorient myself to the vineyard and get more of a feel for the property by taking a self-guided tour. I also needed to contact the owner to let him know I'd arrived early, since it'd been too late for phone calls last night.

My dad's sister, who still lived in the area, knew I was moving here and had tried to convince me to go to church with her. "My daughter's gonna sing on Sunday and it's also a memorial for one of the men from the church. You should come hear your cousin sing, and get to know some of your new neighbors."

I knew from speaking with my parents that my dad's old church was far from accepting. The pastor had been active in resisting legislation that supported LGBTQ+ rights in Tennessee. Being in that man's presence was not how I wanted to spend my first day here, so I politely declined.

"I guess you'll be tired after moving, but you can watch it on TV," she said. "Pastor Atwell's sermons air on channel seven."

Figuring she would ask me about it later, I decided I should probably at least watch my cousin's performance as I went about arranging my apartment. I could tune out any hatred that came flying out of the pastor's mouth, though I couldn't imagine there'd be too much since it was supposed to be a memorial service.

I turned the TV on, just as the service was about to begin, and turned up the volume before going into the kitchen to fix breakfast.

After a while, I heard the choir sing, so I sat myself down on the sofa in case my cousin was about to perform her solo. I'd forgotten to ask when exactly she was singing.

When the choir took their seats, I was about to return to the kitchen when the camera focused on a displayed photograph of the person they were having the memorial for.

"Shit!" I exclaimed when I recognized the face of the old man who'd hired me. I'd spoken to Mr. Brinks just last week and he'd told me to come on down. Now he was dead, and I was watching his memorial? It felt surreal.

I rushed back into the kitchen to turn off the stovetop, my half-cooked bacon be damned, then returned to listen to the memorial service. I partly did so out of respect for Mr. Brinks, but I also hoped to get a glimpse of who my new boss might be. That was assuming one of his family members inherited this place and wanted to keep the vineyard going.

The Bible verse the pastor recited stopped me dead in my tracks. "Romans 1: 26-27," he began, then launched into lambasting the old man's grandson, calling him out on his sins. That sin, of course, was being gay. I sighed, remembering what my dad had said about the church he'd grown up attending. Apparently, it hadn't changed much. Maybe I was dodging a bullet not having to stay in this town after all.

I was about to turn the TV off when what I had to assume was Mr. Brinks's grandson stood up and began walking down the aisle to leave. The man was tall like his grandfather, and appeared to have the same muscular build under the grayish tailored suit he wore.

Unlike his grandfather's weathered face, though, his features were more delicate. And at this moment, as he strode toward a deacon holding a microphone, the expression on that handsome face morphed from one of anger to resolution.

I stood transfixed as the man thwarted the bigoted pastor's hatred, hurling scripture back at him like cannon-fire. His words struck with precision, hitting their target with devastating impact. That the pastor had been caught by the church in no less than four extramarital affairs wasn't even the main point the guy made. He elegantly turned it back around to Pastor Atwell's malicious message, saying the Bible wasn't about hatred and that the pastor was wrong to go after him without facing his own sins.

By the time the man was done and left the entire congregation stunned with mouths agape, I thought I was half in love with him. Maybe before I went back to Nashville, I could meet him. I'd like to thank him personally for being a decent person and standing up to that bully. We as a country needed a lot more of that.

The next morning, I began trying to figure out who I needed to talk to about my place here. I tried calling Mr. Brinks's cell phone, hoping a relative would pick up, but it went straight to voicemail. I also called my dad, who was absolutely no help at all. Then I called the county assessor's office, which informed me the property remained in Mr. Brinks's name because the paperwork was still being processed.

I ended up visiting the newspaper office in Crawford City to get the man's obituary. Apparently his death had been frontpage news in the small-town paper. I learned that in addition to his grandson Matthew, who had to have been the man I'd watched stand up to the pastor, Mr. Brinks had been married to a woman who lived in town.

Fortunately for me, they had been a prominent couple in the community, and the receptionist at the newspaper office was quite the gossip. She was more than happy to tell me all she knew about them, including the widow's address when I slipped the question into our conversation. Unfortunately, when I showed to Ms. Brinks's home, she wasn't there.

The next day, I waited until late morning to once again knock on the widow's door. I sighed when I arrived just as a car was leaving, convinced I'd missed her again. However, an elderly woman came out of the brick house, spotted my car, and waved at me.

I pulled into the driveway and the woman came to my side of the car, stopping me from getting out.

I rolled the window down and she put her hands on her hips. "Folks been saying you've been looking for me." Damn, I guess I hadn't been discreet enough when talking to the gossipy receptionist.

The woman was trying to look intimidating, but couldn't quite pull it off. In fact, even attempting to sound unkind seemed to make her uncomfortable.

"Yes, ma'am, I'm Logan Johnson. Your husband hired me to manage the vineyard. I spoke to him last week and he told me to come."

"Oh, oh, sorry, young man. I forgot all about that. Come on in."

I followed Ms. Brinks into her home and obeyed when she told me to sit down in her very floral living room. She briefly disappeared, then returned with a plate of brownies and what appeared to be a glass of iced tea.

I politely sipped the tea as she settled into another chair and waited for her to start the conversation.

"So, you're wondering what's gonna happen now?" she asked. The woman was direct, I liked that.

"Yes, ma'am, I saw..." I began, then stopped myself, not wanting to bring up the fiasco of her late husband's memorial service. "I heard Mr. Brinks passed away, and I've been trying to track down the new owner since then."

"Well, apparently that's me, at least for a few more days. Do you need me to do something?" she asked.

"Yes, ma'am, I need to know if I'm going to be kept on or if I need to find another job," I said.

"Oh, no, don't go yet. Details about the inheritance are being worked out right now, but you just sit tight and do what you need to do to keep the vineyard running properly."

I nodded. "I'm sorry to ask specifics, but Mr. Brinks offered me a signing bonus, and I was counting on that since my job in California ended early. I also need to know about my salary. We were supposed to hash it out this week."

"Don't you worry about that. I'll have my attorney come by next week and we'll get you paid and ensure all the finances are squared away. If I play my cards right, I won't be the owner come Monday."

I looked at her, surprised. "And the new owner?" I asked.

She grinned, a bit mischievously. "There's a lot going on right now, son. My husband had good intentions, but he made some major mistakes with his will. I'm trying to fix all that, but it takes time. I'm not sure how long I'll be in charge but as long as I am, I promise you'll be taken care of. In the meantime, I'd appreciate if you'd keep his vineyard up to standards. If you have questions, you can ask me, but I'm gonna tell you, I know nothing about growing grapes. Just how to drink wine."

She smiled, but there was sadness in her eyes.

"Yes, ma'am. I know what needs to be done, and if you don't mind, I'll just do what I believe is best. Is it alright if I continue staying in the apartment adjoining the barn?"

"Of course, you can. That's perfect," she said and handed me a pen and pad of paper. "Now, write down your phone number and I'll have my attorney call you tomorrow and set up a time to do all the employee stuff."

I smiled and almost laughed as the older woman then politely kicked me out of her house. I couldn't blame her. She'd just lost her husband, her grandson had caused a major stir by publicly exposing the church's pastor, and here I was trying to get her to manage mundane stuff like keeping me gainfully employed. I felt a bit heartless pushing it, but I didn't have much choice.

I had been counting on the income, and needed to know what the future held for my sake, but I figured she really wasn't in a position to help me with that. For now, I'd need to be happy with the moving bonus and concentrate on work while I still had a job.

I pulled onto the property and gave my parents a call. "Hey, Dad," I said when he answered. "Looks like I'm back at square one."

FIVE

MATT

ATTENDING A MEMORIAL SERVICE in a neighboring town after the showdown at Pastor Atwell's church last Sunday and not have one person say anything negative to me the entire time felt beyond strange.

The service was, in fact, the very opposite of the one last week. Pictures of my grandpa were shown on a revolving screen in the fellowship hall. His friends and our distant family came and sat companionably with us and talked with Ms. Beth and me.

The minister, a woman who appeared to be in her mid-fifties, gave a beautiful talk and spoke about how she'd known my grandpa to be a loving and caring man. She went on to mention how proud he'd been of my artistic abilities, and how he'd told her personally that he thought there'd be a time when people knew my name just because of my paintings.

I knew my grandpa was proud of me, but it helped to hear other people acknowledge it.

When she finished the eulogy, she swiped at a tear that'd slipped from her eye.

"Mr. Brinks has been laid to rest in a private graveyard on his family's ancestral farm. For anyone who'd like to pay their respects at the gravesite, you've been asked to email your request to his widow, Beth Brinks."

Following the service, people came up to Ms. Beth and me in droves for hugs and handshakes. She and Grandpa had been a beloved and highly respected couple in Crawford City. It did my heart good hearing their friends and neighbors recount fond and funny memories about them. The church ladies also put on another impressive potluck, though much less intense than the one last week. Instead, an array of sandwiches and a whole litany of homemade desserts lined the tables.

After everyone had gone, we climbed into Ms. Beth's Lincoln to head back to her house. Before she started the car, I leaned over and hugged her. "Thank you. I needed this chance to say a proper thank you and goodbye to the man who raised me."

She hugged me back. "Well, you should've had that last week. I'm sorry you were put in that position. You must know that was never your grandpa's intention with the will stipulation. He would've been appalled by that pastor's behavior toward you. That man ought to feel ashamed of himself."

I laughed and had to work hard to keep the bitterness out of it. "Trust me, that was exactly how I'd expected that to go. Grandpa always thought that church and its pastor were better people than they were. His own grandfather was a founding member and his daddy preached there, though, so it meant a lot to him. I'm just sad it isn't the welcoming place he'd always wanted it to be."

Ms. Beth nodded as we pulled out of the church parking lot and drove the short distance to her house. "He just always chose to see the best in people, be that misguided or not." After unloading the car, I sat in her kitchen while she put away some of the food the ladies from church had sent home with her.

"Listen, Matt, tomorrow I've set up an appointment with Mr. Conner, the attorney. I'd appreciate it if you'd accompany me."

I nodded, assuming the meeting had to do with my signing away any claim to the inheritance. I wouldn't contest the will. My grandpa had made a mistake—albeit one in good faith—when it came to his church and requiring me to attend. Now that I'd had some days to think on it, his pulling something like that didn't necessarily surprise me, but it still hurt a bit. That being said, knowing that self-righteous pastor wouldn't ever get another penny from Grandpa's estate made it all worth it. I'd sign away my inheritance, then get on with the rest of my life.

I ended up going to Mayville's only bar, even though it was still rather early in the day to be out drinking. More than one person gave me the stink eye, probably because of the church incident. Fortunately, I didn't give a shit about what people in this town thought of me. Their hypocrisy was laughable. They didn't seem to realize that if the good pastor knew they were sitting in a freaking bar, he'd be passing judgement on them too. Regardless, I left less than an hour after I got there.

I stopped back at Ms. Beth's to check in and let her know I was going to drive out to our farm for a final visit. She nodded, and I noticed a strange expression on her face. I assumed it was because I'd said *our farm* like I still owned it, but I wasn't gonna do anything on the land other than say goodbye.

Six

Logan

WITH TIME ON MY hands and my job in limbo, I decided to take a look at the estate. Even if I would have to leave soon, I still wanted to get the lay of the land, and this might be my only opportunity.

My initial tour with Mr. Brinks had been limited to the vineyard, and when I did a search online, I'd seen there was an old mill on the property. I loved history and enjoyed learning about what life had been like in newly settled places and when Indigenous peoples had occupied the lands before Europeans arrived.

It was quite a walk between my apartment alongside the barn and the mill. I ended up wandering down an old dirt road that cut a winding path around trees, crossed a small meandering creek, and ultimately led to a clearing. I could hear the rippling water of the stream before I actually caught sight of the old water wheel.

When the mill came fully into view, I actually gasped at the picturesque sight. The meadow around the old wooden structure hadn't been mowed in a long time, which meant the grass was tall and filled with blooming wildflowers that blew gently in the breeze. Huge trees lined the clearing, providing a backdrop to the post-card-worthy setting. It felt like a magical place, as if I'd been transported back in time a hundred years.

Honey bees buzzed all around me as they zig-zagged amid the wildflowers to collect pollen. The heavy musk-like scent of the flowers reminded me of my dad's stories of when he and his friends collected what he called rabbit tobacco. He'd picked some for me when I was a kid, and the unique musky smell was similar to what wafted through the air now.

As I cut across the clearing toward the mill, giving a black snake that lay in my path a wide berth, I neared a large structure I could tell had once been a log cabin. The long rectangular shape was falling down on one side, and the roof was sagging as well. A retro-looking trailer jutted out from behind the building, and I had to chuckle at the backwoods homeliness of it all.

Despite my curiosity, I didn't dare go inside. I knew like I knew my own name, that structure had either a couple timber rattlers or a copperhead tucked inside.

I was more intrigued by the old mill anyway. It stood five to six hundred feet away. The sound of the stream was much more pronounced here, and I wondered what it must've been like living in a place where you could hear the water tumbling down a rocky stream bed as you slept at night.

The mill was actually in significantly better shape than the old cabin. Although I wouldn't dare climb the stairs to the second story, I felt confident I wasn't going to fall through the first floor. I stepped inside and explored the grinding stone, which sat next to the dilapidated wheel, separated by only a thin piece of wood.

I was just about to take a peek at where they likely used to store the grain when I heard a vehicle pull up.

Wary of snakes lurking in every corner, I gingerly made my way across the wooden floor toward the front door. When I stepped outside, I came upon a man who was turned away from me, looking toward the cabin. I cleared my throat. "Hello," I said tentatively. "Can I help you?"

The man startled, almost to the point of falling down, and whipped around to face me. He appeared so stunned, with his mouth agape, I was surprised he hadn't squealed with fright.

"Um, sorry, I didn't mean to startle you."

The man stared at me a long moment and I returned his assessing gaze, taking mental notes of just how attractive he was. Tall, a little taller than me, and muscular. His dark scruff matched his brown hair, which seemed just a tad too long, like he'd needed a haircut maybe two or three weeks ago, long enough to run my fingers through.

He looked vaguely familiar, but I couldn't place him. He also looked very good in his khaki pants and a button-down shirt, but if I had to guess, I'd say he wasn't altogether comfortable in dress pants even if they were casual. What really struck me, though, were those bright, almost too-green eyes. Was he wearing eyeliner, or were his eyes just that poignant? I could get lost in those emerald pools.

"This is private property," he said, almost stammering. That snapped me back to the here and now right quick.

"Yes, I'm aware of that," I replied, a bit annoyed that he assumed I was the one trespassing. "And you are?"

He hesitated a moment and a flash of emotion crossed his face as he replied, "I'm um... friends with the owner."

"Who is the owner?" I asked, hoping to either catch him in a lie or learn of a change since I'd spoken to the widow.

"Beth Brinks," he said, and I nodded.

"May I ask how you know her?" I asked, feeling like maybe I needed to protect the property. I knew for a fact some of the wood from the old mill would bring in a fortune at the shops that sold reclaimed timber in Nashville.

"I think I should be asking you that," he said, in a tone indicating all civility was coming to an end.

"I'm the new caretaker of this estate. Mr. Brinks hired me before he passed. I wasn't told anyone would be coming out to the property today, so I'm going to have to ask you to leave until I hear from Ms. Brinks."

When the man laughed, it put my back up. Yes, claiming it was my place to protect the property was pushing things a bit. Still, I figured I should stand my ground.

"I doubt Ms. Beth would've called you and if you are who my grandfather hired, I'm guessing he'd have filled me in on that little piece of news as well."

"Grandfather?" I asked. "Mr. Brinks was your grandfather?" He nodded and I could see the sadness in his eyes. "I'm sorry, I didn't realize. You have my condolences."

He looked at me with those intense eyes of his again before sighing. "Ms. Beth inherited the property from my grandpa..." Just as he said that, I remembered why he seemed so familiar.

I missed the last part of what he'd said and shook my head, apologizing. "I'm sorry, I just realized you're the grandson who took that asshat pastor to task for turning your grandpa's memorial into a three-ring circus. I watched the whole thing on TV. You were amazing."

He blushed. "Yeah, well, my grandpa apparently thought dealing with him for a year would be good for my character."

I snorted in amusement. "Not hardly. That man has no business behind a pulpit," I said before the implications of he'd said sunk in. "So, you lost the property because you stood up for yourself?"

He nodded. "Yeah, and now you know a whole bunch about me, and I don't know crap about you."

"Oh, sorry, I'm Logan Johnson, vintner," I said, extending my hand for a shake. "I wasn't supposed to be here for a few more weeks, but since the winery I worked for no longer exists thanks to a fire, I'm now here and supposed to begin making wine. I only heard about your grandpa after I arrived, but he knew I was coming early."

Understanding must have hit him, because he said, "Aah, now I get it." Then he chuckled as he shook my hand. "You're the guy from California that Grandpa told me about, here to manage the insanity he put into the place, otherwise known as his winery."

"Insanity?" I asked.

"Yeah, it's a long story. Well, I wanted to go look around the old homestead one last time before I head back to Lebanon. I'll let you get on with your... um, protecting."

I felt the humor but didn't see a smile. Our conversation had ended on a better note than it started, but I felt the sudden urge to keep it going.

When he turned to walk toward the old cabin, I said, "Mind if I walk with you to the cabin? Then, if you want, you can come have a drink with me. I've got a couple bottles of wine from my last winery in Napa. I was gonna share them with your grandpa, but... well, I'd be happy to share them with you. Besides, after putting that pastor in his place, you deserve a drink."

He looked at me in surprise, as if I was asking him on a date or something. Maybe I was? I honestly hadn't thought that far ahead, I just wanted to keep talking to him for a while.

"Um, sure. Did you walk down?" he asked.

I nodded. "Yep, I wanted to get the lay of the land."

"In that case, I can give you a lift back. Although I'm not gonna take the trail you came down, I'm not sure the old girl can handle it."

I chuckled as I looked at his old nineteen nine-ty-something Nissan. "Yeah, I don't think it'd tackle the creek I crossed to get here very well."

The guy smiled warmly at me, and I decided I liked him. The way my heart flipped around in my chest when he turned those green eyes on me made me think I liked him a whole lot.

"My name's Matt, by the way, and this is where I grew up," he said as he led the way to the old cabin.

Seven

Matt

WITH ALL THAT'D HAPPENED in the past few weeks, I'd forgotten my grandpa had actually hired someone to run the vineyard.

The guy was cute, super cute, and I couldn't help but check him out while we looked around the cabin. He was on the short side, maybe five foot nine if I was being generous, and fit. I could tell by the way his shirt clung to his toned chest and biceps. The man was all muscle, and no doubt developed that lean body by working with his hands rather than toiling in a gym.

If I wasn't careful, I'd start reading too much into Logan's sweet smile and easy conversation. Then again, with my luck, he was probably straight or so deep in the closet, he'd never make his way out. That'd be for the best anyway, as far as I was concerned. Having the hots for Ms. Beth's new employee was the last thing I needed, especially with me being on the verge of splitting town.

I liked him, though, in a soft, warm, comforting sort of way. He was easy to be around. I liked that he was prickly at first, wanting to protect the property. I didn't think there was anything here to protect, not really, but it felt good that someone else did. I mean, this place wasn't mine to worry about anymore, but it had been my home for many years and in some ways, it always would be.

"So, you're from California? How did you get an accent so quick?" I asked, unable to resist a bit of teasing. I was genuinely curious, though.

He chuckled. "I'm from Nashville, and my dad's from around here. College took me way out West. I went to Oregon State University, on a full-ride scholarship for baseball. I immediately fell in love with the vineyards around the school. Next thing I know, I'm graduating with an undergraduate degree in viticulture and enology."

"And you're back now to take up raising vines in Tennessee?" I asked as we finished touring the cabin and climbed into my car.

He sighed. "Yeah, I haven't done too well on the West Coast. I made the mistake of sharing opinions with people who didn't think a country boy with a Southern accent had a lick of sense, let alone knew anything about making wine. I thought I'd finally found a good place in Napa, working with people who respected me and my ideas, then the fire wiped us out. I was coming back home with my tail between my legs when my dad mentioned this place needed help. I visited with your grandpa, and left with the guarantee of a job."

"You must be pretty good then 'cause my grandpa wasn't one to do anything on the spur of the moment. Hell, sometimes I'd think a conversation was over because he was spending so much time thinking about what he said before he said it."

I chuckled at the memory before grief and sadness hit me again out of nowhere. I looked out the driver's side window as I struggled to get myself back under control. If Logan noticed, he didn't say anything.

When I pulled into the barn's new gravel parking lot, he invited me in. "Come on, I'll fix us that wine, then if you want, I can show you what I have planned short-term to get your grandpa's vines prepped for harvest."

"You know I'm not the owner, right?" I asked, and he nodded, looking a little disappointed.

"Yeah, I do, but I've been chomping at the bit to talk to someone about them. They have so much potential, and you can be my sounding board before I actually talk to your grandmother."

I smiled as I followed him into the big tasting room within the barn. "Step-grandmother, actually. They got married when I went to college, but grandmother is a good term for her. She's a great person, and I think you'll really like working for her. My grandpa was a teetotaler before marrying her, opposed to any form of alcohol, and it's her fondness for wine that convinced him to plant and grow vines in order to turn the grapes into *fermented* wine." I laughed at the thought. It was still hard for me to digest completely how far he'd come since he raised me. "Personally, I think it was all an act of love on his part. He loved Ms. Beth something fierce and anything he could do to make his sweetheart happy, he did."

We settled on opposite sides of the long bar and Logan pulled out a bottle with a nice-looking label and poured us both about a quarter of a glass. He also pulled out a bottle of water and what he called a spit bucket. I played along but I wasn't a total hillbilly. I'd been to wine tastings, so I knew what all of it was, I'd just never felt all that connected to the process.

Logan watched me as I took a sip of the wine. "Mmm," I moaned. "This is nice."

That made him smile. "It's okay. Do you drink wine very often?"

I shook my head and blushed. "No, not really. I'm more of a shots guy, if I drink at all. Sorry."

"Don't be sorry, but I want to show you some aspects of your grandpa's wine that might put this vineyard on the map. You game?" he asked.

"Sure, but I don't know that I'll understand."

Logan winked at me. "I'll help you understand."

The flirty look he gave me sent a rush of heat coursing through my body, and the redness in my cheeks had nothing to do with the one sip of alcohol I'd tasted.

"In the glass I just gave you, you'll taste nice fruity flavors on the back of your tongue. You can also taste different overtones, but I'll not push those on you quite yet."

He handed me the water bottle and had me rinse and spit into the bucket while he poured wine from a second bottle. "What do you think about this one?" he asked, handing me a glass. He watched intently as I took a sip.

"Um, well, it feels smoother and causes me to pucker at the back of my throat."

Logan chuckled. "Yes, that's the tannins. You also need them 'cause they help preserve the wine, but it gives it a nice bite."

He had me do the rinse and spit thing again, then handed me a third glass. "Finally, this is your grandpa's wine."

He seemed bemused as I swished it around in my mouth, not completely sure what I was doing, before swallowing. "It's not bad," I said, sounding a little more surprised than I'd intended. Truth be told, I was relieved the stuff was palatable.

"No, it's not bad, but what did you taste? How did it compare to the other two?"

I shrugged. "Well, this one was, um, brighter?" I asked and he smiled.

"Exactly, it's immature," he said. I felt mildly pleased with myself, not so much that I'd said the right thing, but that it met with Logan's approval. And why the hell did that feel good?

"The first bottle you tasted is from Oregon and it's what's known as a table wine. It's perfect for having with dinner or just as a glass before going to bed. But it's not going to win any awards. But then again, it's not meant to. It's made to be sold in bulk." He paused, waiting for my nod of understanding, then continued. "The second one has earned several awards. It's from a vineyard I worked on last year, and even though it's still just a year old, it's already becoming smooth and delicate, taking on lots of different undertones that complement each other nicely. Both wines were made with the same types of grapes your grandpa has planted out there. So, as the viticulturist, my job will be to help the owner decide if we're going to try to become an award-winning wine, or if we want to be a bulk seller."

"What's the difference?" I asked, knowing I was showing my ignorance.

Logan thought for a moment. "It's all about what you're trying to create. In a lot of ways, the bulk wine seller can make more money faster. Going that route, you can often sell other stuff, too, what's called swag." He rolled his eyes at that, so apparently the swag stuff wasn't his department. "But if quality is more important to you, well, that takes a lot of time and energy. Most of it happens within the grapevines themselves, then you make wine and wait. It can take five to ten years before a wine is ready to sell. Which do you think your grandpa would've gone with?"

I laughed. "Seriously? He lectured me time and again, 'Son, we don't do things half-cocked around here.' If it took five years to get a great wine out of the grapes, then five years it'd be. Grandpa wouldn't have settled for anything but the best, especially since this was all for Ms. Beth."

"I had the same feeling about him myself. I think that's why I was so excited about getting the job. I want to make delicious wines. Stuff that outlives you."

The wistful smile he gave led me to become emotional again. "Yeah, that was Grandpa. He wanted things to outlive him," I said, swallowing around the lump in my throat. "I think that's why the church was so important to him. You know, the one I made a fool out of myself at while on live TV?"

A determined look crossed Logan's face and he shook his head. "That pastor was a jerk, and totally out of line. I heard how he taunted you before you grabbed that microphone. You had me practically cheering by the end, standing up to that bully for all to witness."

"That part felt good, I admit, but I didn't pay respects to my grandpa either. His grandfather helped establish that church, and Grandpa's daddy was the preacher there for decades until handing the reins to that jackal Atwell. For my grandpa, I think the church was as much a part of our family legacy as this land... if not more so."

"Your great-grandpa must've been the pastor when my dad was a kid. He's been disappointed for years in how much the church changed since then," Logan said, putting his hand over mine. "I'm sorry about everything, all you've been going through. I can see it hurts to think about. It's obvious how important your family and the land are to you."

I glanced down at his hand and felt heat radiating from where we touched. I tried to conceal my attraction to him, and knew I'd failed because as soon as I met his eyes, his expression changed from concern to desire. That's when he leaned across the bar and kissed me.

I lifted up off my stool and grabbed his shirt as I deepened the kiss, pulling him onto the bar top in the process.

He pulled back laughing when he was nearly sprawled across it.

"Um, sorry about that. I..."

"No, man, don't be sorry. That's the most action I've had in months. Besides, I like you."

Things got awkward for a moment as I became tongue-tied, and Logan smoothed down his rumpled shirt. Then he capped the wine bottles, came around the bar, and took my hand. "Come on," he said, giving me a reassuring smile, "I'll show you the vines."

EIGHT

LOGAN

I WASN'T SURE WHAT got into me. One minute I was trying to comfort the poor guy, the next I was leaning over to kiss him. I blamed it on him looking at me with those intense green eyes. I'd always been a sucker for beautiful eyes.

Matt tasted like the wine he'd just sampled, along with a woodsy, earthy flavor I later realized was actually his aroma. He was delicious. I suddenly wanted to snuggle into him and, well, maybe do a lot more than just snuggling. Seeing shock register on his face after our brief, but passionate lip-lock, I decided it would probably be best if we closed the wine-tasting part of our visit, and got back outside before I did something even more foolish, something like pulling the man back to my apartment to get even-better acquainted.

We walked along the vines, and I talked about what we needed to do to make the most of the grapes we already had growing. Mostly, though, I kept talking to distract myself from his nearness and what I now knew was an incredible mouth.

"We have two months until it's time to harvest. I'd recommend we stop all irrigation until then, stressing the vines and concentrating the sugars in the grapes."

Matt was following closely behind me, and when he didn't respond, I stopped and turned around. Then I almost swallowed my tongue when I saw the expression on his face. Desire blazed bright in his green eyes as they raked over me from top to bottom. Apparently, I wasn't the only one with more than grapes on his mind.

I swallowed thickly as I stepped closer to the row so I could point out how the vines were yellowing along the top of the hill. "These vines are showing signs of potassium deficiency and although we should've applied potassium a few weeks ago, I'm going to apply it this week and hope for the..."

When I stepped back and bumped into Matt, I turned to say excuse me and was pulled into a firm embrace. In an instant, his lips were devouring mine, and all the blood rushed from my head southward. My arms instinctively wrapped around the back of his neck, and I pressed my body flush against his as we kissed.

When he pulled back, his hands sliding down to loosely grip my waist, I couldn't hold back the happy moan that slipped out.

"You... um, you really..." Matt said, stumbling over his words and causing me to chuckle.

"My sentiments exactly," I said, letting him off the hook. "Wanna come back to my place?"

He nodded eagerly, then looked concerned. "Except isn't this some sort of conflict of interest or harassment or something?"

"Not if you don't own the place. We're not crossing any forbidden lines here. Are you going to ask Ms. Brinks to fire me if we don't get it on?" I asked, and he laughed out loud.

"No, I'm not going to mention this to Ms. Beth, and I doubt she'd give a crap what I said anyway. That woman seems to make up her own mind. Besides, she and I don't exactly talk about my... um, relationships."

It was a stretch calling this—whatever *this* was—a relationship, and he sounded nervous even saying it, which was cute as hell. I leaned into him again, desperate to get another taste. "Like I said, I really like you. That speech you gave at the church already had me swooning, then I come to discover you're also hot and sweet and smell nice."

I blushed then, thinking maybe I'd gone a bit too far, but my babbling had Matt grinning. "You fit me," he said, as if that was the best compliment he could give. I thought about it for a moment, taking in the feel of his toned body pressed to mine, and he was right. I did seem to fit him well. He was a few inches taller than me, and my shorter frame seemed to tuck perfectly into his.

"Right, so... my apartment?" I asked again, already knowing his answer. When he nodded and grabbed my hand, we began walking at a brisk pace back down the hill.

Unfortunately, as we rounded the barn, we didn't get far before we saw a black Lexus sitting in the driveway. "Fuck!" Matt said under his breath, dropping my hand.

"What's wrong?" I asked as our pace slowed.

"That's Pastor Atwell's car."

"Why would he be here?" I asked.

"To gloat, probably. Anyway, it doesn't matter. I've given up my claim to the property. I'm meeting with Ms. Beth's attorney tomorrow to sign the deed over to her and be done with it once and for all."

I looked up at him, then back toward the Lexus just as the door opened, and a tall man, probably in his sixties, stepped out. The pastor looked exactly like he had on TV, only more smug.

"Well, guess we better go face him. I'll tell him to leave, though, if that makes you feel better. I meant what I said earlier about protecting this property, especially from anyone looking to do your family harm."

"Nah, he could give you a lot of problems. It's best if you pretend not to know me."

"Um, too late for that. I'm sure he just saw us holding hands. He'll be able to figure out we're... *acquainted*."

"Shit, I didn't think of that," Matt said. "Yeah, you should probably say I came onto you. He'll like that since he hates me so much. He could use that as a way to demonize me even more and you can get off the hook."

I stopped walking and looked up at him. "No, I won't hide who I am, and I won't throw you under the bus just to keep a bigot from causing me trouble. I'd rather move back to California and work in a wine store than hide my identity. Besides," I said, elbowing him in a friendly way, "I'm looking forward to kissing you a lot more. The good pastor can go to hell."

Matt laughed and led the way toward the man. When we reached him, I nodded my acknowledgement, but didn't readily introduce myself. I also made no move to leave, remaining by Matt's side to offer silent support.

"Mr. Atwell, I thought I made it clear I didn't want to see or speak to you again. You're not welcome here. I'm gonna have to ask you to leave," Matt said in a measured tone.

"Well, son, it's my understanding this isn't your property to say who can or can't..."

"However," I interrupted, "...as the caretaker of this property, it most certainly is my concern. Unless you have actual business to conduct here, which I'm guessing not since we're not open today, I suggest you leave before I call the sheriff."

The old man looked affronted, and probably rightly so. He didn't know me, yet here I was ready to call the authorities on him. He must've thought he could just come out here and railroad Matt into something. Not hardly.

"I think your daddy and aunt might have different ideas about that, Mr. Johnson."

That he knew my name shouldn't have surprised me, seeing as several of my family members still attended the church, and I managed to school my expression. Word must've traveled fast, probably courtesy of my Aunt Polly, that I'd taken up residence at the vineyard.

"Sir, I doubt my family care either way. Again, if you don't have business here, please leave."

The man looked like he was about to pop a blood vessel. I could tell the arrogant asshat seldom encountered anyone who'd stand up to him. I'd guess, as the pastor of such a large and influential church, he had a lot of authority. But I'd be damned if I cowered to him after watching the way he'd treated Matt and likely any other gay men who crossed his path. That raised my hackles, and I was in full protective mode.

I turned my back on him, ready to be done with this conversation, and faced Matt. "Are you coming?" I asked.

He sighed. "I will in a moment," he replied.

I nodded, then walked to the barn, but stopped short of going inside. Instead, I stood at the door and watched in case I needed to intervene.

NINE

MATT

"**W**HAT DO YOU WANT?" I asked as soon as Logan had gone.

"Matthew, you and I got off to a bad start. As a Christian, I'd like to make amends."

"As a Christian, I can forgive you, now go and sin no more."

I started to walk away when Atwell put his hand on my shoulder to stop me.

"Sir, you will remove your hand from me," I practically snarled. When he quickly jerked his hand back, he sighed.

"Matthew..."

"Stop referring to me by my first name. You and I are not friends, we are not even friendly acquaintances, and you have shown me no respect whatsoever."

"Fine, Mr. Brinks, your grandfather wanted us to make this work. I admit I may have overstepped during his memorial service, and I'm here to ask forgiveness and for you to come back to church."

I stared at him a long moment, surprised that this idiot would dare to ask that of me. Then it dawned on me why he'd become humble all of a sudden. I laughed at the audacity of why he was really here on bended knee. "You're here because of money. Now that I'm not joining your flock like my grandpa wanted me to, the church won't be getting a dime of the inheritance. Well, sir, I couldn't care less about the money if it requires I listen to your hateful sermons every Sunday. I'll never step foot in your den of snakes ever again."

All the niceties he'd been trying to show me fell away in an instant and the real man came out. "You are on the road straight to hell, Matthew Brinks. I came here to make amends, but you are not a man of God. I just witnessed your depravity with my own eyes. How can you, a degenerate, pervert an innocent young man like Logan Johnson? I will leave you to your own wickedness and pray for your soul."

I was about to lay into him when Logan appeared in front of me again, standing between me and Atwell. "The only soul you need to be praying for, pastor, is your own," he said, sounding as mad as hornet. "You'd best leave this property and not return."

The pastor stared at him with mouth agape, then his mood darkened, and he practically tore his car door off its hinges opening it. Without another word, he got into the Lexus and spun out of the parking lot with gravel flying.

I sighed as the car disappeared from view and Logan turned around to face me. "I wish you hadn't done that. He's going to make your life miserable for it."

"What can he do? Get me fired?" Then he laughed. "I'm here on a shoestring as it is. Ms. Brinks already told me she's lining up a new owner. The likelihood that they'll want to keep anyone in this position who doesn't give a rat's ass what others in this town think, especially that blowhard, is pretty slim. But I won't stand by and let a bully attack someone for who they are, even if I wasn't gay myself, and even if I didn't already like you."

I smiled. "I like you too. Unfortunately, I'm no longer in the mood for fooling around. Can we take a rain check? I'd love to take you out to lunch tomorrow after I'm done with all the legal stuff and before I leave for home."

Logan grinned up at me. "I'd like that a lot. What time do you think?"

"Ms. Beth said we'll be meeting the attorney in the morning, so I'll come out afterward to pick you up. If you give me your number, I'll text you when we're done."

We exchanged numbers and I kissed him again before leaving. If he was right and Ms. Beth sold the place or decided she didn't want Logan to stay on, maybe we could meet up again and see where things led.

I let myself think about him as I drove home. Of course, I felt the usual thrill of meeting someone new, but it ran deeper than that. After only spending a few hours together, I already knew I liked Logan and would enjoy getting to know him better.

That was pretty rare for me. I wasn't very social. In fact, the last couple of years I had all but avoided dating anyone, settling instead for the occasional hookup. And even those had become few and far between. I tended to prefer to stay in my studio and paint, though I'd be lying if I said it wasn't a lonely sort of existence.

The reminder that I'd be losing my art studio soon and had to sell everything caused a fresh wave of pain and grief to crash down on me like a ton of bricks. All the paintings I had stored needed to be packaged and sent off to galleries. The most precious pieces I'd resisted letting go of had to be inventoried and put on offer. As yet, I'd only sold a couple dozen paintings, and even though all the galleries I contracted with had requested more from me, I struggled to part with my artwork.

I knew it was ridiculous, but the paintings felt like my family. Of course, I wanted to share them with the world, to have them seen and appreciated, but I didn't love the idea of selling a piece only to have its buyer hide it away in their living room. I always thought of the ugly velvet painting Grandpa used to have hanging behind the sofa in the old trailer. No, thank you. I'd rather my stuff never became *that* kind of art.

Oh well, now that I was going to have to downsize, I guessed that would all be changing. I'd gotten an email back from every gallery I'd reached out to, all wanting more of my paintings. I should feel honored, but damn, it just felt like yet another loss.

When I pulled into Ms. Beth's driveway, I got out and went inside without knocking. She had given me a key and said to make myself at home, so I had. I removed my shoes, like I'd been told to do by my grandpa when I'd first come to stay with them, and found Ms. Beth waiting for me in the living room.

"I just got a call from Pastor Atwell," she said as I sat on the sofa across from her.

I blushed and sighed. "I'm sorry, Ms. Beth, he came out to the farm while I was there. I would've preferred to avoid him if I could."

"Well, he was irate when he called me, as you can imagine." Then she chuckled. "I've always disliked Mr. Atwell. He's a snake in the grass who likes to prey on the pious members of our community. You know, your grandpa and I almost ended things because I refused to sit in a pew and listen to that unsavory man every Sunday," she said, causing my mouth to drop open. She nodded in confirmation, as if I wouldn't believe her revelation.

"Now, mind you, I don't like disrespect and if you were hateful to him, then I won't condone that, but at the same time, I had a front-row seat when he was disrespecting you and even your grandpa, rest his sweet soul."

Sadness crossed her features at the mention of Grandpa, and once again, I was reminded how much she'd loved him. Despite the conversation, it warmed my heart to see it.

"Anyway, the old coot wanted me to fire Logan and send you packing. Then... oh, and honey, this was the part that set my hair on fire. He wants me to come to church and honor the same requirements your grandpa set out for you in his will."

"He thinks that'll get him the money?" I asked, then laughed. "God, he's something else."

"Yes, he is. I wasn't going to tell you this, not until tomorrow when we see the attorney, but I've decided to leave well enough alone with those ridiculous requirements he put in that will. Instead, once it's all in my name, I'll be giving the whole of your grandpa's estate—the bank account, land, winery, all of it—back to you."

I stared at her with heart and mind racing. "Ms. Beth, I couldn't..."

"You could and you will. That is not my property, and it should remain in the Brinks family. I signed a prenuptial with your grandfather, and he signed mine. We were together because we loved one another, not because either of us wanted to get rich. So, as is your birthright, I'll be signing all of it right back over to you tomorrow morning. Oh, and honey, the best part of all this is that hateful man won't get one red cent."

She leaned back in her chair with a satisfied smirk on her face and laughed. "Oh, to be a fly on the wall when he figures all this out."

I remained too stunned to speak, and tears fell as I digested what was happening. When Ms. Beth glanced my way, she quickly got up and came to sit next to me, pulling me into a hug.

"Oh, baby, please remember your grandpa wasn't doing all this to keep you from inheriting your birthright. He really did think this would help you and that church find common ground."

I sniffed, reached for the box of tissues sitting on her side table, and cleaned myself up. "It's not the money or even the property. I'm not really a person who worries about material things. I'm definitely like Grandpa in that way." I smiled thinking about how he'd taken such pride in fixing and reusing old farm equipment when he could've easily bought new. "But I hated the idea of all that history, our family's history, being lost. I had dreams for the property too. I wanted it to be a place where people could come to paint and relax, like an artists' retreat. It's a special place, Ms. Beth."

"I know, baby, and now you can make that happen. With it all working out this way, you'll have even more money to spend on improvements. Money that would've gone to that hateful man's church like the will dictated will now go toward you realizing your dreams."

When I asked how much money the church would've received, the number of zeros she rattled off took me aback.

"Your grandpa wanted to supplement the church," she said. "He was trying to ensure its future long-term, well after Mr. Atwell's tenure as pastor."

I sat stunned for a long time before I shook my head. "No wonder he came over today with his tail between his legs. I bet the church leadership had words with him about it. That's a lot of money he threw away just to bully me."

"I'm guessing he didn't think he would be throwing it away. That's a huge inheritance you were willing to walk away from, and few people would've done so. I think your grandfather underestimated how much like him you really are," she said, winking at me, then chuckled. "Or how stupid Mr. Atwell is."

I took a deep breath, finally able to wrap my mind around taking ownership of the property, the vineyard, and my family's wealth. "Ms. Beth, are you sure you don't want to keep some of the inheritance? I mean, you *are* a part of this family, plus it's more money than any one person could ever use."

She smiled at that and patted my knee affectionately. "Child, you really are just like your grandpa, and I appreciate you saying that. But I've got plenty, and I'm an old woman on top of that. I don't need or want any more money than I already have. If you really feel that way, though, you could use some of it to improve things for folks around here. Just remember, money isn't what matters in the long run. You can't take it with you."

"But," I said, quoting my grandpa, "...you can sure use it to make the world a better place while you're here." She and I both chuckled.

"I miss him," I said, and wiped away another tear that fell.

"I think we'll both miss him for the rest of our lives," she said, and leaned back against the sofa.

"You don't think this would upset him?" I asked.

She shook her head. "Upset, yes, but not at you. I think he'd be spitting nails at how you were treated, and in his own church, no less. Not in his wildest dreams would he have thought Mr. Atwell would act such a way, and in front of the whole congregation."

"Ms. Beth, I am grateful, and I'll be here if you ever need me. As far as I'm concerned, that money is still yours if you ever need it, and I would never fight you for it. Until then, I'll do what I can to make you and Grandpa proud by using it to benefit the community."

She stood up and leaned over, kissing the top of my head. "I don't doubt that in the least, *Grandson.*" Then she left to go into the kitchen. "I'll have dinner ready in about an hour," she called out. "Why don't you go freshen up, then you can set the table."

I told her I would, but stayed on the sofa for a bit letting our whole conversation sink in. I knew Grandpa had money, but I had no idea how much until talking with Ms. Beth. You'd never know it by looking at him. He kept himself humble. Actually, he kept us both humble throughout my life, and I was grateful for it now.

Even when he moved in with Ms. Beth, the two lived frugally. Ms. Beth had also never called me her grandson before. Something about that warmed my soul. With the exception of my estranged maternal aunt and her husband and daughter, and assorted distant relatives I didn't know, I was without family when Grandpa had died, so I loved thinking of the amazing and powerful

Southern woman as my grandma. It made me feel more grounded somehow.

The next morning, we arrived early at Mr. Conner's office, and I signed all the paperwork rejecting the inheritance, which also made the church's claim to any part of it null and void. That made Ms. Beth, as Grandpa's spouse, the next of kin and thus the next in line to inherit.

As the attorney explained, we didn't have to worry about any state inheritance, estate, or gift taxes, since Tennessee no longer had them. He also assured us that although the estate was considerable, its overall value made it exempt from federal estate taxes, which was a relief. Finances were never my thing, so a lot of the finer details went over my head, but I knew Ms. Beth would've only hired the best of attorneys to sort it out.

"It'll probably still take six months to a year to work all this out in probate court, but I'll petition the courts to let you live on the property and continue to provide you with the stipend your grandpa was sending you," Mr. Conner told us. "Mind you, the church may still try to stake its claim on the inheritance by contesting, but we'll deal with that if and when the time comes."

"Is it okay if I start planning what to do with the property once it's officially mine? I'd like to have an architect come out and look at the buildings and get estimates on what it'll cost to restore them."

"Shouldn't be a problem. Do you plan to physically stay on the property?" he asked.

"I may have to," I admitted. "I already gave notice on my apartment in Lebanon."

"That shouldn't be a problem," he said. "Oh, and, Ms. Brinks, I'll need a complete list of all of the winery's current employees so the estate can continue paying their salaries. That also applies to any new employees hired in the coming months until probate is settled."

Ms. Beth and I both left the attorney's office smiling. I, for one, felt reassured by everything he'd told us. It looked like this might all work out in the end. For the first time since Grandpa's initial stroke, I felt hopeful about the future.

Even as a kid, I'd dreamed of one day renovating the buildings on the property, starting with the old log cabin. I also had grand plans for the old mill, inspired by a beautiful mill restaurant I'd once eaten at in Pigeon Forge. Instead of a restaurant, though, I envisioned using the mill as an artists' retreat. The top floor that had stored grain, I'd turn into my studio, while the whole first floor could be used by another artist or even several.

My mind went a hundred different directions with all of the possibilities. The first step, though, was calling in an architect. I planned on contacting Tom Baskin, a longtime architect in Crawford City. I'd met him several times when I'd hung out with Grandpa at the local restaurant... *Shit!* I'd almost forgotten I had a date with Logan. And holy shit, I was now his boss. *Damn, damn, damn!*

I quickly texted him.

Hey, Logan. Got some major news today. Why don't I bring lunch to you at the farm? We've got a lot to talk about.

Logan texted back less than a minute later, saying that was fine with him.

I called over to the Crawford City Café and asked them to bag me up two lunches to go, whatever was on the daily special. Then I called Tom and asked him if he could meet me at the farm later for a consultation.

When he agreed, I gave Ms. Beth a quick kiss on the cheek, smiling from ear to ear. I told her of my plan to meet with Tom and start the process of saving the old buildings on the farm before it was too late.

She grinned back at me. "I'm glad you are. It's such a historic part of our community, and the state. I told your grandpa more than once it was a shame it'd fallen into such disrepair. He did manage to restore the old barn, though, and it makes a mighty fine winery."

"Agreed, and if it's possible, we'll breathe new life into the other structures too. Keep your fingers crossed they can be saved."

After dropping Ms. Beth at home, I stopped by the café to grab the food order for Logan and me, then headed to the farm. Tom was coming in a couple hours, and I wanted some time to tell Logan that our situation had changed. I guessed now that I was indeed his new boss, the kissing would have to stop, but at least he'd have job security.

I had to admit to feeling disappointed at us having to put the brakes on before we'd even gotten started, but

I couldn't risk this whole venture not working out. Not now, with so much on the line. Truth be told, I didn't have any desire to run a winery, let alone a clue how to go about it, so I'd be relying on Logan's expertise pretty heavily. I knew I already had a friend in him, though, someone who had my back and valued this property, and I'd learn to be content enough with that.

Ten

Logan

I LAUGHED WHEN MATT laid out the smorgasbord of food. He just shrugged. "The ladies down at the café tend to get a little overexcited when you ask for carry out," he said.

I knew he was chewing on some information, and I honestly figured he was going to tell me Ms. Brinks had a buyer, and the new owner didn't want me here. I'd come to terms with it though. This job working out for the long-term had been a long shot, and I'd already reached the conclusion it was too good to be true.

So, we ate in silence as he processed how to tell me.

"Logan, I got some... unexpected news, but I had no idea what was going to happen when I met you yesterday. If I had, I wouldn't have... well, I would've been more professional."

I cocked my eyebrow at him. "I don't think we were unprofessional. I like you and you didn't make the first move, if I remember right."

He didn't smile, which confused me. Had he decided he wasn't that into me? Well, that wouldn't be a first either. Frustrated, I said, "Dude, just spit it out. What's changed?"

"Well, I am the owner of the property, after all. Or at least I'm gonna be, once we clear probate court," he said.

That I hadn't expected. I forced myself to close my mouth and not gape at him. "Well, that's good. You can, um... is that good?" I asked.

He nodded. "Yeah, it's really good. Ms. Beth decided to give it back to me rather than sell it, said the property belongs in the family. And I'd like you to stay on, since I don't know shit about running a winery and even if we... since we kissed, I understand how you might not want to, but if you do want to... I won't come onto you again. I'll be professional."

Matt looked awkward as hell as he stared at me expectantly, and I stared right back. Part of me wanted to pull him into a kiss to stop his babbling, another part really did want this job. It didn't pay to have an affair with your boss, and since my track record with men was horrible anyway, I had no doubt I'd fuck it up sooner rather than later. I needed to rein in my attraction to my new boss and just be happy with the job, period.

"Yeah, that's probably best," I said, glancing away. If I looked at his handsome face right now, I might kiss him despite it being a really bad idea. Instead, I cleared my throat and went for redirection. "So, what're you gonna do with the place?"

The energy shifted then, and Matt smiled brightly. "Well, I've got an architect coming later, and we're gonna look at the old structures on the original homestead to see if we can save them. I want to move my art studio here, and the mill would be the perfect place for it."

That tidbit piqued my interest. "You're an artist?" I asked.

His grin grew wider. "Yeah, although I've not sold much of my stuff. My grandpa gave me an allowance since I graduated from college, so the past few years all I've done is paint. I've got quite a collection now."

"Cool," I said. I had such a thing for artists. While living in California, I'd briefly dated a couple who were living on neighboring wineries. I loved how their minds were able to conceptualize things, capturing the light and the mood.

I sighed. As if I needed another reason to be attracted to the man. "Well, that sounds great," I said, trying to hide the fact that I really wanted to crawl into his lap now more than ever. Before my mind could wander further down that road, I began packaging up what was left of my lunch to distract myself.

"So," I said, "...what I mentioned to you yesterday before, you know..." I tried not to think about the kiss we shared before the jackass pastor arrived. "Do you think it'd be okay if I planned to do those things with the vines?"

Matt nodded with more enthusiasm than I'd expected. "You do whatever you think is right. When you need help, just let me know and I'll donate my back for hard labor."

I chuckled at that. Most winery owners I'd met were good about helping out on the vineyards, but none were good about letting someone else run the vineyard without their direct involvement.

I wondered how long it'd take for Matt to step in and take on a more active role. Regardless, for now, he'd given me the reins, and I wasn't gonna say no to that. I firmly believed we could do amazing things with these vines. I knew some of my ideas were a bit out there, and if he fully understood anything about the process, he might fight me on it. This was my chance to prove my theories. I just hoped it wouldn't all blow up in my face in the end.

ELEVEN

MATT

BREAKING THE NEWS TO Logan went better than I thought it would. I was sure he'd hate me when he found out I was going to be the vineyard's new owner, but he took it in stride. But that's not to say I wasn't a little disappointed he didn't fight me a bit more on the *we can't be lovers now that I'm your boss* thing.

I liked everything there was to like about this guy I'd just met. That in and of itself was a rare feeling for me. Of course, it was just my fucking luck that I'd finally met someone who caused my toes to curl, and I couldn't pursue anything with him. *What shit!*

No matter how I looked at it, it just felt like I'd somehow lost out on something important with Logan. He'd felt so right in my arms when we'd kissed in the vineyard yesterday. I couldn't help but wonder how things might've deepened between us had we made it back to his apartment instead of being interrupted. Maybe we would've been amazing together. Or maybe it would've just made today all the more awkward. The only thing I knew for sure was I couldn't afford to be playing grab ass with the staff, not with everything else on the line, even if that meant sacrificing a potentially meaningful relationship for the both of us.

Tom met me as agreed and we walked around the old log cabin, him using his pocketknife to poke and prod the logs. "The structure is unstable, but most of the hand-hewn logs are still in great shape. I recommend taking the entire structure apart, salvage as many logs as possible, and then rebuild it using modern chinking techniques."

I knew a bit about log cabins. I'd watched enough renovation shows to know chinking meant the stuff that went in between the logs to keep it weatherproof.

We walked over to the mill then, and as Tom walked around it, he showed me several problem areas. "The foundation is limestone and has disintegrated in quite a few areas, which puts the entire structure of this building in jeopardy. All that will have to be replaced sooner rather than later," he said.

As we toured the interior, he seemed pleased. "It's in better shape than you'd think. I remember your great-grandpa put a roof on this when I was a kid, thinking he'd use it as an extra barn. I think that's saved it, to be honest. Although there is definitely some wood rot up on the second floor, so I'd guess most of the siding up there will need to be replaced."

He leaned against the old stone gristmill and sighed. "You're gonna have to sink a heck of a lot of money into these buildings to save them, son. Fixing this place back up, even to the point it was before, will cost a fortune, and putting that log cabin back together will be at least as much. Turning them into modern, livable structures will triple the cost, maybe more. Are you sure you want to do all this?" he asked.

I nodded. "I'm more than sure. I've always wanted to preserve these structures and now I'm in a position to do that."

The old man looked like he wanted to argue. I figured, with him having known my grandpa, he'd want to tell me how much Grandpa would disapprove, but Tom held his tongue.

"I'll work up the drawings. Do you have a contractor in mind?" he asked.

"No, sir, I was hoping you'd know someone I could trust."

"I do. That log cabin is probably outside his area of expertise, but the mill is definitely something he could do. Do you know Todd Thompson?" he asked.

"Well, that name sounds familiar, but... wait, is he about my age, a couple years older?"

Tom shrugged. "He grew up around here. His family lived next to Doc Nash over in Crawford City."

I smiled. "Yeah, he and I went out a couple times. I thought he had a business in Nashville."

"Moved back and is now married to Doc's son, Ash, who's also a doctor in town."

"Cool," I said. "Yeah, if you think Todd would be interested, I've only heard the best things about his work."

"He is the best, better even than his daddy, although you might not want to tell him that. His dad is his business partner now."

"Sounds good to me. Please, have Todd call me and I'll set up a time for him to take a look, then we'll go from there."

Tom left then and I walked back across the property toward the barn, where I'd left Logan. As I walked out of the meadow along the little creek that fed into the stream that powered the mill, I saw the place in the woods I used to sit when I was a kid. My special, secret spot.

It was a small clearing hidden by trees that leveled out about fifteen feet above the road. I could sit up there and see everything that was going on around the farm. I'd often hide from Grandpa up there when he'd come looking for me to finish my chores.

I chuckled to myself as I climbed up the steep path that'd become completely overgrown, careful to avoid the snakes I knew liked to live around this part of the farm.

The nice boulder I used to sit comfortably on was still there, although now covered in moss. It was also a lot smaller than I remembered. After looking around to ensure there were no snakes, I plopped down on it and leaned back against the huge oak tree that stood behind it.

I closed my eyes, letting the melodic flowing of the creek relax me. How was it this was now all mine? Sorrow threatened to swallow me again, thinking of the loss of my grandpa, but I pushed that away. No, this special spot was a happy place. One I'd loved all my life. That's when I remembered my dad had shown this spot to me. It'd been his before it'd been mine. I'd somehow forgotten that, but sitting here now, I could almost feel how it'd been a lot of people's special place over the years. Generations of my family likely sat on this very boulder, listening to the same creek flowing below, finding their own sense of peace.

When I opened my eyes, I could see the homestead, not as it was now, but as it used to be, with gardens planted around the cabin and kids playing in the meadow. The mill's water wheel churned steadily, powering the stone gristmill to grind away at a neighbor's corn or wheat.

I wanted to make that scene real, for this to become that special kind of home again. I was about to get up to leave when I noticed a pretty little rock crystal sparkling in the creek. They weren't really rare, I used to collect them when I was a kid, so it wasn't surprising to see it. But it reminded me of the Thorncrown Chapel that stood so proudly in Eureka Springs, Arkansas.

I'd spent hours painting that chapel. I'd also made a special trip to a Kansas City botanical garden and Bella Vista, Arkansas, to paint chapels there. Their Frank Lloyd Wright style architecture intrigued me as an artist. Now, as I looked out over the vista, I knew how to honor my grandfather and the money he'd attempted to set aside for the church. We could build a chapel up here, for people to use whenever they wanted to feel closer to God, without all the political agendas and vicious rhetoric from people like Atwell.

Both of the architects who'd designed those other chapels were gone, unfortunately, but I could reach out to some of my artist friends to see who was currently working in that same style. I felt hopeful I could find someone who could design what I'd envisioned.

I continued on toward the winery barn, as I'd begun to think of it, feeling full of life. The minute I came out of the trees, though, I saw the dreaded Lexus sitting in the parking lot. Damn, that man wasn't giving up. Only now I understood why he wouldn't.

I reached the barn just in time to see Logan walk away from the man standing next to his car. *Fuck, what has he said to him?* I needed to put an end to this once and for all.

"Mr. Atwell, I thought we'd had our say. What brings you back to *my* property?" I said, knowing full well I was stretching things a bit. I wasn't the owner, not yet. It was still in probate, but if the attorney was correct, it would all be mine... Eventually.

The older man looked surprised to see me. Somehow I must've snuck up on him. Maybe he thought I'd cleared town like I'd intended before my sudden change of plans.

"I've been asked by the church leadership to ask you to reconsider..."

"There's no need, Mr. Atwell. My step-grandmother and I have come to an agreement over my inheritance. As of now, I'm the official heir once again, and with no strings this time. I'm told I won't have to attend your church to inherit my grandpa's estate. Since that's off the table, I think it would be best if you vacate the premises and don't return."

"Well," he huffed. "You'll be hearing from my attorney," he said as he plopped back into the front seat of his ridiculously expensive car and spun out... again.

I quickly called Ms. Beth and told her the windbag had been back causing trouble and that he said he was going to get his attorney involved. She probably needed to have the attorney we met this morning get in touch with me so we could prepare for whatever madness the SOB planned on bringing down on us.

I walked into the barn and found Logan wiping down the counter. "Um, I'm guessing he was harassing you. I'm sorry about that."

"You don't have to apologize for that old windbag. He said he had a talk with my aunt and your step-grand-mother and basically, he's stirring up trouble. I know my aunt and cousin are really attached to the church and all. I hate that he's going to make it difficult for them. He really is a jerk."

"Narcissistic asshole," I said, then sighed. "We need to put up some no trespassing signs and ban him from the property, then call the sheriff if he comes back. He's been told to stay away twice, that's enough, I think, to satisfy the law."

"Maybe not out here, he's a pastor, and the law tends to sidestep preachers, especially one as powerful as him."

I shrugged. "Maybe, but at least we can try."

I got the phone call from Mr. Conner the next day telling me the church had made an objection to the will in probate. Not exactly a complete surprise, but still a giant pain in my ass. "So, do you think they'll win?"

The attorney chuckled. "Seriously doubtful. As you well know, your grandpa's will was very specific. You were to attend his church and your fellow churchgoers were to nurture and support you. Since the pastor publicly embarrassed you and made you feel uncomfortable, you have a very legitimate reason for leaving. At worst, they'll prolong the probate process, but I doubt they'll win in court."

I breathed a sigh of relief at that, but our conversation still had me feeling uneasy. "Thanks, Mr. Conner. I know you're Ms. Beth's attorney and handling the probate stuff, but do I need to hire someone to represent me?" I asked.

"You sure are welcome to and, quite frankly, it's not a bad idea. I don't know how hard the church will come at you personally, but if they push, it might be wise to have someone in your corner who can stand up to them."

I thought about that for a moment, then decided I would pursue it. I called a friend, an attorney in

Nashville, and he immediately referred me to Mr. Erickson, who agreed to represent me.

I guessed I should've been more prepared for the worst. I mean, nothing had worked out since my grandpa's death. Not that I was really blaming him. I got it, I did. He wanted to believe in his church, but just couldn't see them for what they were, but there was no sense in getting worked up over it now. Atwell was an ass, always had been, and he'd do what he could to bring me down. *He really did represent Satan so much more than he represented Christ*, I thought. Then said out loud, "Get thee behind me, Satan," and wished like hell I'd said that when the asshole had come around last time.

Oh well. There was nothing I could do now but put my nose to the grindstone here on the farm. I'd help Logan with the vineyard, move forward with the homestead restoration planning, and let my new attorney worry about the rest.

Twelve

Logan

T HE FEW TIMES MATT came to the farm since telling me he'd likely inherit the property, I only caught glimpses of him before he was carried away with plans or meetings with contractors. He remained friendly, but noticeably kept his distance.

Although not pursuing more with him was disheartening, it's not like I could blame him for the decision. He had a lot to lose. The jackass pastor coming after him with a vengeance didn't help matters. So, I resigned myself to pine for the handsome artist from a distance and go on with my daily chores, trying to think about him as my boss. Memories of the mind-blowing kisses we'd shared and how feeling his lips on mine had lit me up inside were hard to forget though.

Probate worked out well for me. I got paid as agreed by Mr. Brinks before he died, and basically had free license to do anything I wanted as long as it didn't cost too much. My experimentation with stressing the vines was paying off too. The grapes were much sweeter already after lowering the irrigation. I kept my fingers crossed that we wouldn't get hit with too much rain between now and the harvest.

One morning when Matt stopped by to tell me there would be strangers on the property looking at the cabin, he stood close enough that I could smell the soap on him. He also had a little smudge of what I assumed was paint on his neck. God, it really did take everything in me not to reach over and wipe it off with my thumb. I desperately wanted to ask what he'd been painting, too, but held my tongue. The more I stuck to only discussing vineyard matters with Matt, the better.

So, I just nodded and walked away, but not before catching another delicious whiff of him that left me buzzing. I knew if I didn't burn off some of this pent-up energy, I might explode. I ended up crawling into the brand new vats that lined the side of the winery and cleaned them thoroughly. "Stupid rules..." I said, and heard the echo around me inside the vat.

Next, I cleaned the grape-processing machines in the lean-to part of the barn, since we couldn't afford any foreign matter getting into the juice and disrupting the fermentation process. By the time I finished, I'd worked up a sweat and burned off some of the frustration churning inside me. At least the sorry state of my would-be love life ensured I gave all of the equipment a good going over. As the weeks flew by, with little else to do but work,

I forced myself to focus more and more of my mental and physical energy on the grapes. If I had to sacrifice a relationship with Matt for this winery, I'd be damned if I wasn't going to do all I could to ensure its success.

There are basically five things to look for in grape ripeness. The color of the grapes and the color of the stems were paramount. It's also important the grapes plumped up as the sugar increased in the final stage of ripening.

Another telltale sign was when the grape seeds became chewable. I didn't really like that method of evaluating ripeness, because each variety could be tricky. The thing I tended to pay the closest attention to was the taste of the grapes. Not only would the tangy flavor of the peel or flesh go away, but the special overtones each vintner strived for would show up in those last few days of ripening. Picking your grapes too early or too late, and you'd lose flavor.

I managed to mostly avoid my hunk of a boss, until the week before I thought the grapes would ripen. I found him by the homestead speaking to a very handsome contractor. I pushed down the jealousy I had no right to feel, and rushed over before he left.

Matt looked up and smiled before the guarded look he always seemed to have around me crossed his face. "Hi, Matt. I need to speak to you when you have a chance."

He nodded, then remembering the man standing next to him, said, "Todd, this is our resident winemaker, Logan Johnson. Logan, this is Todd Thompson, who may be doing the work out here to preserve the mill... If I win in probate court, that is."

I instantly wanted to comfort Matt when a look of sadness passed over his face. I could imagine how much stress he'd been under this whole time. Todd, however, nodded at the both of us before excusing himself. "I'm going to check out the foundation of the mill and talk to my dad to see if we're both on the same page. Matt, I'll also check with the log-cabin guys and see how much they're going to charge to undo that mess over there," he said, pointing at the half-fallen-down cabin.

Todd left us alone then and I couldn't help but watch the beautiful man walk away. When my eyes snapped back to Matt, a dark shadow had crossed his face. "What?" I asked.

"Nothing," Matt said, sounding a little annoyed. Then he took a deep breath and rubbed at the back of his neck. He seemed uncomfortable all of a sudden. "Just so you know, Todd's married to the local doctor."

I laughed nervously. "What?" I asked again, and wondered if maybe he'd caught me checking Todd out. When Matt's expression didn't change, I sighed and looked down, before muttering under my breath, "I wasn't gonna go attack him or anything."

"So, anyway," I said, making eye contact with him again, "...next week, I think we need to harvest the grapes. As far as I can tell, the grapes are close to being ripe. Can you help me harvest? It'll take us at least a week unless you've got some buddies who'll donate some of their time to help."

Matt's face finally cleared, and he smiled. "This is exciting. Um, yeah, I've got some friends who might help, but they're gonna harass us for free wine when it's done. If we need more hands, I should be able to hire a couple of seasonal workers, but need to check with the attorney about their pay beforehand. I'm not sure what I can get lined up in a week, but I'll try."

I matched his smile. These mostly solitary weeks on the vineyard had been... well, pretty damn lonely. All I did was work, and I didn't have any friends around here to help blow off steam or otherwise distract me from thinking about the guy I couldn't have. Despite my best efforts to pack down my feelings about Matt, my desires were only growing stronger. So, yeah, having more people on the farm for a while to help with the harvest would be a welcome change.

"I'm excited, too," I said. "These grapes have the feel of being a good batch. It hasn't hurt that we've had a drought. When I first got here, they were so overwatered, they were already splitting. Not good for wine. But, they're looking perfect, knock on wood."

"I'll start making some calls to my friends and the attorney after I'm done with Todd and his dad. I'll let you know who I get lined up to help us."

As Matt walked away, I drank in the sight of him, watching the way his body moved with every step. It'd been almost three months since I'd arrived. To be honest, I loved running the show by myself, but being part of a team also felt good. Matt might not be my partner in any sense of the word, but we were still very much in this together. If my instincts and approach were right, we'd soon be producing wine good enough to rival the wineries I'd worked at in California and Oregon. That goal hadn't changed, and reminding myself of that helped keep my emotions in check... most of the time, anyway.

THIRTEEN

MATT

A S FRUSTRATING AS FANTASIZING about Logan had become, it was still better than trying to sort through my actual feelings. When he showed up while Todd was here surveying the mill, and all but eye fucked the man, I felt a wave of jealousy wash over me. I kept having to remind myself, Logan wasn't mine, but damn, it was hard to convince my heart.

When he told me the grapes were ready to be harvested, or at least they would be soon, his excitement rubbed off on me. This wine-making venture was all my grandpa's doing, but the way just telling me about the harvest caused Logan to light up, that was enough for me.

I'd offered the help of friends to pick the grapes, but in truth, I didn't know anyone who could actually help. My friends were all other artists, the kind who stayed holed up in their studios creating new work and rarely went out into nature unless it was for their art. Collectively, they were about the furthest thing from gym rats or even weekend workout warriors.

Honestly, the only reason I'd told Logan otherwise was because I'd become momentarily intoxicated by him. When the breeze shifted, I'd caught a whiff of him… smoky with a little tinge of the alcohol from the wine. He'd smelled the same the first time I'd kissed him, and all I wanted to do in that moment was nuzzle into his neck and breathe deeply. Ugh, I was so screwed.

When Logan left, all but skipping back down the lane, I went over to where Todd and his daddy, Amos, stood. "Do you know anyone who'd be willing to come help harvest our grapes next week?" I asked.

The men looked at me like I'd grown a horn and I shrugged. "I sort of got stuck with all these grapes when my grandpa died, and I don't really know that many people around here who could help. There's probably a fair number who wouldn't give me the time of day anyway, not after the church fiasco."

Amos nodded. "Yeah, we heard a bit about your troubles in Mayville. My husband and I could probably come help. How about you, son?" Amos asked, looking at Todd.

"I'm happy to lend a hand too. I can ask Ash if he's available, but I think it all depends on when you need help. He'll be working at the clinic during the day."

"I know y'all are busy," I said. "I hate to be a bother."

"Nonsense," Amos said. "It's a small town, you got to rely on your neighbors when you can, and knowing what you've been through, I'm guessing your network is pretty small. Emanual and I will call around and see who else we can find."

His kindness had me blushing. I wasn't someone who asked for help, and if I'd allowed myself to think a bit, I wouldn't have asked now. I could almost hear my grandpa mumbling under his breath about taking charity from neighbors. I just got carried away with Logan and the way his face lit up so cute and sweet when he was telling me about the harvest. I didn't want to let him down either.

"Well, thank you. I'll welcome all the help I can get, and you've got my number. I doubt I'll be able to afford to pay more than a couple people at most, though. It'll be different next year, but until the probate is settled, I'm afraid things are a little short over here."

"Nobody will ask to be paid, you can count on that. Just share some wine with us when it's done and we'll be happy as can be," Todd said, causing me to blush again, but I couldn't help but smile as well.

I felt hopeful as they left. Finally, something was going right. I mean, I tried not to complain too much. I'd had a very pleasant life and my grandpa's stipend had helped a lot in making my life pretty easy. However, aside from the probate mess, things had recently taken another shitty turn when, after giving my notice on my apartment in Lebanon, the landlady sold the building. That meant I had to clear out sooner than planned. It also shortened my timeline for photographing, cataloging, and parting with my paintings–my babies, really–as I sent them off to galleries.

In all, eighty paintings, the summation of my life for the past seven years, were packaged and shipped. When the studio was empty, I allowed myself a week to wallow in self-pity. This was why I'd always struggled with selling my artwork. Parting with each painting felt like giving up pieces of my soul. I hadn't found much solace at the farm either, since everywhere I turned, I saw Logan.

Spending every day working with the sexy vintner I'd not been able to get my hands on was difficult. I tried avoiding him as much as possible without being obvious. No matter how hard I tried, though, I couldn't shake the memories of him in my arms, the feeling of our lips brushing together. *Damn*, I thought, then let out a heavy sigh.

I sighed repeatedly that week and muttered, "oh well," under my breath just as often. *You can't cry over spilled milk. Life goes on and you do the best you can.* I summoned up several more of my grandpa's old sayings too, none of which made me feel better. I really liked Logan, and was tempted to sell the freaking winery just so I could date him. It wasn't like I needed a winery anyway. But then I remembered the promise I'd made to Ms. Beth and to myself to give this my all, and knew I didn't have it in me to just walk away now.

The objection to Grandpa's will filed by the church was... well, let's just say, it took all my raising to not go full-out postal on the pastor's self-righteous ass. He claimed that my grandfather had told him if I rejected the will, all the money was to go to the church. Knowing Grandpa as well as I had, I knew for a fact he would never have given it all to the church even if I refused. If he had truly wanted that, he'd have spelled it out in writing, and talked about it with Ms. Beth besides.

I admit, I didn't understand why Grandpa had chosen to set things up the way he did. I suspected he just trusted that Ms. Beth would make it all right in the end, but dang, he'd certainly misjudged that horrible pastor.

During my self-pity week, I spent time remembering my childhood, the good and the bad. I remembered the pastor coming into youth meetings and yelling at me in particular about how sinful I'd behaved, even when I wasn't doing much of anything. He seemed to hate me from the start. I never really understood why.

I'd asked my grandpa about that once, and he'd simply shaken his head. Curiously, though, he didn't seem surprised by the question. "The pastor was sweet on your mom for a while, before she married your daddy," he'd told me. "I don't think he ever really got over it, but your parents only had eyes for each other. They started dating their freshman year, and that was it for the both of them. High school sweethearts to the end."

I recalled how Grandpa got a bit misty-eyed telling me that story. He'd never held back talking about my parents whenever I asked, but I knew he felt their loss as acutely as I did up to the day he died. I'd almost asked him if I was possibly the pastor's son, but one glance at my grandpa quelled that notion. Seeing his wild nest of hair that matched my own, and remembering that my daddy had it too, along with the same green eyes we all had, left no doubt. I definitely descended from the Brinks family line.

Since surveying the mill, Todd and Amos had been running numbers along with Tom as we discussed renovation cost projections. Ms. Beth's attorney, Mr. Conner, had assured me and my new attorney over and over that the church's claims were unlikely to win, so I just plowed forward with the plans.

Ultimately, I loved what Tom had come up with for the design. Since the log cabin would have to be completely taken apart, then rebuilt, he suggested we add it onto the rear of the mill. He had drawn the plans so the log cabin's wide front porch would overlook the stream that powered the water wheel. The side door that at one time probably led to a summer kitchen would be used to attach the log home to the mill.

The redesign allowed for adding a little apartment to the top floor for the artist in residence I'd hoped to sponsor each year. I'd already decided I wanted to spend some of Grandpa's money on sponsoring young gifted artists. No artist could ask for a more inspirational place than this beautiful property, at least that was how I felt, and I wanted to share it with the world in that way.

Logan continued to star in my daydreams. I thought of him way more than I should've, but nothing I did seemed to curtail my fantasizing. All I could do was try to avoid him even more, because it was getting increasingly difficult to keep my hands off him. I was truly committed to staying professional, but dang, it was a true test of willpower.

At one point, my mind was so full of Logan that I considered mentioning it to my attorney, but that was when Atwell started lying about what he said Grandpa had told him. It just felt wrong to pile something else onto the legal mess I was already dealing with.

Not only that, but I also didn't want to share my feelings about Logan with other people. Like my feelings for him were special... private, and deserved to be protected. And hell, if I was going to tell anyone about my feelings, Logan deserved to be the first to hear it. Not that I even knew how he felt about me at this point, maybe he just thought of me as his boss now. Letting my own thoughts fall down that depressing rabbit hole wouldn't help anything, though, least of all my productivity.

So, I kept myself busy with the many changes taking place in my life.

With my apartment gone, I ended up moving back into the old trailer behind the log cabin. My grandpa had maintained it as well as anyone could maintain a sixty-year-old trailer, but it was far from perfect. Rust coated the outside, the carpet was as old as the house, and the dark paneling was still as ugly as the day it was made. The place was clean and functional, but dated and dreary.

Ms. Beth had offered to let me move in with her, but I'd refused. She didn't need the burden of putting me up for who knew how long, though I did make a note to myself to visit her more often. No, I grew up in this old sack of rust, and I could tolerate it until the spaces I actually cared about were renovated and turned into my new home.

Of course, what I hadn't anticipated was that living less than half a mile from Logan would test my willpower to resist him all the more. The long nights where all I'd been able to think about was him and how easy it would be to walk down that old road to his doorstep and offer myself to him were agony.

The first night, visions of wrapping my arms around a naked Logan got so overwhelming that I got up, got dressed, and almost went over to the barn. I had my hand on the trailer door to leave when I remembered I'd promised to be professional. Being a man of my word, I stripped, climbed back in bed, and spent the rest of the night staring at my ceiling. *God*, I thought, *I might not be able to do this after all.*

After another restless night and a morning making phone calls about the property, I walked over to the barn to see if Logan could use my help, and found him dancing in front of a grill to Lady Gaga's "Stupid Love." I thought it pretty cute and wasn't at all prepared for when he began to really move his body to the music. Seeing his hips gyrating in perfect rhythm to the beat had me mesmerized.

When he looked over and saw me, I froze. My brain was totally short-circuited by how sexy this man was, how much I wanted him. He blushed and quickly grabbed his phone to turn the sound down.

"Did you want something, Matt?" he asked, and I swallowed around the lump in my throat.

"Yeah. Where did you learn to dance like that?" I asked.

He chuckled as his adorable blush deepened. "Well, Richy Jackson, Lady Gaga's choreographer, has YouTube videos on how to do it. Wanna learn?"

I slowly shook my head, then blurted out, "I'm sorry, Logan. I'm too attracted to you for all this. You're all I think about. I'm not sure how to deal with it, especially since I'm living here now."

Logan looked startled and the weight of what I had said settled between us. He began absently tapping the side of his phone with his finger, like he was suddenly restless, and I could've sworn his breath quickened. Was he nervous? Finally, Logan cleared his throat, and asked, "You're moving into the barn with me?"

It was my turn to look startled. "No, I moved back into the old trailer. Sorry, I should've mentioned it sooner."

He seemed to relax at that, then his face screwed up, and he asked, "The old dead trailer behind the fallen-down log cabin?"

Him not even trying to hide his understandable disgust for the old rust bucket eased some of the tension between us and made me chuckle. "Yeah, I grew up in it, so I don't mind. At least, not too much."

"Damn, does it even have electricity?" he asked, clearly ignoring my word vomit moments ago about him living rent-free in my head.

"Yeah," I said, feeling a little defensive. His question brought up memories of when I was a kid and a couple bullies picked on me for being trailer trash. "It's just temporary. It'll be fine."

Logan seemed to pick up on my defensiveness. "I didn't mean to judge, it's just that you shouldn't be staying in that run-down place when there's plenty of room here."

"What? With you in the barn?"

He nodded hesitantly. "I mean, it's a two-bedroom apartment, so it's not like we'd be living on top of one another," he said, then quickly added, "Or, we could pull a bed into one of the tasting rooms, since the winery isn't open, if that feels better to you."

"Did you miss the part about me being too attracted to live half a mile down the old road? You're already driving me to distraction. I can't *live* with you."

Logan turned the grill off and walked over to where I stood. "I never told you to stop liking me. I'm attracted to you too, that hasn't changed. But you became more distant, more professional I guess, and I just thought you weren't that interested in me anymore."

I almost choked. "What, the drooling tongue hanging out every time I'm around you wasn't a clear indication of how I felt?"

He laughed. "You haven't been obvious at all, and certainly not as much as me. It seems like we're both struggling for nothing." He took a deep breath, letting it out slowly.

"So, I'm fixing steak and it's a monster, too much for just me. I'm also baking a huge potato with some leftover baked beans. Why don't you join me for dinner, and we can chat. We can't be the first coworkers to pursue a relationship... I mean, if that's what you want."

"Yes, in fact, hell yes!" I said, and we both laughed.

He closed the distance between us, leaned up on his toes, and gave me a chaste kiss on the lips. "I've been wanting to do that for a long time," he admitted.

"Man, you and me both."

I leaned down and kissed him again. This time there was nothing chaste about it.

When he pulled back, I could see the longing that matched mine, and I'd have happily taken it to the next level when he put the skids on. "I like you, Matt, more than I've liked anyone in... well, ever really, but we both have a lot to lose here. Neither one of us can afford to screw things up."

I nodded, understanding where he was going. "So, we should take it slow?"

"Should, yes. Want to? No!" he practically shouted, causing me to chuckle with him.

"Okay, you've convinced me, but I get to kiss you, right?"

"Mmm," he moaned in answer, and that was almost enough for me to throw caution to the wind.

"So, slow it is..." I said, and ever so slowly began pressing soft kisses to the side of his neck. As I wrapped my arms around his back and he leaned into my touch, his body pressed flush against mine, all the jagged emotions floating inside me seemed to settle into place.

LOGAN

MATT AND THE FOOD were equally delicious. Rather than having an in-depth chat over dinner as planned, we ended up kissing and touching our way through the meal. After he headed back to his trailer, I locked the door because getting caught dancing once was enough, then squealed like a teenager and danced around the big room of the barn. *OMG, he wants me! And I swear, kissing him again was better than the first time. How is that possible?*

But leave it to me to be my own cockblocker, putting the brakes on what could've easily been a magical night spent in his arms. I didn't think dating my boss would be a problem, so long as we didn't let it interfere with work or cloud our judgment. Well, that and there had to be more to it than just fucking. Knowing myself too dang well, I knew that I couldn't be casual about Matt Brinks.

The past few weeks had been proof enough of that. Nope, I was already a bit crazy about him and needed to ensure we were on same page before anything serious happened between us.

The following week was chaos. I went out on Wednesday morning, tasted the grapes, and they were perfect. I pulled the refractometer out and it just confirmed what I already knew.

I texted Matt, saying it was time to harvest.

By noon, Matt, Todd, Amos, Amos's husband, who everyone called Doc, and several others showed up to help. I showed everyone what to do, including which grapes to choose.

"Listen, there's a bit of an art to all this. You only want to pick the best grapes. Feel free to pick around bunches where the grapes aren't looking as good. At the end of the day, we want the best tasting juice because that'll make the best tasting wine."

I followed the group around for the first hour and was surprised at how fast they seemed to be catching on to which grapes were the best. When I was confident they didn't need supervision, I took a row myself and quickly began harvesting the grapes. I worked a lot faster than anyone else in the group, of course, having years of experience behind me. By dinnertime, we'd finished over sixty percent of the harvest. Everyone hauled their grapes to the barn, and I showed them how to pour them into the sorting machine.

The sorter Mr. Brinks had bought was way too fancy and expensive for this type of operation. The fact was, the vineyards I'd worked at before did a lot of this stuff by hand. But I wasn't going to complain about his having invested in the equipment since it saved literally hundreds of man-hours.

Everyone gathered around as I turned the machine on, and watched in amazement as it destemmed the grapes, then automatically sorted them for optimal production.

Within a very short time, all the grapes had gone through the machine and were ready for processing. "Wow, that was fast," Matt said when I flipped the machine off.

"Yeah, your grandpa bought a top-of-the-line sorter. It processes three tons per hour."

"Really?" he asked. "It's a bit overkill, huh?"

I chuckled. "Yeah, and it's unusual for this size operation to have such fancy equipment, but it would've taken a lot longer if we hadn't had it."

Matt nodded but looked confused. From what I could tell, his grandpa wasn't one for extravagance, but knowing there was a definite lack of wine-making experts in this part of the country made me think he might've been savvier than we were giving him credit for.

Regardless, the almost two-hundred-thousand dollars he'd spent on the machine was outside most vintners' reach. However, as I explored the machinery, I was convinced we could extend the vineyard to five or ten times the size in the coming years and still not overload the equipment.

I explained to the novices that, "Because we're making a red wine, we have to crush and ferment the grapes before they are pressed. We need the peelings to help with sugar content, color, and even natural yeast. I'll finish off the harvest, add it to these, then I'll add the yeast."

"How long before you press them?" Doc asked.

I smiled, enjoying explaining it all. I'd always been a bit of an extrovert, especially when it came to the wine-making process. Discussing the finer points of it with vineyard workers brought my inner wine geek out to play.

"Well, it's a detailed process. We call this stage maceration. And we want to allow the grapes to remain in contact with the skins as long as possible. Our operation is way more advanced than it should be for its size, but because Mr. Brinks thought ahead and gave me some good cold storage to work with, I can manage the temperatures of these grapes so well that I'm going to try to keep them macerating for at least two weeks. I might even try for three before I start to ferment."

The process was complicated, and as I went about my routine, checking sulfur content and reassessing sugar levels, I left most of the details out. I couldn't begin those finer details of management until I had the rest of the grapes harvested and added to the mix anyway, so mostly I just enjoyed letting the group ask me questions.

I noticed that Matt was the most attentive of the bunch during my descriptions of the process. I guessed I couldn't blame him. In the end, this would all be his and learning every step of the process would be imperative even if he didn't want to be actively involved.

When I was confident the unfermented grape juice, which was called the must, was secure for the evening, I rinsed off the equipment as Matt treated everyone to pizza he'd ordered earlier. Knowing tomorrow would be another day of processing, I used the large broom to sweep the excess grapes and discarded elements to the side. I'd need to talk to Matt about composting at some point. I had ideas about that too, but seeing how overwhelmed the poor man was already, I didn't want to push things too fast.

When I was done, everyone was getting ready to leave. I thanked them all profusely for their help. Knowing that without them, I'd be a lot further behind than I was now.

I kicked my boots off at the door and joined Matt on the porch swing along the barn's patio. He handed me a couple slices of pizza that he'd apparently set aside for me since I'd missed the group dinner. *So sweet*, I thought. Matt slowly rocked the swing back and forth while I devoured the pizza.

"That was intense. I mean processing the grapes, not you inhaling your food just now," he said, causing me to laugh.

"Dude, this is a small vineyard. Wait until it gets bigger."

He looked at me funny. "You think we should get bigger?" he asked.

"I do, and judging by the equipment your grandpa purchased, I'm guessing he planned on growing it significantly as well."

"Dang, I really am green when it comes to all this."

I reached over and patted his knee. "Don't beat yourself up, it takes time to learn and understand it all. Meanwhile, your grandpa hired me to make sure everything works out."

Matt's eyes traveled from my hand on his knee up to my face, and I could see his expression had softened. "Thanks for being here," he said quietly.

I leaned into his side, and said, "Thanks for having me here."

Anticipation fluttered around inside me like butterflies as our lips touched, then Matt moved in to deepen the kiss. When he pulled back, I almost groaned from the loss of contact.

Oh my God, I wanted him. And letting things go at this point caused my chest to burn with desire.

We'd both decided just a few days before to keep things cool for now. I had to remind myself we had both decided to take it slow. It wouldn't be fair of me to push those boundaries at this point.

So, after accepting things as they were, I curled into him. His firm body, with his long torso and strong arms, was so perfect for cuddling. He wrapped his arm around me, and before I knew it, I was sound asleep.

Fifteen

Matt

T HE DAY HAD BEEN exhausting, confusing, amazing, and rewarding all at the same time. It was beyond awesome to have help from the community. Amos and Todd had been excited to help, and when I met Doc, I realized just how much I liked all of them. Once everything settled down, I wanted to have them all out for a huge cookout. I could easily see them becoming close friends of mine, and I hoped they viewed me the same.

Everyone left around seven that evening and just as they were getting ready to go, Logan came out of the backroom, literally covered in grape juice. He looked exhausted, but pleased. I felt the same about the incredibly productive day we'd had.

He plopped down next to me on the big, oversized swing on the barn's patio, ate the pizza I'd saved him, and kissed me. It wasn't chaste, but I could tell there wasn't much energy left in him. When we broke apart, he let out a contented sigh and snuggled into my side before falling asleep in my arms.

My heart did bizarre things then, like the feeling of rightness of having this man nestled against me meant he was mine. He smelled so good, a mixture of the grapes we'd just picked and a floral smell that must've been his shampoo, along with a strong masculine scent. Not wanting to wake him, I leaned in ever so slightly and breathed deeply. The contrast of the three smells mixed together kicked my libido into high gear.

There was just so much to lose with a romance between the two of us. Luckily, he wasn't pushing for a lot more, and I still wasn't sure how much I should pursue someone who worked for me. There were just so many potential pitfalls to consider.

I wasn't one for creating a life plan, preferring instead to let life happen as it would, but that didn't mean I couldn't imagine what it would be like to have Logan as a long-term lover. Would it always be this tender, this sweet? Was there more to it than just that? Would our sex life be... less? I kissed the top of his head and knew that wasn't going to be the case here. There was just too much attraction between us for our love life to be anything short of amazing.

I swung back and forth on the swing for a long time, letting him rest. When my legs began to fall asleep, I lifted up, waking him.

"Oh, shit, I fell asleep," he said, sitting up and rubbing at his still tired-looking eyes. "Sorry, I tend to do that during harvest time." He reached over to kiss me good-night, and I pulled him into an embrace.

"I really like you, Logan," I said in a whisper, causing him to shiver.

He swallowed hard and nodded. "Yeah, me too," he said.

I grabbed his hand and led him to his apartment door, then waited as he unlocked it. When he turned back around to face me, I kissed him passionately, which made my head spin, before saying goodnight.

I would've much rather gone in with him and spent the rest of the night ravishing his body, but it wasn't time. I wasn't sure when it would be, but it certainly wasn't now.

I got onto the used ATV I'd bought a couple days before and drove back along the forest road to the trailer. Logan had offered to let me stay with him in the barn, and although that was intensely appealing for various reasons, I wasn't ready to move in with him just yet. Also, being tucked into the old run-down place made me think of Grandpa and my childhood, and there was an odd comfort in that. I grew up with a freedom most kids don't have. I knew every nook and cranny of this farm, plus a few other neighboring farms, because after coming to live with Grandpa, I spent every summer exploring the area.

Being here reminded me how the simple things in life could often be the best. We'd lived like paupers, but in more ways than one that made me rich in experiences. It was hard at the time, but I wouldn't trade it for anything now. Had I been given everything I ever wanted in life, like video games, computers, and other things my grandpa thought a boy shouldn't be using during summer breaks, I'd have missed the world around me. That, of course, generally made me an oddball among other people my age, except maybe Logan. His love of the vineyard seemed to be as intense as my love of nature.

I was restless when I got back to the trailer, and even though I no longer had an art studio, I felt the need to channel my energy into my art. I'd turned my old bedroom into a makeshift studio, complete with an easel, canvas, and paint sitting on my old beat-up dresser. As soon as I'd changed my clothes, I began to paint.

I got lost in the work, and when I finally came back down to earth, the sun was rising. I looked at the painted canvas and smiled. It was abstract, but I'd basically captured the grape harvest. I'd represented every person who was there in some form or another.

I didn't do a lot of abstract painting, but somehow it seemed like the entire wine-making process was abstract in my head, like it was blurry, something I couldn't quite see, but loved nonetheless. The painting still needed more work, but I knew I was going to hang it in the winery barn and name it *Day One*.

I fell into bed the minute I finished rinsing out my brushes. I slept hard and deep, but I had recurring dreams of picking grapes and kissing Logan.

We were figures inside a painting with intense colors awash on the canvas, like something out of the Renais-

sance. Logan and I stood along rows of grape vines, and I could sense I was in my own vineyard.

People were around us, but they were blurred out, and I couldn't quite make out who they were, but they were friendly, accepting...

The dream kept coming back to Logan standing in front of me, me kissing him, and him laughing happily before pulling back and disappearing down the rows again.

It was like being in the vineyard and kissing Logan somehow belonged together.

Logan

I WAS DISAPPOINTED WHEN Matt didn't show up for work the next day. Although we hadn't really discussed it, I certainly thought he would. Instead, when I came out of the barn with my coffee in hand to see who'd just pulled up, Doc and Amos climbed out of the vehicle. "We figured you might need a little more help finishing off those grapes."

"You figured correctly, but you sure you wanna tackle another day?"

"We want to learn more about the process, and figured if you got another day of free labor out of us, you'd be willing to teach us more."

I laughed. "That sounds like a really great trade."

After we had coffee and omelets I quickly threw together, the two men and I got to work finishing off the harvest. I expected them to leave at noon, putting in four hours like they had the day before, but to my pleasant surprise, they continued helping until we had finished the last row.

"Y'all, I'm beat. Should I call for another pizza to be delivered?"

Both men laughed. "No, let us take you out to the local diner."

I looked at my clothes, and said, "I'd welcome that, but I'm still a mess and need to finish off the grapes before going to bed."

"Listen," Doc said. "This is a blue-collar town. Seeing a man come into the diner after a long day's work will earn you more respect than if you're clean as a whistle. We aren't gonna change, and you don't need to either. We promise to get you back in plenty of time to finish off the grapes. Besides, we're wanting to watch you do it and we're both old men who need their evening meal."

I laughed. "You're both harder workers than most of the young people I've worked with before. So, no more old men stuff. And you win, but I really can't be out long."

Amos put his hand up and said, "Scout's honor. We'll have you back quick as a wink."

I chuckled and followed the men out to their truck and let them drive me into town.

I hadn't seen much of Crawford City, to be honest, but I'd noticed how cute the town was when I'd come looking for Ms. Brinks. It was smaller than Mayville, and because I grew up coming to visit my aunt, I knew where a few of the necessary shops were, but I hadn't spent any real time exploring the area since moving here.

I wasn't in the least bit surprised when the two men pulled up in front of the Crawford City Café and parked. The same place Matt had picked up our delicious lunch the day he told me he'd be inheriting the property after all.

The diner was sweet and very traditional. People sat in booths and at tables that seemed haphazardly placed around the building. In the middle of it all was a huge plywood buffet line that stretched from one side of the place to the other. On one end were salad fixings, and everything from fried fish to roast on the other. The entire thing was bursting at the seams with sides. This buffet was over the top.

The only food we'd had all day were our morning omelets and the bologna sandwiches I'd thrown together for lunch. The three of us dug into our meals like starved animals.

"That kind of physical labor can make you really hungry," I said when I finally came up for air.

"It's good for a person to work hard from time to time," Doc said.

"Well, you're the doc," I said.

"He is, or at least was," said a voice behind me that had me startled. "Now he's a retired layabout forcing his son to do all the work he refuses to do." I turned around to see a drop-dead gorgeous man dressed in scrubs.

When he saw me, he smiled. "Hi, I don't think we've met. I'm Ashton Nash."

"Oh, you're Todd's husband?" I asked, shaking the man's hand.

"The one and only. Please, call me Ash. And speaking of my handsome hubby..."

Todd came in behind Ash and patted my back. "So, did you get the rest of the harvest in?" he asked.

"I did, thanks to your dad and Doc," I replied happily. "They talked me into coming here to stuff my face before I go back and show them the wine-making process."

Ash shook his head. "Dads, neither one of you need to get any ideas about starting a winery. You've got more on your plate now than you did before the two of you retired."

Both men sitting across from me laughed. "We do like our hobbies. It's more fun when you're doing stuff because you want to versus doing it for a living."

When I looked confused, Todd said, "After retiring, Dad became my business partner, has opened a hardware store, and Doc over there has become mayor."

"They have potential as vintners as well," I said, and when the two younger men frowned, I shrugged. "Hey, just calling it as I see it."

All four men laughed, then Ash and Todd went to get their plates, while Doc, Amos and I found the dessert section. "Oh my goodness, I haven't had homemade banana pudding in so long. I hope it's as good as my aunt used to make," I said when I sat down, then took a bite and moaned happily. "It's so much better than I remember."

The men smiled at me, and Todd said, "There isn't much better than Southern country cookin'. It'll make you fat as a pig, but it's so good."

I finished off the pudding, then leaned back, letting my full protruding belly testify to Todd's statement.

Ash was as nice as the rest of this family, personable, friendly, and not like most others in the medical profession I'd met over the years. He was much more down-to-earth and relatable than the doctors who'd come to the vineyards out West with their spouses. I always thought it looked like they were all terrified someone might ask them something about their health, and they were constantly on guard against it. It'd be a tough way to live your life.

When we were done eating, we said goodbye to Todd and Ash, and headed back to the farm. As we pulled up, I immediately noticed the Lexus sitting out front. "Shit," I said, causing Doc to turn around.

"What's wrong? Who is that?" he asked.

"A pastor from Mayville who's been giving Matt a lot of crap lately."

"Oh, is that Pastor Atwell?" he asked.

I nodded and we all three climbed out of the truck. I expected Atwell to get out of the car then, but when we walked around, he wasn't in the vehicle. I immediately began scanning for the old man, not trusting what he might be up to out here alone.

When I didn't see him outside, I walked toward the barn just as the man walked out.

"Why were you inside my home when I'm not here?" I asked, not even trying to hide the accusation in my voice.

"Oh, sorry," Atwell said with a smirk. "I thought this was a public winery."

"Nothing says this place is public," I heard Doc say behind me, and the older man jumped when he noticed I wasn't alone.

"I'm going to call the sheriff," I said. "You can explain to her what you're doing trespassing in my home."

"My phone is already ringing," Amos said.

I heard him talking to the sheriff's office as I stood facing the man who'd come out here and made himself at home.

"Sheriff Cross is on her way," Amos said. "Now, Mr. Atwell, I'd recommend that you get in your vehicle and wait for her to arrive. It probably wouldn't do for you to leave until she's had a chance to discuss this with you. I'm guessing word of you fleeing from the sheriff wouldn't sit well with your congregation either."

Atwell's face got redder and redder as Amos spoke. I could see his sense of entitlement as he stared at me. Like somehow, he had the right to come and go as he pleased.

Doc and Amos stayed outside watching Atwell's car as I went in the barn to see what, if anything, had been taken or vandalized. When he'd walked out, he hadn't been carrying anything, so I didn't think he'd stolen from me, but I didn't put it past him to try to break something or do damage to the property in another way.

The entire place looked unaffected, though, and when I came out, the sheriff was standing with the three men.

I walked up to them and when they turned toward me, I said, "It doesn't appear anything's been taken or damaged, but I'd like to know why this man thinks he has the right to walk into my home uninvited when I'm not here."

Atwell huffed and said, "This isn't your home. You are just a freaking *employee*." He snarled out the last word like he was referring to trash.

"This is, in fact, his home," the sheriff countered. "He has every right to be here, but he isn't why I've been called out here. You should know better than to be going in and out of other people's property without permission."

"Well, I do have permission. Mr. Brinks allowed me access to the property whenever I wanted."

"I highly doubt that, but even so, my grandfather is no longer with us," I heard Matt say as he walked toward the group. He looked as angry as I'd ever seen him, tired too. "Why is that man here?" he asked all of us, probably emboldened by the sheriff's presence.

I looked over at Matt, and said, "We just finished the harvest a couple hours ago. Doc and Amos took me to town for dinner and when we got back, Mr. Atwell was coming out of the barn."

"I have every right to be here. This property is in dispute."

"It is not in dispute. You are petitioning the court for a portion of my grandfather's will. That still doesn't give you rights to this property."

With that, Atwell spat at Matt's feet. "Sheriff, all four of these men are degenerate sodomites. I would think you'd be more interested in keeping the likes of them away from good God-fearing folk like myself than harassing me for coming and going on a property I've always been welcome on."

Matt looked at the sheriff. "I have *No Trespassing* signs all over this property, posted as required by the county. I've also already told this man he's not welcome here. Can I press charges for trespassing?"

The sheriff's eyes grew big, but she nodded. "It'll likely cause you some troubles, but you certainly can."

"Troubles or not, Sheriff, these boys have a right to their privacy, and to not having a stranger lurking around and going through their private things," Doc said.

"Yes, Mayor, I agree."

Mr. Atwell, I'll need to have you come with me. I'll allow you to follow me in your vehicle if you can promise me you won't be trying to get away."

"You are not going to arrest me, Sheriff. I haven't done anything wrong."

"Last chance, Mr. Atwell. Can you follow me, or do I need to arrest you and put you in the back of the cruiser?"

Atwell's face darkened as he looked between Matt and me. "You will regret this," he growled.

"Sheriff, that man just threatened these two plain as day," Doc said. "I do believe it's time for him to leave and–" Doc looked at the pastor. "–never return again."

The sheriff let Atwell leave first, then she followed him, I assumed, to the station.

Both Crawford City and Mayville were in the same county, and the jail was located in Mayville, since that was the county seat.

"What the hell was that about?" Amos asked.

"He's been harassing me since I got here. The man hates me. Always has."

"Well, don't feel bad. He was indirectly involved with the burning down of a historical building in Crawford City, though we've got no hard proof. The former mayor and one of Todd's former employees were directly involved. Neither one would incriminate him, but we've all come to suspect the pastor had a hand in it too. I'd be very careful from here on out where that man is concerned. Matt, do you have video surveillance out here?"

Matt laughed. "No, and never thought we'd need it."

"I'd highly suggest you get some sooner rather than later. If you wish, I'll ask Todd about it, since he's the one who rehabbed the barn here. He might know how best to build in the surveillance."

"Really? I hadn't known who did all this for Grandpa. I guess it makes sense it was Todd, since he's the best around."

Amos smiled. "That he is. So, I'll ask Todd to come out tomorrow and help you with the cameras. I don't like you boys being out here in the sticks alone, especially when word gets out that you're pressing charges against the old son of a bitch."

"I'm not going to press charges. I just wanted him removed from the property and to flex a little muscle. I was hoping he'd get the idea and leave us alone."

"I'm gonna tell you, Matt," I said. "I doubt that man is ever going to leave you alone. He's a bully and maybe a bit of a sociopath. Doc and Amos are right, we need to put surveillance in. I'm still not sure he didn't do something in the barn. He could've contaminated the grapes for all I know. I'll keep the batches separate for now, just in case, because it goes without saying the man can't be trusted."

SEVENTEEN

MATT

TODD CAME OUT FIRST thing the next morning to install the security cameras, which was a relief. As soon as he left, though, the crap hit the fan. I had Mindy Cross, a reporter with the *Crawford Independent*, call me about Atwell's run-in with us and the sheriff.

"He didn't break in, Mindy, he was trespassing and was caught coming out of the property caretaker's home when he wasn't there. We don't think he stole anything, but we also can't be certain what all he was doing in there."

Mindy kept trying to spin things until I'd finally had enough. "Mindy, if you need me to come down there and proofread the damned article, I will. I told you already what happened, now don't go spinning this like you're some cable TV personality spewing a fake news story."

She hmphed and then hung up on me. I immediately called over to Ms. Beth and told her what was happening, and the backlash likely coming her way, too, once Mindy's mess of an article hit the paper.

"Oh no, she won't. I'll call Dan, who owns the damned paper, and he'll put an end to that," she said, causing me to smile. I loved being back in a small town, especially one where I knew people who could make things happen, including putting an end to the actions of a troublemaker that served no purpose other than creating drama. I wondered how much better the world would be if some of the large media outlets had a Ms. Beth to keep them from spinning lies.

The next day, I got a call from a man I knew from Grandpa's church. They asked if I could meet with them.

"Absolutely not. In fact, since you are all basically suing to take my inheritance from me, and I'm considering pressing charges against your pastor, I think this call is inappropriate. You can direct any further inquiries to my attorney."

I was just about to hang up, when the man said, "That's what we want to talk to you about. Feel free to bring a witness along, or your attorney. Just, we want to clear the air before things get more out of control."

He told me the time and place they wanted to meet. I guessed it was serious, since the guy didn't even try to convince me to come back to the church. I immediately called my attorney, Mr. Erickson, gave him the name of the man who'd just called, and informed him they wanted to chat.

He wasn't encouraging, saying it could be a trap to make me look bad. I agreed to let him call over to get the lay of the land before I stepped into a possible landmine.

I got a phone call back an hour later, and Mr. Erickson said he thought the meeting would be fine and that he was going to have them meet me at his office, which was just down the road from the church. "Good idea. I should've thought of meeting in a more neutral place myself. What made you change your mind?" I asked.

"The church's Administrative Committee is officially recommending Mr. Atwell be relieved of his pastoral duties," he said.

I was so shocked I didn't really know how to respond. "They want to fire him? Really?"

"Apparently, they are going to announce it to the congregation on Sunday, and wanted to square things with you before they did."

"Square things with me? What's there to square with me?"

"Not sure," he said. "But if they're going to create another stink over your inheritance, I'd say we had better hear it from them. You can let them do all the talking. I'll speak for you, and we can record the whole thing as well, just to protect you from any potential problems."

I agreed to go, then quickly gave Doc a call and asked if he could join me. I told him that despite my attorney's reassurances, I was still a little concerned about it being a trap. I figured, even if this all went to crap, having Crawford City's mayor on my side as a witness could sway things a bit in my favor.

He quickly agreed, and I thanked him over and over. "I'm so sorry for asking this, but I'm an outsider here, especially in Mayville. I'd just feel so much better knowing I've got an advocate there tomorrow."

"Of course, son, I'm happy to help," he said.

I was supposed to meet Logan tonight and watch him work the juice, but I ended up calling and canceling. My head was beginning to hurt, and I just wanted to get the next day over with so I could get on with my life.

Logan was completely understanding, but I could hear the disappointment in his voice. When did I get to the point where I couldn't stand the thought of disappointing this man?

But, no, I didn't want to drag him into this more than I already had. It was definitely better to spend the night alone. I wasn't usually alarmed by things, but I knew how quickly people could turn against you around here. My grandpa had taught me how important it was to be prepared, especially living out on the farm alone, where it could take a long time for law enforcement to get to you. So, I was ready for anything that came my way, but would Logan be okay? I had to assume he would be, especially with Todd having generously put up cameras all around the barn, including one aimed at Logan's apartment door.

Grandpa hadn't really ever been into dogs. He said they cost a lot to feed, and just brought fleas and ticks up to the house. But I sort of wish I had a dog to keep watch over the place. It'd be nice to have some warning before someone was on top of me.

I contemplated visiting the local animal shelter and popped some Tylenol for my headache, then walked back toward the bedroom. Passing by my old one, I noticed work in progress sitting unfinished since the night I'd painted it. I walked in, prepped the paint, and began to add the finishing touches.

As I painted, I remembered the camaraderie the day of the harvest. Neighbors helping neighbors, not for a reward of some kind, but just 'cause they wanted to help. Grandpa would've been against it. *Don't ask for charity.* But I knew for a fact, if any of the people who came out that day needed my help... hell, if anyone on the properties around mine needed help, I'd go without hesitation. Wasn't that what it meant to be neighborly?

When I finished the painting, I felt better. Like I'd reached back into the memory of that experience and pulled all the happiness from it into the darker feelings I had tonight, somehow lightening them.

Feeling the painting was done, I quickly signed it and cleaned up my brushes before heading to bed. Although it wasn't the best or even the most unique example of my work, it probably meant more to me than any of the others had. Somehow it was the beginning of a new life. I chuckled when I remembered what I'd already named it, and said aloud, "*Day One.*"

The next day, Doc showed up in front of my trailer and picked me up. I'd forgone the tailored suit I kept for special occasions and dressed in my only other set of nice clothes, a pair of khaki slacks and a black button-down shirt I wore when I had a gallery showing. I wasn't sure why it felt important to be dressed up, but somehow it did.

Doc was in a good mood, and teased me, saying I cleaned up nice. "Maybe I should introduce you to my barber, though," he said, causing me to laugh.

"Yeah, I've not been paying too much attention to my appearance lately. When I was living in Lebanon, I had a barber just down the road and made routine visits. Otherwise, I'd have let it grow out like this."

"Well, it don't look bad," he said. "It makes you look like the bohemian artist that you are."

I chuckled before getting serious. "So, today could get weird."

"I doubt your attorney will let it get too weird," he said. "Did you know Erickson was a judge for a while? The man was always a hard-ass, which most folks around here prefer."

"So, you think I can trust him?" I asked. I'd been referred to Mr. Erickson by my school buddy, Eric, from Nashville. He thought a local attorney would work better under the circumstances.

"I'm almost sure you can. Besides, if what you told me is correct, I'm guessing the church is trying to save face."

I sighed. "I hope so."

Doc and I arrived thirty minutes early, and Mr. Erickson greeted us like he'd expected Doc to be there. He talked to me about how important it was to let him do the talking, and if something needed to be discussed, we could step out into the hall, or put them off until a decision was made. "You don't want to give them any ammunition in case this is some sort of trap," he'd advised.

I nodded and was happy to sit back quietly while he did all the talking. Trepidation about how things would go naturally kept me quiet, and it wasn't like I was overly eager to chat with these men anyway. I had to remind myself I wasn't the one on trial here, but I still didn't want to accidentally say the wrong thing and make the situation worse.

When the entire Administrative Committee of the church came into the room, I was shocked. These were the same men I'd seen time and time again sitting in the old trailer's living room discussing church stuff with Grandpa. He'd been a member of this committee my entire life. And besides a few who'd passed away, they were all basically the same men who'd always been around.

The men looked over at Doc when Mr. Erickson said he'd be acting as a witness to the discussion. I could tell they wanted to argue, but the committee chair, Mr. Louis Reece, shook his head at the rest of them before they could complain.

"Mr. Brinks, let us get down to why we asked you to come. As we told your attorney, we have relieved Pastor Atwell of his duties as pastor of our church. Of course, this will require a vote of those in attendance on Sunday, but once we lay out the charges, we assume they will accept our recommendation to let him go."

I nodded, but didn't respond. I thought they should've booted the leech years ago, but no one had ever cared about my opinion before.

When it was clear I wasn't going to respond with words, Mr. Reece cleared his throat, and continued, "Most of the leadership knew of the pastor's infidelity, and although we are instructed by Christ to forgive and forget, there is only so much we would tolerate before we'd have to let him go. We were willing to look past even your exposing those truths to the congregation, but when Atwell sued you for the money he'd caused the church to lose by antagonizing you, we had more than six families remove the church from their wills. They were all afraid the church would sue their families for more money."

The old man took a deep breath and shook his head, speaking mostly to himself, as he continued, "The church has never been one to be aggressive against parishioners. We've had a few family members fight us, and we've backed down instead of trying to force an endowment upon them, but never anything like this."

He paused again. I could tell he wanted to see what my reaction would be. But as advised, I remained silent. Finally, after a couple awkward moments, he shook his head again, and continued, "Mr. Atwell was told to back down by this committee, and he refused, saying it was our duty to..." The man trailed off, looking embarrassed. I could guess what he was going to say. Atwell never made any bones about what he thought of me and my "lifestyle" as he called it.

I wanted to fill in the blank. I wanted to yell it at these men who sat by all these years and let that horrible man say hateful things about me and other gay people, but I made eye contact with Mr. Erickson and knew I needed to remain silent.

"Well, it doesn't matter what he thought. In the end, Mr. Atwell disobeyed a direct order from this committee, which he had some limited authority to do as pastor. But when he was found coming out of your property, trespassing, and being charged for it, that was the last straw. Mr. Brinks, please understand we are strong advocates of a man's personal rights, and property rights especially. We didn't condone the actions of Mr. Atwell, and when he pushed things too far, we had to step in and make it right."

He looked toward his fellow committee members and several of them nodded at him.

Mr. Reece took another long, deep breath, then looked me in the eye, and said, "You have deep roots in this church. Maybe more than anyone else, you have a birthright here. I feel as if the pastor has taken that away from you. We would love to have you back in our fold if you ever wish to return."

There wasn't enough money on the planet to get me to return to that church. It felt good that they offered, though, even if the offer was likely loaded on so many different levels.

I looked at Mr. Erickson, whose nod gave me permission to respond.

"I appreciate your offer, and I more than appreciate you distancing yourself from the harassment that Mr. Atwell has been inflicting on me and my employee. I take it this means you will be dropping the claim against my inheritance?"

All five men on the committee nodded at the same time.

"I won't be coming back to the church, and we all know the reasons for that. They extend much further than just what Mr. Atwell has done and has always done to me and to others like me." The men in front of me squirmed a bit. They were all anti-gay and I'd heard them say so repeatedly over the years. But my grandpa did love the church, and I did have deep roots there.

I internally debated how much I was willing to share with these men, but decided, for Grandpa's sake, I'd share what I had intended. "My grandfather wanted to leave a legacy to this area and to the church. After a lot of consideration, I've decided how I'd like to honor his desires. I recently got in contact with an architect, and he is drawing up designs for a chapel that'll be placed on my property once the probate court rules the inheritance is mine. I would very much like for whomever your new pastor is to be the person who dedicates the chapel once it is completed."

I saw the hard-shell expressions momentarily lapse from the faces of the men in front of me. Unlike Atwell, who I always knew was in it for himself, these men were pious people.

We disagreed on a lot of things. Some things were so strongly disagreed upon, there would never be a way to bridge the gap. But these men all had good hearts. I'd known them all my life, and I'd seen their true natures show time and again, and hearing that I was going to establish a chapel in my grandpa's honor was something all the men in front of me could get behind.

"We'd very much like that, son," Mr. Reece said. "You do your grandpa proud. We're all very sorry things have gone the way they have."

Before they left, Mr. Erickson told them that he'd have Mr. Conner, Ms. Beth's attorney, get in touch with them soon about dropping the claim on my inheritance.

Once they were gone, Doc sighed. "That was hard for them to do. Those guys haven't had many times in their lives where they've had to humble themselves in front of anyone, especially a gay man. The fact you brought me, another gay man, as his witness was doubly difficult."

Mr. Erickson chuckled. "Well, and in front of a gay attorney. A trifecta."

Both Doc and I raised an eyebrow at Mr. Erickson. He smiled as he turned the picture on his desk around, revealing a much younger version of himself embraced by an extremely attractive man.

"How did I not ever know?" Doc asked.

"Well, not many people know, I guess. When I was judge, I had to run for office. Those five men that just left would've done everything in their power, which in this county is significant, to keep me from winning each and every election."

Doc frowned. "Yeah, I didn't come out until after I retired for the same reason. Hey, you and your..."

"Husband," Mr. Erickson clarified.

"You and your husband should come over for drinks and meet my husband, Amos," he said.

"Oh, we know Amos. He redid our house twenty years ago."

"Did he know about y'all?" Doc asked.

"He probably suspected, but we built a home with mother-in-law quarters, so anyone who asked would've likely thought we were roommates living in the different sections of the house."

"It's ridiculous looking back at how we had to hide things," Doc said on a sigh. He glanced back at the door where the five men had just left, then back at me. "I hope your generation never have to know what it's like to hide who you are and who you love, just to satisfy self-righteous men like those."

"Tennessee is still pretty backward, at least this part of it, but yeah, it's nothing like it was back in the day," I said.

Both Mr. Erickson and Doc chuckled at my comment. "Back in the day, huh?" Doc said, teasing me again.

I smiled, because all of a sudden, I felt like the kid in the room. I guessed I was, but now I felt like I had real advocates too. I was already friends with Doc, and I now wanted to get to know my attorney on a personal level too. It seemed this part of the state had a lot of great people I'd yet to get to know. Now that I had that jackass pastor off my back, I felt more excited about moving back to this area than I ever had.

Eighteen

Logan

I CHECKED EVERY WAY possible to determine if the jackass pastor had sabotaged the grapes when he'd trespassed in the barn. It didn't seem that he had. I even drank a whole glass after it was processed to make sure there was no cyanide in it, which, in hindsight, might've been a stupid idea. Regardless, there was no indication that anything was wrong or even different between the two juices. I taste-tested them side by side and used the refractometer on both batches, and they were almost identical. Similar enough that I knew the two batches were the same and there was no indication anything would cause the wine to go off. That was a huge relief, though I still couldn't shake an uneasy feeling about the whole situation.

I combined the juices and began the process of monitoring them, hoping to get the full three weeks of maceration. I knew I was pushing things. The humidity here was over the top, and the temperature was higher than in California or Oregon this time of year. There were many unknowns, but I was driven to succeed.

I could imagine taking our wines to competitions, showing the judges what we'd coaxed out of the ground and the environment of my home state. I could almost hear the critics complain when they learned the first-prize winner came from a part of the world known more for moonshine than wine. I took great pleasure just in that possibility.

I wanted to compete and win. Not only with other American winemakers, but on an international level. I wanted to pull out all the stops. Sure, this was the first year the winery had officially made wine, but we had the capability, and I didn't mind pushing the envelope. If the wine went off, it wasn't like there was a lot to lose. Not yet. I convinced myself the beginning was the time to try things, when no one was attached to the outcomes. Hell, Matt didn't even officially own the winery yet. Had his grandfather been alive, it would've been different. But, if it all went south, well, we could always point to the circumstances.

I shook my head. I was justifying things. I decided it was time to stop acting like a bad guy in my own story and come clean with Matt. Tell him about the risk I was taking. I needed to respect my boss enough to trust him. Ultimately, this was or would be his winery, and he needed the opportunity to make up his own mind about my lofty goals for it. So, I texted Matt later that evening, telling him I needed to speak to him about the process.

I'd spent several days cleaning the equipment, ensuring that it'd be ready when we harvested again next year, then I covered the equipment with plastic. No point in allowing a year's worth of dirt to get into it and potentially destroy future batches.

I closed and locked the processing room, determined not to take any more chances with anyone tampering with the wine. One scare was enough to last me a lifetime. If he'd tampered with the grapes, over forty percent of our first batch would've been put out of commission. That wouldn't do, especially with us being such a small winery to begin with.

I was just about to go back to the apartment and clean up when Matt arrived. It felt strange to have the owner knocking on his own front door, but I'd gotten in the habit of locking every door now, even when I was there.

I opened the door and smiled as Matt walked in. "Do you not have keys to the place?" I asked.

Matt shook his head. "No, I doubt my grandpa even kept an extra set. If he did, I have no idea where they'd be."

"Well, we should find out or have copies made, because I think all doors should remain locked anytime we're not open to the public."

"Is that why you wanted me to come over? Has something else happened?" he asked, and I could see he was becoming more agitated. Without even thinking, I reached out and placed my hand on his arm in reassurance.

"No, nothing like that, it's just we have some pretty important stuff fermenting back there, and any tampering could easily destroy our efforts. Your grandpa invested a lot of money into this place. We shouldn't let it all go to waste."

"Agreed," he said. "So, I planned on talking with you too. I have news. In fact, let's go out and celebrate."

"Celebrate what?"

"Well, lots of things. The harvest is done, the grapes are being turned into wine, and the church is backing down. They're no longer coming after the inheritance."

"Really? That's great news. That's totally worth celebrating!"

I felt genuinely excited for Matt, then looked around and shrugged. "Even with locking everything up, I'm really nervous about leaving this place unattended. Maybe you should consider getting a couple really nasty guard dogs."

Matt smiled at me so warmly that it lit up his handsome face, and sent flutters through my stomach. "You really are committed to this, aren't you?" he asked.

"Well, yeah, it's what I've built my life and career around. I really think we have the potential for something amazing with these grapes. I'd like to see that through to the end."

He nodded, but didn't seem to fully get what I was getting at. Remembering he was an artist, I said, "Imagine, you spent the past six years learning how to paint, painting under masters, then you have the opportunity to paint all on your own, doing it your way, the way you think would make masterpieces."

When I saw I'd hit a nerve, I continued, "Now, imagine all your paintings were sitting in a vulnerable place and you came home to find some stranger walking out of your studio like he owned it. Wouldn't you be petrified he'd gone in and destroyed all that you'd worked for?"

Matt slowly nodded and sighed. "Yeah, I'd be beyond terrified. But you can't live your life here staring at the wine, Logan. I'll tell you what, I'll run into town and get spares made, provided Ms. Beth doesn't have the keys lying around, so that it's not all on you. Better yet, I could just get new, better locks for all the doors. If I do that, would you feel comfortable going out to dinner with me?"

"Maybe," I said halfheartedly. To be honest, nothing less than barring the doors with screws and two-by-sixes would make me feel comfortable at this point. Todd had wired up enough of the surveillance system that I figured we could put more cameras on the front, perhaps one aimed at the driveway to keep an eye on who was literally coming and going. That would help as well.

Matt turned to leave, then spun back around and tugged me into a kiss. "Things are looking up, Logan. I can feel it."

Then he dashed out the door. He seemed so excited I couldn't help but catch some of it myself. I didn't know whether things were looking up or not, but he was right about me sitting here like some old mother hen protecting her clutch of eggs.

At this point, we were fairly safe. Safe enough that I wouldn't hyperventilate thinking about it at least. We had a surveillance system, could add more cameras where needed, and we'd be getting better locks on all the doors. I had to hope and trust that would all be enough.

Nineteen

Matt

I FOUND GRANDPA'S SPARE keys in his old coin toss bucket inside Ms. Beth's coat closet. When she told me he tossed everything in there at night when he got home, I guessed they'd be there. He'd done the same thing every evening when I was growing up and his keys always landed in the bucket.

I had just pulled in front of the hardware store to see about buying new locks when I got a phone call from Chattanooga. "Hello?" I answered.

"Hello, is this Matthew Brinks?" the lady asked. I didn't recognize her voice.

"Yes, this is Matt."

"Hi, Matt, I'm Veronica Lewis. I work at the Riverview Art Gallery in Chattanooga, where you have your paintings. I have a buyer who wants to see more of your work, and I told her I'd contact you for that information."

"Hi, yes, thanks for calling. Actually, I've got my paintings spread throughout the southeast. Is she looking for something in particular?"

"Well, she represents several collectors, and yes, I think many of them are looking for specific things. Do you happen to have a website where they can view your full catalog of available pieces?"

I chuckled. "No, I don't have a website, but if they're really interested, I could send an email with photos of my work being sold at other galleries and how to contact them. It'll take me a couple days, though."

Veronica put me on hold, I assumed to speak to the interested buyer. When she came back, she was ecstatic. "That's perfect," she said. "She is going to be back in Chattanooga next weekend. If you can send me the pictures and location details, I can put them on a website that'll allow her clients to see your collection."

"Okay, that would be great. But how will you get them?"

"Oh, honey, most galleries have relationships with each other, and the ones that don't will work with you if you've got active buyers. You get those pictures to me, and I'll handle all the rest," she said confidently before hanging up.

I didn't see that coming. I was so glad I'd inventoried and taken photos of all my paintings before I sent them off. Of course, I'd done that for me so I could have something to remember them all by. I'd already sold several pieces here and there, but not on a large scale. To be honest, I'd priced everything unreasonably high, or at least I thought so, trying to deter buyers. I knew that was stupid, but it'd been so difficult letting them all go.

My artist friends teased me, saying I was a hillbilly painter watching my stuff like a dragon protecting its hoard. I knew I should want to get my art out into the world, but I also had visions of displaying my paintings in the old mill after its renovation. Showcasing my artwork in my own space—the very place that'd inspired me to pick up a paintbrush in the first place—was a dream I didn't even knew I had until now.

By the time I got to the barn and tried Grandpa's spare key, I was floating on air. This really had been a great day. Logan met me at the door dressed in dark jeans and a sexy-as-hell, tight-fitting, white pullover.

"You look really hot," I said when I saw him, and he blushed. "Wanna blow off going out and just celebrate here instead?"

Logan's expression turned heated as he gave me a once-over, my skin prickling under his close inspection. The thought of holing up here was clearly as appealing to him as it was to me, but he quickly got himself under control. "Nope, you promised me a courtin' meal, and you're gonna have to pay up now."

"A courtin' meal, is it?" I chuckled at his old-fashioned talk. "I'll show you courtin'," I said, and pulled him into my arms, kissing him passionately.

He melted in my embrace and deepened the kiss, which just made me long for him more. He'd already snuggled into me a couple of times, which did funny things to my heart. But yielding to me, especially when he looked so sexy and smelled so delicious, did a number on an organ located significantly lower than my heart. When Logan's hands slid lower to cup my ass, I knew I had to pump the brakes, or we really wouldn't be going anywhere.

"Come on before I attack you here on the floor," I said, grabbing his hand and pulling him along with me.

"Where are we going?" he asked.

"You like Italian?" I asked, and he nodded. "There's a little place in Lebanon that is really amazing. It's sort of the go-to place for fancy food."

No sooner had I said the words than his stomach growled, and he laughed. "Well, I'm hungry enough to eat a horse. I've been so preoccupied with making sure everything is perfect with the wine, I sorta forgot to eat today."

"Man, that's not healthy. Although, when I get caught up in painting, I'm the same way."

We chatted companionably as I drove us toward my old home. Lebanon wasn't very big population-wise. Interstate 40 went through it, and lots of Nashville folks would show up from time to time. Still, compared to the tiny towns of Crawford City and Mayville, Lebanon felt like a big city.

I pulled into the restaurant's parking lot and Logan looked at me with a cocked eyebrow. The place looked like a dive, but the food really was delicious. "Trust me," I said. He just shook his head, got out, and followed me inside.

Sometimes at this time of year, it could be really busy on a Saturday night, so I felt like I'd hit the lottery when the hostess seated us right away. When she asked if we wanted the house wine, it was on the tip of my tongue to say no. But I'd forgotten I was with a wine expert, so I sat back and listened to Logan question the young woman about their selection.

Her knowledge of their wines was quickly exhausted, though, and she left to find the restaurant owner. A few minutes later, a handsome middle-aged man came over to answer Logan's questions.

The two chatted about wine and I didn't understand any of it, which left me feeling out of place. Finally, it was decided that someone with as refined a palette as Logan should have the two-thousand-sixteen Antinori Tignanello.

"You should pair that with the lasagna," the man said. "We stuff ours with all sorts of different meats—beef, pork, and lamb, all from around this part of Tennessee. It's very flavorful and the Antinori compliments it beautifully."

"Then, by all means, that's what I'll have," Logan said.

"Me too," I added.

"I will bring the two of you the bottle then, so you will have plenty for your dinner." Logan nodded appreciatively before the man walked away.

"I'm gonna guess that bottle is going to set us back a little," I said.

"You are a vineyard owner, my friend. That man will remember us now, and when it's time for us to sell our wine, he'll be referring people to yours instead of a wine from Italy. So, yes, it'll cost a little, but it'll be worth it. Besides, I've had the wine he's bringing us, and it's delicious. Not as good as ours will be, but delicious nonetheless."

I chuckled. Logan was already adorable, and melted my butter in so many ways, but that strange, fluttery feeling in my chest returned seeing him all geeked out about wine. He had a little snobby feel about him, too, but his sincere love of wine-making made it endearing. I really did fancy this guy.

I told him about my strange meeting with my grandpa's church group, and he was happy for me. When his face turned serious, though, I knew he had something important to say. My heart began to beat faster when I thought maybe he was going to tell me he'd found another job, one that didn't require him to watch over the wine he was making like a soldier keeping guard.

"So, Matt, I've been going at things like I own the winery. I started feeling guilty about all that today. I really should be going over things with you before I just plow through them."

I laughed. "You must know by now that I'm relying on your expertise. I have no idea about most of this, and that goes for wine and the wine-making business. It'd be like me trying to explain to you why I chose radiant white versus titanium."

Logan's smile returned, which helped ease some of the seriousness in his expression. "Well, it's my job to keep you informed. These are bad habits for me to learn so early in my career. If I go to work for someone else, they'll expect me to keep them fully apprised of the process."

My heart was in my throat as I swallowed hard. The thought of him going anywhere else struck up the same panicked feeling I was having before. I pushed it down, though, not wanting to spoil our nice evening. "So, okay, tell me what you're doing, and I'll pretend like I understand."

The restaurant owner came back then with a bottle of wine, and poured a glass for Logan to taste, which he did and approved. "Shall I pour for you as well?" the man asked me.

When I nodded, he poured me a glass. I expected him to wait for me to taste it, too, and was surprised when he just left.

"I guess he knew I didn't know what the hell I was doing," I said with a shrug.

Logan smiled. "No offense to you, but the person who orders the wine is usually the one who must approve the bottle. Taste it and let me know what you think."

I wasn't a lover of dry wines. In fact, I was dreading it, because I didn't want to disappoint the man sitting across from me. He watched intently as I brought the wine glass to my lips. When I took a sip, the flavor exploded in my mouth. "Oh, wow, that's really different," I said, causing Logan to laugh out loud.

"Yeah, that's why it cost a bit more. Now, tell me what you taste."

"Um, well, I can taste the juice. Although it's bitter, it's not unpleasant."

"Tell me what's going on with your tongue. How does it feel on the sides, in the back? Do you taste any other flavors that weren't there before?" Logan asked, sounding excited. God, he was so damn cute.

I took another drink and swished it around before swallowing. "Is it cherry? Yeah, I taste cherry, and my tongue feels like it's got a coating of something good on it. I can't really explain it."

Logan looked pleased and took another swig. "I taste the cherry, too, but people would say it has fruity overtones. I can also taste a little smokiness as well, on the back of the tongue. Those are also called overtones, and in a great wine, that's what you want to complement the food with."

"Cool," I said, still feeling out of my element, but thoroughly enjoying seeing Logan's passion on full display. "And all this time, I just thought wine was something to make you look important while you're getting drunk."

"Oh, you have a long way to go," he said with a wink, making me laugh.

"So, back to what you wanted to tell me," I said, and attempted to steel myself with another glass.

"I'm pushing the process a lot because I'm waiting three full weeks before I press the wine from the peels, and there's a good chance I could cause it to spoil. Your grandpa has refrigeration set up and I'm watching the pH balance, but you should know I'm taking a chance with your grapes."

"What's the purpose of that?" I asked, suddenly relieved and confused at the same time. He wasn't leaving.

"Color, texture, not unlike the smoothness you mentioned. The best vintners keep the juice on the peelings for that long."

"Have you done it before?" I asked, and he shook his head.

"No, the other wineries I worked for weren't really award winners. The last one, the one that burned in the fire, would push the boundaries. That's sort of why they hired me, but I didn't get much of a chance to work with them before the vines were destroyed."

"So, you're wanting to push the boundaries here, with the hope it works out?" I asked.

He nodded. "I mean, it's a lot to ask, but at the same time, I figure we have the least to lose right now since the winery is in probate, and it's the first batch. It seems to me, if we're gonna take chances, this is the time to do it."

Logan stared at me with eyebrows furrowed, biting his bottom lip. He seemed concerned about what I'd say, and I wanted to reach across the table and kiss away his worry. "I think I agree. If it bombs, no one will bat an eye, but if we start making a name for ourselves, and then bomb, it'll be harder to recover."

"Exactly," he said excitedly. "I'd like your permission to push the boundaries here and create the best possible wine we can. I mean, I can pull part of the juice out early, just in case, and make a smaller batch of the later wine to reduce the risk, but I'd have to get more equipment to do that."

"No, my grandpa hired you, and I trust you to do what you think is right. Next year, when I actually own the place, I might wanna be more cautious. But right now, I say go for it."

He lifted his glass, and said, "Here's to taking chances." I clinked my glass with his just as a server arrived with our meals. We spent the rest of the evening talking about wine and food pairings and such things. Logan's enthusiasm for it all was contagious.

When we pulled up to the barn, I jumped out of the car telling Logan not to move a muscle. "Since this is officially a courtin' meal," I said as I opened his door like a gentleman, causing him to laugh.

I walked him to the front door of his apartment and kissed him deeply, then let him snuggle into me. "Thank you, Logan," I said softly.

He pulled back slightly from my embrace to look up at me. "For what?" he asked.

"For making tonight special. I needed it after today. I mean, it was all good news, but it's been hard putting all that ugly church business to bed."

He leaned back into me for a moment, and I tightened my hold. When he pulled back again, he said, "You make me happy, Matt Brinks, really happy." Then he smirked. "And I'm not just saying that 'cause I like your grapes."

He waggled his eyebrows and I laughed as he turned to unlock the door. "Thank you too. Dinner with you tonight was the perfect way to end a perfect week," he said before kissing me again. "See you tomorrow?"

"Yeah, see you tomorrow," I said, and watched him disappear from view.

I realized once I was back in my car that I'd forgotten to tell him my news of the interested art buyer. *Oh well, don't count your chickens before they hatch*, as Grandpa used to say. I'd best not do that with my growing relationship with Logan either.

TWENTY

LOGAN

ONCE I'D CLOSED THE door behind me, I twirled around the room like Anna dancing through the castle in *Frozen*. God, that man made me all kinds of crazy happy.

It also felt like I'd taken a weight off by coming clean with Matt about my wine-making plans. I thought I made clear the level of risk involved, and although he agreed to it, I doubted he fully understood the chance we were taking. Regardless, I would do what I could to minimize that risk. He'd put his trust in me, and by God, I wasn't going to let him down.

After our courtin' night, Matt began stopping by most afternoons or evenings. Sometimes we'd have dinner, and sometimes we'd just make out until we were both so hot and bothered we were about to burst. Somehow, we'd manage to force ourselves to pull apart, believing taking things all the way—at least right now—could spell disaster.

At day twenty, I decided to begin the fermenting process. I had tasted the juice, and could tell it was now or never. Not wanting to take even more of a chance, I prepped the yeast. When Matt came in, I led him to the back and let him pour the yeast in after taking one more measurement with the refractometer.

"So, now what?" he asked.

"Well, it's a maintenance thing. I've been working the mixture several times a day, ensuring that the peels and seeds don't cap on the top and prevent oxygen from getting in. Now I'll let the vat warm up a bit, so the yeast can do its job, then, and in two or three days, we'll press the wine and prep it for clarification. It's a complex process but, for the most part, we just need to get it to the point we can put it into those white oak barrels over there," I told him, pointing at the barrels sitting empty along the back wall of the barn.

"Cool," he said, and I chuckled.

"You really are very sophisticated, Matt."

He stuck his tongue out at me, and I acted like I was going to bite it. That caused him to tickle me until I cried uncle.

We were both laughing as I covered the grape must back up and set the timer on my phone to remind me when I needed to stir it again, then we went to my apartment to cuddle and explore other ticklish places on my body I hadn't even known about.

The nights were getting cooler, and I loved the wood-burning fireplace in the corner of the apartment's living room. I'd used it a couple times, and tonight, I didn't even have to ask. Matt got up from where we were snuggled on the sofa and started a fire, most likely to chase off the chill.

"So, are you happy here?" Matt asked me out of the blue.

"Yeah, I love this kind of work, and I'm happier now that I've got something to work with. The wine seems to be progressing perfectly."

"I'm glad to hear it, but I wasn't referring to the wine. I asked if you are happy *here?*"

His question took me aback. I honestly hadn't thought about that. "Well, I'm happy about a lot of things." I turned toward him when he rejoined me on the sofa, and asked, "What's brought this question on?"

He sighed. "I'm liking you more and more, Logan, but this is a far cry from California. Small-town Tennessee will never be Wine Country. I have to wonder if, at some point, you won't leave and go back West."

I shook my head. "I don't know, to be honest. I grew up in Nashville and visited this area during the summers. It's a beautiful part of the country. I never imagined I'd be able to make a living as a winemaker here but, obviously, that's changed."

"What kind of social life did you have in California? Did you date much?" he asked.

"That's sort of loaded since we're dating, don't you think?"

"Nah, whether you dated a different guy every day, or didn't date anyone, I'm cool with it. We can't change the past anyway, right?"

I leaned into Matt's side and fixed my gaze on the fireplace, preferring to watch the flickering flames while recounting my unremarkable dating history than stare into his penetrating green eyes. He wrapped his arm around my shoulders and pulled me close. "No, I didn't date a lot back in California. I was working a lot, probably too much, and focused on building my career. Besides, even in California, the rural areas are still pretty conservative. Not as conservative as here, of course, but finding men to date would've taken more effort and energy than I wanted to give."

"Did you date much in college?" he asked, skating his fingertips up and down my arm as the fire crackled.

"Not a lot. I had a couple boyfriends, but they didn't last long. I mean, I'm basically a glorified farmer. That didn't scream 'life mate' to the guys I dated." I chuckled at the memory. "There was one guy whose father owned a winery, so he at least understood what I was usually blathering on about, but he wanted to be an attorney. In the end, we weren't really compatible anyway. His sights were set on working in state government, and I just wanted to make wine. We split up when I took a job working for his dad."

"So, why don't you still work for his dad?" he asked.

I shrugged. "I had ideas that didn't jive with the manager's. I think it also had to do with the fact I'd dated the owner's son and that we'd remained friends, which didn't sit well with my coworkers."

"You're still friends with him?" Matt asked, a note of concern in his voice.

I chuckled. "Don't be jealous. Gren and I weren't compatible in any way, Matt. Even if he'd had an interest in the winery, we both understood we made better friends than lovers."

Matt sighed. "What about men who worked around the wineries? There's got to be a lot of gay men lurking around the profession, right?"

"Not a lot, but a few, and most of them are married with kids, at least in my experience."

"So, you never hooked up?" he asked.

"I feel like I'm getting the third degree here." I smirked at him, so he knew I was joking. Had anyone else started this line of questioning, I'd have already bolted, but not with Matt. I knew he genuinely wanted to learn more about me, and truth be told, I relished being the focus of all his attention. "Of course, I hooked up. I'm a guy with needs, after all. Hookups are easy, and being as close to San Francisco as I was, there was opportunity. But there's a lot of difference between a hookup and dating someone."

Matt thought for a moment, then said, "I hate dating. My last boyfriend lasted three years. He was an artist too, and I think he liked living with me 'cause I had such a huge studio space attached to the apartment I rented. I swear he had more sex with other guys while we were dating than we had together, though."

"He cheated on you?" I asked indignantly, unable to hide my annoyance at his ex-boyfriend. Matt's lips quirked, probably from amusement at my inexplicable need to defend him, and he kissed my nose.

"Nah, we had an open relationship. But when I realized he was spending more time and energy outside our relationship than in it, I began questioning the point of being together. That's when I broke it off."

I nodded. "Yeah, I'm not good with the open thing. Or at least I don't think I would be. I can be possessive over things and people I consider mine."

"Is that right?" Matt asked as he leaned over and kissed me on the lips. "Are you feeling possessive over me?"

I smiled. "Not yet, but I should probably warn you, if we take this to the next level, I can be a jealous bitch!"

"No, not you!" he teased, and I stuck my tongue out at him. When he lunged toward me like he was going to bite it like I'd done to him earlier, I used the momentum to pull him on top of me and stretched out under him. Matt wasted no time capturing my mouth in his and I couldn't hold back a moan as our tongues tangled. I slid my hands underneath his shirt, loving the feel of his bare skin under my palms, while our bodies ground against each other.

Things were heating up when my phone began to ring. I ignored it, literally too wrapped up in Matt to care about anything else. After our talk, it felt like we were on the same page and finally moving things to the next level.

When it rang again for the third time, I gave up. "I'm sorry, Matt, it might be my parents. I should check on it."

He moved off me so I could sit up. When I saw it was my aunt calling, I quickly answered. "Hi, Aunt Polly, what's up?"

She sounded irate, telling me her pastor visited her home and he'd told her that Matt had stolen over a million dollars from the church and was even conspiring to get him fired. He'd also informed her I was somehow involved in all of it and that she needed to get me away from Matt and the winery to save my soul.

"Aunt Polly," I interrupted, barely able to get a word in edgewise. "I don't have a say in where Matt does or doesn't go to church, but it's the other way around regarding the money. He hasn't stolen anything. The church was suing *him* for his own inheritance."

Matt looked up at me then, and I shrugged.

"No, Aunt Polly, I'm not gonna quit. I like it here and I like Matt too. He's a good man."

I had to take the phone away from my ear as she began screaming at me. When she started in on calling me names, I disconnected the call.

"Wow, that was intense," I said. "She's never talked to me that way."

"I'm guessing Atwell strikes again?" Matt asked.

I nodded. "Hey, Matt, I need to call my dad and try to stem the tide here a bit."

"Yeah, I understand. Just so you know, things could get a lot worse on that front. The church will be voting to fire him on Sunday."

I nodded and set my phone down before pulling him into a hug. "I know this has been hard on you, Matt, and I want you to know this won't influence how I feel about you. My Aunt Polly has never been okay with me being gay, and she's made her opinion about that very clear in the past. Her reaction likely has more to do with that than anything, okay?"

He nodded and leaned into me, before whispering, "It feels good to have an advocate. Even if it means you getting caught up in the middle of it. Grandpa used to be my shield between the church's hatred and me, but now that he's gone..."

Matt's voice cracked at the mention of his grandpa, and I kissed and hugged him tightly. My phone ringing behind me drew me back to the situation at hand. I pulled away, saw my dad's name on the caller ID, and sighed. "I'll talk to you tomorrow, Matt."

"Talk to you tomorrow," he replied, and left my apartment.

TWENTY-ONE

MATT

I KNEW IT WAS probably petty of me, but I watched the live broadcast of the church service to see how the congregation reacted to the news. Mr. Reece stood up after the announcements were made and explained that Pastor Atwell had been asked not to attend today. A low murmur swept through the crowd, and I could see but not hear dozens of congregants whispering to each other as the camera panned the audience.

"Following the service, which will be conducted today by Assistant Pastor Greene from the Community Church of Larksburg, the congregation will vote to either keep Pastor Atwell as the spiritual leader of our church, or honor the unanimous vote of the Administrative Committee to terminate his contract."

Mr. Reece stepped aside then as the guest pastor took to the pulpit and began his sermon. I lightly tuned him out, but kept the TV on, intent on not missing the congregation's vote at the end. I got lost in my head, thinking about all that'd happened with the church over the past several weeks and the emotional toll it'd taken.

I had always expressed myself with my art, and I was surprised to realize I hadn't used it to deal with all my upset about the way the church had treated me. While the service droned on, I pulled another canvas into the living room and propped it in front of the TV. I decided it was best to paint in oils, and like the vineyard piece, I felt a pull toward abstract.

As I picked up my paintbrush, feelings of anger, hurt, and disappointment in the church for its intolerance, going as far back as my childhood, hit me full force. With emotions swirling, my brush flew over the canvas in bold strokes. I painted the church I'd grown up attending, using reds to signify my feelings of being drowned in the blood of hatred in a place that should've been a sanctuary. I chuckled when I painted Atwell behind the pulpit and gave him horns and a tail.

Being an abstract piece, you wouldn't be able to tell what it was if you didn't know to look for it, but I'd know. Every time I looked at this painting, I'd know the meaning behind it all. *Be gone, Satan*, he'd hollered at me at Grandpa's first memorial service. Titling this piece *Be gone, Atwell* seemed rather fitting.

My attention whipped back to the TV as the assistant pastor finished his sermon. The service was concluded when Mr. Reece stepped back up on the pulpit to begin the voting process. He announced that congregants attending virtually could vote through the church's website, or call in to the switchboard.

"Before ya'll cast your vote, know that the Administrative Committee isn't making this recommendation without due cause. We've had very disturbing information come to light about Pastor Atwell, and even though we lean toward forgiveness for many things, there are limits to what can be tolerated among church leadership."

Mr. Reece then described Atwell's infidelity with four married women that I'd brought up at Grandpa's memorial debacle, and even mentioned me by name. I cringed at that, concerned it could come back to bite me. "What we haven't disclosed until now is that three other women have contacted the church since Mr. Brinks divulged Mr. Atwell's indiscretions to the congregation, all stating our former pastor propositioned them as well."

You could hear the restlessness among the congregants grow the more he spoke. He waited until things calmed before continuing.

"But our recommendation to terminate goes beyond personal improprieties. We are concerned that Mr. Atwell chose to bring legal action against Mr. Brinks for his inheritance. This church has several members who have endowed the church with gifts. It has always been our position not to fight the family over endowments. However, Mr. Atwell ignored our policy, and used the church's name against our wishes to pursue this legal quagmire. We have removed our names from the legal dispute, and have personally apologized to Mr. Brinks for the inconvenience and undue stress the church has inadvertently caused him."

Mr. Reece paused and stared hard into the camera, as if he knew I was watching and willing me to feel the sincerity in his words. His mea culpa on behalf of the church was unprecedented, and airing the church's dirty laundry so publicly would no doubt feed the small-town gossip mill for decades to come.

"We would be remiss not to tell the congregation today that because of Mr. Atwell's actions, people have withdrawn their endowments from the church. As a result, programs we've held sacred for decades are at risk of being lost. The final straw for us as a committee, however, came when Mr. Atwell was arrested for trespassing on Mr. Brinks's property. Not only that, but the trespass was caught personally by the mayor of Crawford City. When the committee confronted Mr. Atwell, he said the property was rightfully his. We assure you, nothing in Mr. Josiah Brinks's will indicated any inheritance, property or otherwise, to Mr. Atwell."

Mr. Reece took his glasses off then, and rubbed between his eyes. The older man looked utterly exhausted, as if delivering this speech physically and emotionally hurt him. Being a man of God, perhaps it did in some ways.

"Mr. Atwell's actions continue to become more and more of a liability, both spiritually and legally. Therefore," he said with a sigh, "we, as the Administrative Committee, feel it's impossible to allow him to remain as leader of our church. I will now open the floor for discussion."

I continued painting as congregants lined up and testified either for or against their pastor. More than one woman voiced concern about leaving their daughters alone with the pastor and that they thought the committee had made the right decision.

After everyone said their piece, the congregation voted seventy-five percent to twenty-five percent to terminate Atwell's contract. I stood before my canvas, holding my paintbrush aloft as it dripped onto the floor, unsure how to react. It felt so wrong that for all these years, the church protected that predator, and it took the threat of losing money for them to finally act.

Regardless, hopefully this would mean Atwell was out of my life for good.

After the shock passed, I picked up the paintbrush, wiped it clean and finished the painting before putting it in the makeshift studio of my old bedroom to dry, and left to visit Logan. I was sure he'd be interested in hearing the outcome of the vote.

I texted him on my way out the door to see if he wanted pizza, and he said no, asking if I wanted to join him for sandwiches instead. I texted back a thumbs up.

We had just sat down at his kitchen table with our sandwiches and chips when we heard a vehicle pull up outside. Both of us groaned at the same time.

"If it's Atwell, we need to stay in here and call the sheriff," I said, and he nodded.

Logan walked toward the door and peeked out the window. When he saw who it was, a look of recognition crossed his face, and he opened the door and stepped outside without a word.

I immediately got up and crossed to the door in time to see Logan hesitantly approaching a woman I vaguely recognized. Another woman, quite younger than the first, climbed out of the car's passenger side. Both women appeared dressed in their Sunday best, and both were crying.

I automatically assumed they were Logan's aunt and cousin. I was considering slipping out the back door of the apartment to give them some privacy when Logan brought the women inside.

"Matt, this is my Aunt Polly and my cousin Millie. Y'all, this is Matt Brinks."

Ms. Polly wiped her eyes, and said, "I knew your grandpa really well, Matt. I'm sorry for your loss."

I nodded, but didn't really know how else to respond. She had called and screamed so loudly at Logan the day before, I was able to hear her from several feet away. Now, in person, I felt the need to maintain some distance.

When she realized I wasn't going to say anything, she said, "I was a fool, boys. I was so taken in by what Past... I mean, Mr. Atwell said that I didn't even consider he was the one being inappropriate. I can't apologize enough for how I acted on the phone yesterday."

"I should leave you all alone to talk. Logan, please call me later, if you don't mind," I said, and was about to excuse myself when Ms. Polly stopped me.

"I didn't mean to interrupt you. But, after what we learned today at church, I just couldn't let another moment go without Logan knowing how sorry I am."

I turned to Logan and winked at him. "I'm sure he's very appreciative, Ms. Polly. In fact, I am too. It takes a true Christian to admit when we're wrong and try to make amends."

I nodded to Logan and took my leave. Although our being interrupted again frustrated me, I was glad Logan's aunt had come to make things right. I hoped he would go easy on her.

Family could be a lot to deal with, but having the kind of family that made good on bad situations was admirable, to me at least. Polly's phone tirade had revealed her intolerance of gay people, but here she was trying to redeem herself in the eyes of her gay nephew. I hoped she was actually moving closer toward acceptance, which would bode well for her fellow congregants too, even if dealing with their prejudice in the meantime stung a bit.

Twenty-Two

Logan

I WANTED TO ARGUE that Matt should stay and finish his lunch, but he was probably right to give us some space. After he'd gone, I asked Aunt Polly and Millie to sit down. Aunt Polly told me what had happened at church that morning, and explained how horrible she felt the entire time she listened to the case against her now-former pastor. "I had no idea that Mr. Atwell was involved in so many shenanigans. He was always such a righteous man, or at least he acted like one."

"Aunt Polly, I'm no expert on religious matters, but doesn't the Bible say something about wolves in sheep's clothing? Don't beat yourself up too much. It sounds like he's been pulling the wool over everyone's eyes for a long time."

She looked at me for a long moment with tears threatening to flow again. "I know I've not been accepting of your lifestyle, but I've always loved you, Logan. Since you came out... well, I've done a lot of studying the Bible and reading what people say on both sides of the issue. I don't really believe it's a sin to love anyone, even if you love them in a gay way. But every time I'd come to that conclusion, Pastor Atwell would have weeks of sermons on how it was a sin. I let myself get led astray, baby. As a result, I've done a lot to hurt you."

I got up and knelt in front of my aunt. "It didn't really hurt me, Aunt Polly. I just didn't come around you, that's all."

"But that's not how family is supposed to act. I mean, you've been here for months now, and I've not even come by to see your place. I just don't know how to ask for forgiveness, Logan. I wouldn't blame you if you did hate me."

"Listen, I'm who I am, and that's not gonna change. Even if I could, I wouldn't. I don't blame you or hate you. It's a lot to come to terms with when you've been raised to think it's wrong, but it means a lot to me that you're here today. It'd mean even more if you'd come around more often and let me get to know you as an adult. Maybe we could even be friends." I looked over at Millie as tears rolled down her cheeks. "Besides, I haven't gotten to be around my baby cousin much at all. I bet I could teach her a lot about making wine."

Aunt Polly sat up straighter and I could tell she wanted to argue about that. This was still the rural South, after all, and lots of old Southern folks still saw any sort of alcohol as the devil's drink. However, she let it pass and smiled. I knew for a fact she'd be telling Millie not to ever touch wine, here or anywhere. Still, I had to work to hide my humor as I thought about my twenty-two-year-old cousin who was in her senior year at the University of Tennessee. She had, more likely than not, partaken of it plenty.

"I need to call your daddy and apologize to him too. He was so mad at me last night. I haven't seen him that spittin' mad at me since we were kids." She chuckled to herself. "Did I ever tell you how I snuck up on your parents when they were making out back behind Daddy's old shed? I was only eleven and thought kissing made a baby. Well, I went screaming into the kitchen, crying and telling Mama that Raymond was gettin' Jennie pregnant. After that, Mama and Daddy made him and Jennie sit in the living room where they could keep an eye on them. He used to give me the stink eye every Sunday after church when they were able to be alone."

We all chuckled at the story, then Aunt Polly sighed heavily. "I've really screwed things up," she said. "The family has been pulled apart, and it's 'cause I let that hateful man influence me, even though I knew better."

She got up then and kissed the top of my head. "I know that Brinks boy is good as they get, Logan. All the Brinkses were good people. I remember old man Brinks from when he was the pastor. Oh, he gave the best sermons, and they were almost always about loving your neighbor, following the teachings of Christ, and remembering to love first and not judge. We've forgotten that message, I'm afraid."

She gave me a tight hug before she and Millie left. Millie didn't really say anything until after her mom went out the door, then she gave me a hug too. "I'm sorry about all this, Logan. We need to get together soon 'cause I've got news you should know."

When I gave her a curious look, she winked at me. I'd always thought my cousin swung toward the lesbian side of things. She never seemed to have a boyfriend, which was strange for these parts. She'd also majored in Women's Studies and, last I knew, was planning to be a journalist or attorney.

Millie was such a strange contrast to her mother, who was, in every way possible, the perfect Southern housewife and conservative, churchgoing woman. When her husband left her ten years earlier, she'd refused to even look at another man, saying in the eyes of God, she remained married until he passed away. Then, as now, it struck me as a damn lonely way to go through life, devoting yourself to a man who wasn't any damn good in the first place.

Thankfully, my dad had drifted away from the conservative teachings of his childhood and he and my mom had joined a United Church of Christ. Being a history professor, he bragged about how he was a liberated Puritan these days. The UCC was mostly gay-friendly, so when I came out, it was no big deal. The church even had a party to celebrate. That's how different things were between my cousin and me.

I texted Matt when they left, saying he should come back to finish his sandwich.

He texted back a moment later, saying we should forget our stale lunch and go to eat at the Crawford City Café.

Me: *Dude, I'm already gaining weight and can't afford to go out to that place very often.*

The text he sent back included a smiley face emoji that looked bloated.

Matt: *I'll be by to pick you up in ten.*

Me: *I'll drive. Your piece of crap car will die on the way there.*

I could hear him laughing in my mind. It was a crappy car. I didn't really understand how it hadn't died a miserable death long before now. I was sure the old thing was over twenty years old, and it smelled like exhaust whenever we rode in it. As soon as his inheritance came through, I'd try persuading him to get a vehicle from this century at least.

Twenty-Three

Matt

L OGAN PICKED ME UP and drove toward Crawford City. He was in a good mood, so I knew the conversation with his aunt and cousin had gone well, but I still asked, "So, things okay with the family?"

"More than. As you mostly heard."

I put my hand on his leg and squeezed, mostly to comfort, but also to flirt a little. "You're lucky to still have family. My mom's relatives are so hateful. I've not seen them for years, and even before I came out, they didn't like us. I guess it's a good thing she was never close to them anyway."

I chuckled bitterly at the memory. "They actually used to go to a church that was even more conservative than ours was, if you can believe it. I remember as a kid, her telling Mom that she was going to hell for going to *that* church."

"Really?" Logan asked, sounding surprised, and I nodded.

"No joke... you know it's the South when one hellfire and brimstone church is convinced everyone who doesn't attend their hellfire and brimstone church is going to hell. Anyway, their church closed down after the pastor was murdered by his wife, or some such thing, and they started going to Grandpa's."

"Yeah, sorry, dude. You don't have a chance."

"What up with the 'dude' thing?" I asked, and he laughed.

"California..." was all he said, and both of us chuckled, letting the horrors of bigoted hypocrites slip from our minds.

Logan and I had a nice second lunch at the café. He regaled me with stories about growing up in Nashville, and the culture shock of moving out to Oregon for college. I told him more about my artwork, like where I drew my inspiration and the sorts of things I most enjoyed about being an artist. He seemed genuinely interested, and I wondered if he'd ever let me paint him. He dropped me off at my trailer a few hours later, pulling me in for a kiss and then playfully swatting my ass as I climbed out of his car. I went to bed that night smiling, thinking about the best ways to capture Logan on canvas.

I got a call the following week from Veronica Lewis at Riverview Art Gallery, saying the art buyer she'd been in contact with wanted my entire inventory. "What?" I asked. "All my pieces? Why? What is she going to do with them?"

"A group from Murfreesboro plans to convert an old historic home into an art museum. They viewed the photos you sent me and love your art, and because you're local, they thought you'd be the best first purchase for the museum."

I was shocked. "Wow, okay. That's... that's overwhelming."

She giggled. "It's amazing, right?"

"Yeah, I can't believe it. I feel like I should talk to them or something, to say thank you."

"No need. They've already put down a deposit. The property is already being renovated, and when it's done, the paintings will be moved into their permanent home."

"Is it just my art that's being displayed?" I asked, still overwhelmed and a little confused.

"Oh, no," the woman said. "They'll have several artists on display, but yours will be the only contemporary art. At least for now."

I really didn't know what to say. I thanked her before hanging up and sat in Grandpa's old chair, staring at the wall. She'd told me the group hadn't tried to negotiate a discount for the collection, which should've surprised me in and of itself, considering how high I'd priced each piece. Even though I considered them priceless, I never imagined anyone would willingly pay top dollar for my artwork.

My heart hammered before a calmness settled over me, as if my grandpa were here. I said quietly, "I guess all your investment finally paid off. Most of my art will be displayed in a new museum in Murfreesboro, of all places." I could almost feel the clap on my shoulder in congratulations like Grandpa used to do.

I'm proud of you, Grandson. His unspoken words echoed in my mind, pulling the tears from my eyes.

"I miss you, Grandpa. I miss you so much."

The moment lasted for a few seconds more, and just like that the air was lighter and I felt alone again. It seemed fitting that my grandpa would've come back to celebrate this moment with me. Without him, I'd never have had this kind of success.

A knock at the door caused me to swipe at my eyes. I quickly went to open it and was pleased to find Logan on the other side. "Hey, come in," I said. Logan must've noticed my red-rimmed eyes because he instantly looked concerned and asked if I was okay. "Yeah, baby. I feel fantastic."

I explained what'd just happened with the art sale, and he jumped into my arms, then twirled me around the living room in circles. "Oh my God, Matt, that's amazing! When do I get to see some of it?" he asked.

I immediately thought of the piece I'd painted of our first day in the vineyard and decided it wasn't the right time to show him that one. Not yet. I wanted that to be a special surprise.

"Wait here," I said, and dashed back to my old bedroom and pulled out the painting I'd done when the church voted to let Atwell go.

"Here," I said, handing the abstract piece to him and feeling insecure all of a sudden. "I just finished this one."

He stared at it for a long time, studying it in detail, before he said, "It's the church, isn't it?"

I was shocked he recognized it. "Yeah, but how could you tell?" I asked.

He pointed at the blob of paint at the top of the canvas and said, "I recognize the demon behind the pulpit."

I cringed. "Dang, I probably shouldn't show this one around, huh?"

He smirked, then shrugged. "I doubt most people would get it, but after all you've been through, I caught on pretty quick. You had to release all that negative energy somewhere, makes sense it'd be on canvas. No, you definitely *should* display it. In fact, let's put it in the winery barn where it'll be on full display after we open."

"Nah, I've got other ideas for that. For now, let's hold off on this one."

Feeling naughty, I chuckled and said, "Maybe I can put it in the new chapel I'm gonna have built in my grandpa's name."

"Wow, that's cool. Where at?" he asked.

"Between here and the barn. It'll be right off the main road, so we can put in a little parking lot and people will be able to visit without disturbing anyone who lives along there. It's also right next to the little creek that feeds the bigger stream that once powered the mill, which will make for some peaceful outdoor places to meditate as well."

"That's going to be amazing, Matt. We'll have to take a walk there later so you can show me the spot."

I nodded. "So, what brings you here?" I asked.

"You mean other than wanting to see your handsome face?" he asked, giving me a quick peck on the lips. "I got a phone call from my friend Gren. He's coming to Nashville and wants to swing by to see the winery."

"Like your ex-boyfriend, Gren?" I asked, then caught myself. "No, don't answer that, it's not my business."

Logan grinned, and said, "Yes, he is my ex, and yes, it *is* your business since we're dating, but Gren and I are just friends and have only been just friends for several years."

His reassuring smile settled my unease at the thought of him hanging out with an ex-boyfriend. Logan had never given me a reason not to trust his word. "When's he coming?"

"Week after next," he said. "I'm excited about his visit, actually. It's been a while since I've seen Gren, and I want to get his opinion on the wine at this stage to see if he thinks we're on the right track."

"I thought you said he wasn't into wine."

He coughed at that. "No, I said he wasn't into running a winery. He's probably one of the most talented sommeliers around, he just isn't interested in the business side of it."

"Sommelier?" I asked.

"Expert in wine. He's a sought-after judge for competitions around the country because he can pick up on some of the most subtle elements of wines."

"I hate him already," I said, causing Logan to laugh.

I kissed him then, and he melted into me. When he pulled back, he said, "You have no cause to be jealous.

You'll see just how incompatible we are once you meet him. Besides, I'm gonna be the jealous one 'cause I know for a fact he's gonna be trying to get into your pants."

It was my turn to bark out a laugh. "Seriously, you're gonna bring your ex here and you think he'll be trying to hit on *me*?"

"Yep, he's a shameless flirt, but I trust him not to actually try anything. You'll understand when you meet him."

"What if I decide to run off with him and leave you to run the winery on your own?"

"Then I'll feel sorry for you. Gren is not an easy lover for anyone, and he'd drive a free spirit like you to insanity."

"Aah, and here I thought I'd found a way to make you jealous," I said with a smirk.

"You'll have to do better than Gren, I'm afraid."

Twenty-Four

Logan

G REN SHOWED UP AS planned, but Matt wasn't here. He'd ventured to Murfreesboro to meet the museum group buying his art collection. I'd ended up going with him to get his hair cut and then forced him to wear his suit instead of slacks. "This is important. You need to dress to impress," I'd told him.

"You're acting like an old mother hen," he'd said, laughing at my words. "They're interested in my paintings, not the fact that I'll be wearing a tie."

I punched him lightly on the arm. "Well, I could go get Ms. Beth to give you what for. She'll show you motherly fussing."

He cringed and said he was sorry and that he'd gladly wear the suit to avoid his step-grandmother getting after him. She had given us her blessing to date, not that we needed it, but I think it eased Matt's mind, on the condition that I stopped calling her Ms. Brinks. So, Ms. Beth it was from now on.

Gren arrived about an hour after Matt left. As we toured the property, I ignored the way he wrinkled his nose at our small operation. When he made some offhanded comment, I reminded him that when his great-grandfather started the vineyards his family owned, it was on less than an acre and situated behind a little nineteen twenties bungalow.

Gren laughed. "Yes, but that was a century ago."

"Everyone has to start somewhere, you pretentious snob."

Gren's smile showed me he had just been pulling my chain. He was a snob, no doubt, but he was a good guy overall. Despite knowing that, I was glad Matt wasn't here to see Gren give me grief. Gren and his sense of humor took a little getting used to, but I had a feeling the two would get along well given half a chance.

Gren tasted the wine, and he seemed impressed. At his family-owned vineyards, they grew seven different kinds of grapes. Their winery also sold various other merchandise, making it a significant operation. Despite that, their wines weren't renowned. Rather than enter competitions, they were content making large quantities of lower-priced wines to sell in bulk to grocery stores. That's what had gotten me in trouble with the manager years ago. I'd recommended making minor changes to increase the quality of their wines, but that had never been their focus.

"This is quite good," Gren said. "You've done well and if it matures as it seems to be doing already, you'll have a legit little wine here."

That made me smile with relief. "I thought so as well."

We hung out, talked about the winery, and I showed him the equipment Matt's grandpa had invested in. "That's pretty good stuff for a winery this size," he said. "I'm impressed."

"I think the original owner wanted the best, but I also think he wasn't planning on hiring much help. My guess is the equipment reps assured him he could do this on his own, or mostly on his own, by investing in automated processes."

Both of us had dealt with equipment reps, and Gren nodded his agreement.

"Regardless, it was nice to have it during harvest season. It saved us a lot of time and energy. It might've saved the wines too."

"Young whippersnappers think they gotta go with this new-fangled stuff," he said, and I could almost hear his father saying that, which made me laugh out loud.

"The man who bought all this wasn't a young whippersnapper," I said, chuckling. "His grandson now running the place is, though, assuming we all still fit in that category."

I set Gren up in my guest bedroom, and Matt joined us the next morning for breakfast. As I suspected, Gren and Matt hit it off well enough. But, in truth, because Matt was so laid-back, I figured he got along with most people.

The three of us walked among the vines as I explained my plans for them. When we came to the forest, I said, "I'm trying to convince Matt that we should expand here, doubling the vineyard with the vines he's already growing."

"You should add a white wine to your grouping too, since most of the folks around here will prefer a sweeter wine."

I made a face and Gren chuckled. "Now who's the snob?" he asked.

"Well, me, of course. But he's right, Matt, we should add a white wine. And we should diversify the reds as well. I found a nursery just down the road in Warren County that supplies Merlot as well as several white wine varieties already grafted and ready to plant."

Matt just smiled. I knew he didn't really care either way, but ultimately, it was his decision to make. I made a mental note to speak to him about it later.

"How much land do you own?" Gren asked him.

"A lot. Along with the current vineyard, there's the wooded areas all the way up to that hillside above the tree line."

"That's good grape-growing land all facing south," Gren said, pointing to the hillsides facing us. "You could leave the wooded area intact and just move the vineyards up there, if you wanted. Once you get established, you'll get a lot of tourists who want to wander around the vineyards. We make almost as much off tourism as we do wine sales. Keeping little wooded areas like this undeveloped is perfect for picnics and family gatherings."

I hadn't really thought about the winery operation long-term. Gren came from generations of winegrowers, so he'd know that sort of thing better than me. Ultimately, I was all about the grapes. The money-generating tourism stuff was better left to that sort of expert.

When I turned to Matt, I could tell he was pretty-much lost to the entire conversation and, making eye contact with Gren, I realized he knew it too.

Novices were always coming in and out of the wine-making business. Technically, I'd still be considered a novice by most people in the industry, but at least I'd studied and had a degree and some hands-on knowledge to back it up. Folks like Matt who fell into it, well, that was another thing altogether. Regardless, his grandfather had hired me, and he'd kept me on, and I felt I could bring some value to the discussion.

That night, after Matt left, Gren asked, "So, you've moved to a part of the country not known for its wine and are working for a complete novice? I mean, I know you were being snubbed back home, but this is a bit extreme."

I shrugged. "You gotta make a name for yourself somewhere, and I *am* from here, Gren. When the fire destroyed the only winery that'd really respected me, I almost gave up altogether. This landed in my lap, and it just feels right."

"Well, the wine tastes right, at least for its age. Maybe you'll surprise me."

"Maybe I don't give a damn what you think," I said, chuckling.

He rolled his eyes, knowing better. "Maybe. But, once your wine is aged and properly vetted, I'd be happy to introduce it to a few of my colleagues. It might garner you just the right amount of attention to get you back to a real winery, where you belong."

I hadn't thought of that, to be honest. I'd just figured I'd be here at least until I was either let go or the winery closed altogether. In any case, we were a long way from that. No need to consider what might be until I had more to share with people than a green immature wine with potential.

TWENTY-FIVE

MATT

I WAS JUST ABOUT to go run some errands when Logan texted asking if I would mind entertaining Gren for a few hours. Logan's aunt wanted to spend time with him, and he didn't want to rebuff her offer since their relationship was still a bit fragile. So, I stopped by the apartment, and that's when Gren talked me into showing him around town.

"That'll take about ten minutes," I said, and he laughed.

We ended up getting breakfast at the Crawford City Café. Gren's face morphed into a smile when he saw the huge buffet laid out with all sorts of breakfast goodies. The café was always packed in the mornings, and we had to wait fifteen minutes before we could get a seat, but we met several folks who came and went, which I think Gren enjoyed. I didn't know much about Oregon, where he was from, but I did know there was something unique about a small town in the rural South. Good and bad, people seemed to be involved in your life.

When we finally got our plates and he began to eat, he moaned like he was having an orgasm. "My God, this cinnamon roll is like eating a cloud," he said, causing me and several people sitting around us to laugh.

"It's really a great place to eat. Most popular place in town."

"So," he said after swallowing down another mouthful, "...you plan on being a winery owner then?"

"No, I plan to be a landowner who lets Logan work his magic while I stay the hell out of his way," I said, just a little defensively.

"You're not after the prestige of owning a winery?"

The mouthful of coffee I'd been about to swallow almost shot up through my nose, and I coughed. "Around here, I'm considered something between a moonshiner and an uppity snob because of that winery. I'm not even sure why my grandpa started it other than maybe to appease his wife. But I can assure you, he didn't give a damn about prestige, and I'm too ignorant to know or care about it either."

Gren studied me for a long time before he laughed. "I think you're probably telling me the truth. So, Logan says you're an artist?"

With that, our conversation turned to more benign topics. I could tell that Gren didn't really approve of me as a winegrower, and I didn't really give a crap what he thought, so any further discussion about the winery would likely end up with one of us not liking the other. Best to avoid such landmines for both our sakes.

As it turned out, Gren had a very proficient knowledge of art, and even liked some of the more obscure artists that I did. I told him about my art collection going into a new museum in Murfreesboro and from that moment on, we spent our morning chatting about that and what it meant for my career as an artist.

It was funny that my art would be the easier subject between us. I usually didn't like sharing what I did or why. But like Logan, Gren was easy to talk to and I could tell he was genuinely interested.

On our drive back to the winery, he asked, "So, I was thinking it'd be nice to bottle up your first official bottles of wine as a present to Logan. This really is a big deal to him, no matter how you feel about it."

We were back to the wine conversation and his slight, intentional or not, about the first bottle being important to Logan, but probably not to me, got my back up.

"I realize it's important to him. And *he* is important to me."

I could feel Gren's eyes on me as I kept mine fixed on the road. "I suspected there was more going on between the two of you."

His comment hung in the air as I drove down the driveway and parked in the makeshift parking lot alongside the barn.

"Logan is special," he continued. "Even if we'd been compatible as lovers, I knew I'd end up hurting him in the long run. We're much better off as friends. I think you might be the perfect match for him, though."

I couldn't hold back a blush at Gren's directness, though the sentiment felt good to hear from someone who knew Logan so well. My skin felt hot, and he must've noticed the tips of my ears had turned pink because he smirked. "I'll tell you what, I'm going to help you out while doing something special for Logan too. Tell him you sold me a barrel of wine. He's gonna be mad at you, but at the same time, it'll stroke his ego a bit. I'll bottle the wine back in Oregon and put it under your own label and you can give it to him as a reminder of his first batch of wine as well as your winery's. What do you say?"

It was a very generous offer, but I still had to think about it for a moment. "I wouldn't sell the wine without Logan's permission. He'd know that, so he'd figure it out quickly enough. But I can tell him you asked, and I can pretend like I need the money since my inheritance is still in probate. That way he'll be more likely to say yes out of sympathy."

Gren laughed out loud. "Yes, that's better, and getting him to agree will likely keep you out of the hot seat too. See, that's one of the biggest reasons I wasn't good for him. I'd have just pushed forward instead of asking him. You really are a good match."

As I predicted, Logan was visibly disappointed when I mentioned the sale, but he agreed it would be a good way to create a little income until the inheritance came through. Seeing his nearly crestfallen expression almost made me back out, but I also believed once he held his very first bottle of wine in his hand, he'd be pleased.

The next day, as Logan worked on some stuff with the equipment and wine, I pulled Gren aside, and said, "He's agreed we can send the barrel to you. I've been researching wine labels and I think I'd like to create it myself."

When he cringed, I laughed. "I'm an artist, and I know how important minimalization is for advertising. I read all about that last night, but I'd like this batch to be special and the label to be special too."

When he nodded in agreement, I added, "I think we should call it Logan's First."

Gren smiled at that. "You really are a romantic, aren't you?"

I winked at him. "Maybe, or maybe I'm just taken with that guy in there."

Gren helped me prepare the wine for shipping to prevent it from being damaged, and it was in the mail to Oregon before he left.

That night, as I cuddled with Logan in front of his fireplace, he asked, "So, did you ask Gren to buy the wine, or did he offer?"

I shrugged. "He said he'd like to have a sample of your wine and I agreed, provided you didn't mind. Are you regretting it now?"

"No, I was just curious. I guess I'm not too surprised he was interested. He's been wanting to create an award-winning wine since I've known him. His father isn't really interested in such things, but I have to wonder if maybe he wanted the wine to help promote his interest."

"You think he'd pass your wine off as his?" I asked, suddenly worried. I'd only known Gren a couple of days, but the man didn't strike me as any sort of swindler.

"No, he's too honest for that, but he might serve it to some of his contacts and say he's found a supplier that has potential. That in and of itself would elevate him with some of his wine aficionados."

"So, as long as he doesn't claim it as his, why do you care?" I asked.

"I don't really. It's just, I think we need to get credit for the work we're doing here. The people who taste that wine will assume it's either from Oregon or California. I seriously doubt he'd tell anyone it's from Tennessee."

For a moment, I wondered if maybe the smooth man had outwitted me into thinking I was doing something good for Logan. I couldn't figure how it would matter in the long run, though. Besides, Gren hadn't paid me for the wine, I'd sent it on my own accord by paying for the shipping, and I'd agreed to pay for the bottling as well. I guess it was possible he could cheat us and put crappy wine in the bottles, but that wouldn't really serve his interests and he seemed genuinely concerned about Logan's future success. I guessed time would tell just how good of a friend Gren was to Logan.

Twenty-Six

Logan

T HE WEEK BEFORE THANKSGIVING, Matt got word from his attorney that the probate case had been closed and he was the official owner of the property. There was a lot more to it than that, but basically, the place was his, and all the legal hoopla was behind him.

I assumed the church pulling out of the running for his inheritance had sped up the process.

"Hey," I said to Matt one evening as we were both just about to doze off in front of the TV, "...wanna come to Thanksgiving with my family?"

He was quiet for a moment until I turned around to see his nervous expression. "What? Were you planning to spend the holiday with Ms. Beth?" I asked.

"No, she's been invited to dinner with friends. It's just, that's a big step, meeting your parents. I mean, we haven't even, you know..."

I chuckled and resumed my position on the sofa, laying against his chest. "You can't avoid my family forever, and besides, they will love you. Mom's been giving me grief for weeks to bring you by to meet her. Ever since Aunt Polly visited and spilled the beans about us being a thing."

"I guess, but it's not fair that I don't have a family to force you to endure the holidays with," he said, and then tickled me when I pretended to be angry. "But yes, I'll come to dinner and meet your parents. Thank you for inviting me."

As it was with most American families, Thanksgiving at my parents' house was always a huge hog fest. Mom and Aunt Polly cooked like fiends. In my attempt to arrive as late as possible to avoid being roped into helping, we showed up about twenty minutes before the meal was served. That didn't stop Mom from pulling Matt into the kitchen to whip homemade topping when he ignorantly offered to help. "He'll learn," I told Dad when I found him hiding in his office playing solitaire on the computer.

"So, you seem to really like this one," Dad said in his totally obvious but trying to be sly way.

"I like him fine," I replied, then quickly changed the subject. "So, what's happening at school? Anything interesting happening this term?"

He chuckled. "Nice try, but if you want that poor boy to avoid getting the third degree, you'd better give me something to feed your mom before we all sit around the dinner table."

I sighed deeply, reminding myself of the times I'd sat here having to confess my sins to my dad throughout my teen years.

"I do like him. He's smart and funny and incredibly talented."

"He's also your boss," Dad said, and when I blushed, he turned from his computer and squared his chair with mine.

"He wasn't really until like a few days ago, not officially. He inherited the place from his grandpa, who hired me."

Dad put his hand up, and said, "Son, I'm not judging. I'm stating a fact. You like him, and *now* he's your boss."

"Yeah, I do, and he is. We're not making a secret of it."

"Is that gonna cause trouble in the future?"

"I mean, possibly, but Dad, the wine we're making is good. Like, really good. If I manage to help him pull off an award-winning wine, even if our relationship goes south and he ends up firing me, I will have shown what I'm capable of. That's something, and it could open other career doors if need be."

Dad nodded. "I think I'm more worried about your heart. You aren't one to let people in. Do you realize this is the first guy you've ever brought home for us to meet?"

I stared at him in surprise because no, I hadn't realized that. "It's not like I meant it to be like that. He lost his grandpa and didn't have anywhere to go for Thanksgiving."

Dad laughed. "Well, regardless of your intentions or reasons, he's here now and your mom and aunt are like buzzards circling their prey."

"Oh God," I said, and jumped up. "I left him in the kitchen with them. They must be interrogating him by now."

"Oh, no doubt of that, but if you go in there, you'll just make it worse. I suggest you sit back down, and we'll battle it out with one of your old video games. That always seemed to put you at ease."

I chuckled and we went through some of the games we'd played together when I was in high school. I hadn't seen some of them since I left home for college. I rarely had time or energy to game any longer, not that I'd be using these old ones anyway.

Regardless, it was fun kicking Dad's butt again. True to form, he still sucked at gaming, and he never really cared all that much either. I knew it was just his way of spending time with me.

Dinner wasn't nearly as uncomfortable as it could've been, probably because my mom and aunt had already drilled Matt for information in the kitchen. Aunt Polly really did seem different since the day she'd come to my apartment to apologize.

She was a lot more fun and laid-back now. She even teased Matt about being a handsome single man stuck in the middle of nowhere. "It's a wonder some man hasn't swept you off your feet," she said, then giggled when she looked over at me. I'd, of course, blushed from head to toe.

I was pondering getting even, when my cousin said, "Speaking of that, Mom and I would like to go ahead and let ya'll know, I'm coming out of the closet."

We all stared at Millie like she'd grown a second head before I glanced over at my aunt, who was smiling. Beneath that pasted smile, I could see the grimace that wanted to come out, but I was proud of her for holding it back.

"Well, in that case, we need to have a party to celebrate!" I said, and Dad and Mom agreed. "You know, the church threw me a party when I came out."

Millie chuckled. "I seriously doubt that'll be happening back in Mayville. But I did want y'all to know."

"Are you dating anyone?" Mom asked, as if Millie had just told everyone she liked wholewheat instead of white bread.

"Yeah, sort of." She looked over at Matt and blushed. "Lia Edison and I have been going out for a while."

Matt choked on a bite of mashed potatoes. When he got his composure back, he said, "Lia Edison, as in daughter of Lidia and Jim?" Millie nodded. "I'm happy for you both. Now, if you don't mind, please tell my cousin she needs to call me!" he said.

"Oh, how had I forgotten you were related to the Edisons? That's your mama's folks, isn't it?" Aunt Polly asked.

Matt smiled. "Yes, ma'am. Lia is my first cousin on my mom's side."

He looked over at Millie and winked. "She's also ornery as they come. I wish you all the luck," he said, causing the entire table to laugh, even Aunt Polly.

When the conversation shifted to other things, I leaned over to my aunt and whispered, "I'm proud of you."

She looked surprised and said, "It's you who is the hero in this story. If I hadn't had you to lead the charge, I might've said or done something to drive off my baby girl."

She leaned over and kissed my cheek before wiping at a tear that'd run down her cheek. "Thank you, nephew," she said.

"What are you two whispering about over there?" my mom asked.

Aunt Polly replied, "You were always the nosiest person, Jennie. I swear you're always lurking about."

Both Mom and Dad blushed then, causing the rest of us to belt out a laugh. When Aunt Polly confessed that she'd told us the story of Dad making Mom pregnant behind the shed by kissing her, they both blushed even deeper. "It was humiliating," Mom said. "I swear they all thought we were really making babies back there. The most I ever got in the shed was a hickey."

We all ended up laughing then. I looked over at my Aunt Polly and could hardly believe she'd come so far in such a short time. I couldn't really take credit for it, though. The incredible man sitting next to me who'd stood up in church and rightfully called out a hypocrite in front of God and the world, he was what had made this all possible.

The coming-out party turned into plans for a bigger celebration marking Millie's coming out, Matt getting his inheritance, and the vineyard producing our first batch of wine. Matt kindly offered up his farm as a venue.

"It'll be cold before Christmas, but if we get enough fires going, people can hang out around there. The tasting rooms are big enough that we can get quite a few people in there," Matt said. "We can have our official ribbon-cutting before Todd and Amos begin refurbishing the mill and cabin, which won't happen until spring. The plans for the chapel are done, so we can set that up so people can see what it'll look like too."

Excitement vibrated through the room. My mom and aunt loved to plan a party, as was evidenced in the extravagant parties they used to throw Millie and me for our birthdays growing up. The rest of Thanksgiving dinner was spent brainstorming for the celebration.

As I watched my family and Matt deep in discussion, I realized just how lucky I was. Not only did I have an amazing family, but my boyfriend had been pulled into the fray with little to no effort, at least now that Aunt Polly was free of the hateful preacher who'd once clouded her common sense. If I could've designed the perfect family holiday, I wouldn't have even imagined it being this good.

TWENTY-SEVEN

MATT

PREPARATIONS FOR THE PARTY proved to be as big a job as harvesting and making the wine had been. I mostly took a back seat to Ms. Polly and Ms. Jennie, though. Logan's mom must've been staying at his aunt's house in town, because they'd literally showed up every day since Thanksgiving, measuring spaces and bringing in decorations. Lord, this was going to be a heck of a lot bigger affair than I'd anticipated.

I met Todd, Ash, Doc, and Amos for dinner that Saturday, and explained how Logan's mom and aunt had taken over the party planning. I didn't add that it was also Millie's coming-out party, since that was something she needed to announce herself. As far as my cousin was concerned, that was another story altogether.

My aunt and uncle had been even more distant, if that was possible, since I'd come out. I hadn't heard from them once after Grandpa died, then the fiasco at their church happened. I'd texted Lia twice since Thanksgiving, but as yet, she hadn't texted me back. I'd corner Millie once she returned home from school on winter break and ask her what she knew. I knew enough to keep my distance, though. Mom's family were more conservative than Grandpa had been, and that was saying a whole lot, considering the man helped run a megachurch in the middle of nowhere, Tennessee.

The guys were all excited for me, and planned to attend the festivities. Doc, especially, had a ton of ideas about what we could do once we got the winery up and running.

"We've got a while before the Mercantile Building is done. You ought to consider renting a small space from Todd and have tastings there. We're gonna have the boutique hotel on the upper floors, so a nice wine shop would really tie in well."

"Y'all need to be talking to Logan about all this," I said with my hands up. "I'm clueless about it all. Just the suggestions you've made make me want to hide under the buffet table."

All four men laughed at me. "Oh, a little birdie told me you've sold your art to the Bailey Mansion Art Gallery going up in Murfreesboro," Ash said. I must've looked shocked, because he looked sheepish in return. "I probably shouldn't have said that. I know a couple people who've donated to the museum, and they're all ecstatic about having so much of your art in its permanent collection."

I sighed. "It's still a shock to me. You know, I've only sold a handful of pieces myself. I was forced into listing those, so having them go into such a prestigious place, I'm just coming to terms with it."

Ash smiled. "Well, we're looking forward to seeing your work once the museum is all set up."

"Speaking of getting stuff set up, did you decide if you're gonna go ahead and include the chapel in the building plan?" Todd asked.

"Yeah, I think I'd like to. I know it's sort of overkill to do all three buildings at once, but like Amos told me, it could save a lot of money if I include it now."

"I think it's quite a nice tribute too. I went to the chapel in Eureka Springs, and man, it's something. Makes you feel like you're standing next to God while you're in it."

I smiled. "Yeah, and the site it's gonna be on is a special place for me, and has been for my family for a long time, I think."

As we were chatting, the other town doctor, a man I hadn't met yet, came in with his husband and daughters in tow. The men were introduced to me as Doc Gib and Doc Allen. I hadn't realized they were both doctors. "There seems to be a whole bunch of doctors in the room all of a sudden. Are y'all trying to tell me something?" I asked.

The group laughed. "This is still a two-doctor town. Doc Allen works in Nashville, and I'm retired," Ash's dad quickly said.

"Not quite, if you're the mayor."

Doc laughed. "Touché," he replied.

I ended up inviting them to the party as well. They lived in the big Victorian mansion at the end of one of Crawford City's main streets. It was one of the town's oldest and most impressive buildings, and it made me happy that their young family now owned it.

By the time the day of the celebration arrived, I was ready for it to be over. Artist I might be, and the two women kept reminding me of that, but decorating wasn't my thing. I was not a designer, or a crafty person by any stretch.

However, the party was a major hit. People from both Mayville and Crawford City came out to celebrate. My grandpa had produced several bottles of wine himself, which we put out for people to drink. They'd been part of his initial experiment in wine-growing, and Logan said it tasted pretty good since Grandpa had let him sample some on his first visit. Logan held a few bottles back, though, and stored them in a dark glass-covered shelf under Grandpa's picture that we'd hung in the big tasting room.

Ms. Beth took a full bottle and stuck it in her gigantic purse, saying she was out, then laughed when I opened another bottle and poured her a glass. She took a long drink and sighed. "I'm so happy you've done all this, boys," she said. "I can almost hear Josiah saying how proud he is of y'all."

"Ms. Beth, it wouldn't be happening if it wasn't for you," I said, and she tut-tutted me.

"I told you to call me Grandma. I am legally, you know."

"Yes, ma'am," I said. "Thank you, Grandma."

She smiled a cute, tipsy little smile at that, and dashed off to find her girlfriends she'd brought with her.

Outside, people were gathered around several bonfires set near the barn, safely away from the building, forest, and vines. We'd had a warm spell and it was sixty degrees out, which was a huge blessing. Often by now, daytime temperatures could drop to freezing.

Christmas music drifted through the barn and beyond as our guests drank cider and Grandpa's wine, ate food brought in as a potluck, and enjoyed each other's company. At three thirty, Ms. Polly announced that everyone needed to head over to the ribbon-cutting ceremony. Folks had the option of walking or taking a hayride to the old homestead.

I hopped on the hayride alongside Doc and Amos, who'd come to support us. Doc was set to give a speech about the history of the old mill, and how it used to be the only mill serving Crawford City and the surrounding areas, then I'd cut the ribbon to make it official we'd soon be bringing the mill back to life.

Twenty-Eight

Logan

I MOSTLY HUNG OUT in the wine-making room, answering questions about the process. Mom and Aunt Polly had bought some box wine and made wassail for people to drink. I thought it was ridiculous and totally not a wine connoisseur's thing to do, but one didn't win any arguments when it came to Mom and Aunt Polly's holiday party plans.

"It's a centuries-old Christmas tradition, honey. Get behind it," Mom chastised me when I wrinkled my nose at the mulled wine.

I was one of the last to leave for the ribbon-cutting. Mostly, I hung back to lock up to make sure the wine wasn't left vulnerable again. I was far from getting over that incident, and even though we hadn't seen hide nor hair of the nasty old bigot, I still didn't trust he wouldn't try something if given half a chance.

After blowing out the candles my aunt had lit around the prep room, I locked up and used the ancient ATV that Matt had left behind. I picked up a few stragglers along the way and was approaching the mill when I realized I'd forgotten to blow out the candles Aunt Polly had placed on the tables we'd set up inside the barn. I dropped off my passengers and rushed back.

When I got there and opened the main door, a young man wearing a backpack came walking out. "How did you get in there?" I asked.

"Sorry, I was already in here. I had to use the restroom."

It sounded plausible, since I hadn't thought to check the restroom before locking up, but I was going to get his information anyway. That he was beginning to act nervous about something only raised my suspicions.

Just then, Millie walked around the corner of the building with a young woman about her age. I could tell from the blush on their faces, this was probably Lia.

"Oh, hi, Leland," Millie said.

The boy blushed. "Hi, Millie. Hi, Lia."

Both girls knowing the boy eased my mind a little, particularly since they seemed friendly toward him. No sense in making a scene that wasn't warranted. I'd need to remember to ask my cousin about him later, though.

"Are y'all going to the ribbon-cutting?" I asked.

The three of them nodded, and after I blew out the table candles, we piled into the ATV and headed that way.

The ceremony was perfect. Doc, in his official capacity as mayor, gave a short but informative speech about how important the mill was to all of Crawford City and the county, and how it would be again after the renovation.

I looked around the crowd gathered and guessed we had well over a hundred people present. Had this been a year ago, I bet few people would've come to Matt's ribbon-cutting, out of concern for angering the hateful preacher. Heck, my Aunt Polly being here and chatting with my cousin and her girlfriend was testament enough that things really were changing for the better.

Twenty-Nine

Matt

L IA HAD SHOWN UP for the party and we'd spoken briefly, but really only enough for her to confirm that her parents were causing a lot of upset about her coming out.

She shut down quickly, though, when Millie came over, clearly not wanting her girlfriend to know about family problems. I was disappointed for my cousin in having to deal with it, but not surprised. Her parents had practically made it their mission to cause me grief when I'd come out, and I wasn't even their kid. I didn't envy Lia growing up under their self-righteous thumbs.

Millie and Lia stayed to help clean up as the crowds dispersed. I was outside with Todd, helping to douse what was left of the bonfires, when my aunt and uncle drove up. "Shit," I said under my breath. "This ain't gonna be good."

Todd heard me and asked if everything was okay.

"Yeah, sorry, it's my aunt and uncle. I'm going to go meet them and see what's up." By the time I got to their truck, I saw them dumping furniture and boxes onto my driveway. "What's going on?" I asked.

Both of them ignored me and continued unloading the truck.

I didn't really know what to do until Lia walked up and stood next to me. Her dad looked at her with such hatred, my heart sank. "You are no longer our daughter. This is what you had left at our house. Never come back," he spat out as he threw a lamp onto the pile. Her mom wouldn't even look at her as she climbed into the passenger side of the truck. My uncle slammed his door shut and peeled out of the parking lot, sending dust and gravel flying.

"Lia, I'm so sorry," I said. She began to cry, and I wrapped her into a hug. "Oh, honey, I'm so sorry."

A few minutes later, Logan's family were all outside, each taking turns comforting her. Millie cried, too, telling her she was sorry for getting her into this.

"Baby, do you not have a place to stay?" Logan's mom asked her. Lia shook her head. "Well, you'll stay with us then. Boys," she said to me and Logan, "...y'all put her things in the back of our truck."

Lia was overcome with grief, so I stepped in, and said, "It's probably best if she stays with me for a while. I'm guessing her mom will come to her senses soon enough and will want to make amends. If she's here with family, it'll be easier for her to do that."

Ms. Polly nodded sadly, as if realizing that could've easily been her and Millie had she not come to her senses already.

When Lia nodded her approval to that plan, I said to the group, "If y'all could help us move this stuff into the back of the tasting room, that'd be very helpful." Within moments, all of Lia's possessions were neatly piled in the barn, where they'd be safe. Logan took Millie and Lia to his apartment to give them space to talk, then came back to resume the cleanup.

"I've got the extra bedroom, Matt," Logan said as we finished cleaning. "Why doesn't she stay with me? No offense, but I don't think she'll feel too comfortable staying with you in that... well, your place."

I almost flipped him the bird, but remembered his family was standing around. So, I gave him a look instead. "You're probably right, although you're also very rude," I said, causing him and most everyone still there to laugh.

When the laughter died down, I said, "If you don't mind her staying here, she *will* be more comfortable."

We didn't see Millie or Lia for the rest of the evening. Logan's parents left a bit before nine, and Ms. Polly went in to check on the girls. When she returned, both of them were with her.

"Millie and I'll be back tomorrow morning to fix y'all breakfast in appreciation for all you've done," she said, but I knew it was more for Lia and Millie's sake than ours.

After they left, Logan went to get Lia's room ready, and I sat down with her and asked if everything was okay.

She nodded, but didn't look it. "They've been really edgy since you confronted Pastor Atwell. Mom knew I liked girls, and she must've told Dad because they've been shoving scripture down my throat every chance they get. Millie and I both agreed we were gonna tell our parents over Thanksgiving, so we did, and apparently, you were there when she told her family. Y'all even had a party for her. Mom and Dad weren't so great about it."

She wiped at the tears that were falling again. "They told me I had to go to conversion therapy if I wanted to remain a part of their family. Of course, I refused, saying I was an adult, and they couldn't force me to go. We've argued back and forth since then. They must've somehow known about the party 'cause they confronted me before I came here, saying that if I did they'd kick me out for good. I know I probably shouldn't have come, but, Matt, I can't live under their thumb anymore. I can't pay for college next semester, but I have a good job in Knoxville and my rent's paid up until May."

"You *can* afford college. I'll pay for it," I said, the anger at my idiotic aunt and uncle slipping out before I could rein it in.

"No, you can't do that. I have some money saved. I can get by and then next year, I'll qualify for scholarships and grants."

"Cousin," I said. "You've got one more semester, right?" She nodded. "I've inherited a good amount of money, and I'll be damned if I let your parents cut you off at the knees for being true to yourself. Fuck that and fuck them!" That earned me a small smile from her. "I love you, Lia, so stop being stubborn. You'll stay here. You, Millie, Logan and I are going to have a fucking amazing Christmas, then you and Millie will go back to school. You'll graduate and make me proud to call you my cousin, even though I'm already proud as hell of you."

Lia chuckled and wiped her eyes dry. "You were always so bossy," she said.

"Me?" I asked. "You've been trying to boss me around since you came out of the womb."

"You need someone to boss you around. You'd turn into a pile of bones if someone didn't."

We'd switched back to the teasing we'd done all our lives. Lia was several years younger than me, but despite her parents, we'd been close growing up. She was as close to a sibling as I'd ever had. At least, until I came out and my mom's side of the family had disowned me.

By the time I was ready to head back over to the trailer, Lia appeared in better spirits. She rummaged through her things, beginning to take some back to her new bedroom while I kissed Logan goodnight.

"Thank you for letting her stay," I said.

"It's your place," he replied, and I chuckled.

"Hardly, it's yours and you know it. I really do appreciate it. She'd have really hated staying in the trailer. She's always called it hillbilly junk," I said.

"She's not wrong, and you should've taken me up on my offer for you to stay here."

"Nope, this worked out perfectly. Now, good luck having any place to put your toothbrush," I said when I saw Lia coming toward us.

"Hey, I'm a great roommate," she said.

"You're a girl. Girls are known to take over a whole bathroom. I speak from experience, since I've had two such roommates who did exactly that."

"You're a hillbilly brat is what you are," she said, and stuck her tongue out at me.

I laughed and flipped her off as I headed out the door.

"Night, cousin. Night, Logan," I hollered behind me.

At least by harassing Lia a little, I could make her laugh. I just wish I could've erased some of the hate her parents had thrown at her last night. I knew I'd never forget the look on my uncle's face. I couldn't imagine she would either.

Thirty

Logan

T HE REST OF THE holiday season was spent shopping and prepping for spring. I hired a kid with a drone to take pictures of the property, then using a property map I found online, I was able to outline the borders of the estate, at least close enough that I could draw up my plans for the winery.

I planned to present it all to Matt after the new year and wanted to be prepared, especially after Gren had planted the thoughts into Matt's head already. *What's that saying, strike while the iron's hot?* That was my goal, at least.

Lia proved to be a perfect roommate. She was incredibly tidy, probably because she didn't want to disturb me, but since I spent most of my time creating those plans and collecting soil samples in different areas of the farm, I wasn't around much.

Millie tended to come by every day, and I accused her of moving in too. It was strange that my first cousin was dating Matt's. Of course, it was a small world, and Lia and Millie had gone to school together, and now they were going to the same university. I guessed that wasn't too big a surprise.

On Christmas Eve, we accompanied Matt's step-grandmother to her church in Crawford City for a candlelight service. It'd been a long time since I'd gone to one of those, but I loved how peaceful it was. It was also like we were taking the time away from all the commercialism and focusing on the sweet meanings of Christmas.

The next day, Lia, Matt, and I piled into my pickup and drove to Nashville to spend the holiday with my folks and Aunt Polly. Lia was reticent, and I could tell she was more than a little nervous, but having Matt with her seemed to take a little of the pressure off.

The minute we showed up, Lia was pulled into the fray that was my family, and I leaned over and whispered in Matt's ear, "You are so lucky that Lia took the heat off you."

He smiled guiltily. "Is it bad that I'd already thought of that?"

I elbowed him and he chuckled as he put his arm around me. The kitchen was too full, so even though both Matt and I offered to help, Mom and Aunt Polly asked us to set the table, then stay out of their way.

"So much for trying to undo sex-based stereotypes," I teased, and got *the look* from both my aunt and mother.

Dad was spending the morning with a friend who'd lost his wife recently, so it was just Matt and me in the living room. It felt so good to cuddle up with him. "What's going on with us?" I asked Matt, surprising both of us with the question.

"What do you mean?" he asked.

I leaned up to look at him, and kept my voice low. "I think we both know what I mean. You and I seem to be dancing around taking things to the next level."

Matt nodded. "It seems like we keep moving in that direction, then stuff happens to cockblock us. I mean, I like you and you make me feel all fuzzy inside when I see you or cuddle with you. Not to mention when I kiss you..."

"So, what are we, friends?" I asked.

"Sure," he said with a chuckle. "Friends that cuddle?"

"And kiss," I quickly added.

He laughed a bit, and said, "Yeah, friends that cuddle *and* kiss."

I leaned up and kissed him just as Dad came through the front door. I could tell he'd seen the kiss because he was smiling, and I inwardly groaned at the harassment it was going to cause me later.

Luckily, he didn't say anything when he came over and sat across from us.

"So, how's the wine business?" he asked.

I shrugged. "Slow at the moment, but I've been working on some plans I'm gonna present to my boss after the new year."

"And just what might those be?" Matt asked, clearly surprised.

"Can't tell you. You'll just tell my boss before I'm ready for him to know."

Matt just hmphed and pulled me closer to him. Dad changed the subject and began asking Matt questions about his work with the new art museum and when his collection would be ready to view.

I listened as he told him about the museum coordinating a big event for the grand opening. "April first is their projected opening," he said.

"Really?" I asked. "I didn't know they'd set a date."

"I heard that from Doc, so it's not official. They've had some problems with the contractor so they aren't one hundred percent sure they can pull that day off. But the benefactors are getting antsy, according to Doc, so if it's at all possible, that's the date."

"Matt, that's so cool. I can't wait to see all your art in person."

I'd harassed him into showing me pictures after hearing the announcement that the museum was buying nearly his entire collection. His art was beautiful and so different from anything I'd seen before. Since wine and art went hand in hand, I'd been dragged to many gallery openings over the years, and I could tell Matt's paintings were special and unique.

"Just know that isn't gonna get you out of working on the vineyard," I teased him. "There's quite a lot of work to do come spring."

"I'm sure we'll be fine, and if we aren't, we've got Lia for free labor."

I turned around and saw Lia come around the corner and sit in the recliner next to us.

"Um, what am I free labor for?" she asked.

Matt shrugged. "Not sure, that'll be up to the great winery manager here."

"Not really," I said. "It depends on whether the winery owner likes my ideas or not."

"I'm pretty sure he will," Matt said, and kissed me on the cheek.

Mom and Aunt Polly came out of the kitchen and called us all into the dining room for dinner. As usual, it was over the top with food. Just like during Thanksgiving, I looked around at my family and couldn't help but feel happy that I had these people in my life. The fact that Matt and Lia were now part of it just felt right.

I thought about that as I ate. Matt and I were definitely keeping things cooled down, but he already felt like family. What did that mean? I had a hard time putting my finger on how that might impact the future and my time on the farm.

"Cousin, you seem deep in thought over there," Millie said.

I glanced at Matt and blushed. No way was I gonna share what I'd been thinking about to him, much less the rest of the family.

"Yeah, just pondering on how lucky we are to have each other." I felt myself get emotional, which surprised me. I took a moment to choke back the tears that threatened to spill and get myself back under control. "I'm just feeling blessed," I said, and got a few aahs from the folks around the table.

Matt reached under the table, took my hand, and squeezed it. The sweet, discreet gesture just warmed my heart for the man that much more. And, of course, it made me that much more reticent about our relationship, or lack thereof.

After dinner, the men had clean-up duty. "You brought it on yourself with your stereotype statement earlier," my mom said when I complained.

I didn't really care, but it was fun to act like I was still a grumpy teenager when I was at home.

It didn't take as long as I thought it would, and before long, the food was put away, the dishwasher was full and running, and all the pots and pans that were caked with gunk were soaking in the sink.

When Dad, Matt and I finally came into the living room, Millie began passing out presents. I could immediately identify the one Matt had given me. It was wrapped, but its size and shape indicated a painting. I could hardly contain my excitement. If he was gifting me one of his paintings, I didn't even know how I'd react.

We all unwrapped our gifts one at a time, so photos could be taken, and everyone could ooh and aah over what we'd gotten—another family tradition of ours.

I saved Matt's gift for the very last. I slowly unwrapped it, and I could see Matt was anxious, which made me more excited, to be honest.

Tossing the wrapping paper aside, I held in my hands one of the most amazing paintings I'd ever seen. It was abstract, but as I studied the lines, shapes, and colors, it became clear this piece represented the vineyard. When I pulled the card out and read *Day One*, I realized its significance.

"Is this the first day we harvested the grapes?" I asked Matt.

He nodded, and I was embarrassed by the sudden flow of tears that'd slipped out of my eyes. "This is the most amazing gift, Matt. I don't even know what to say. It's perfect." My emotions overwhelmed me, and Matt wrapped me in a comforting embrace as I buried my face in his chest.

That was it. I was officially in love with the man. I felt closer and more connected to him than I ever had to a partner. How could that be when we'd never even had sex?

THIRTY-ONE

MATT

I'D DEBATED WITH MYSELF whether or not to give Logan the painting. It felt right, but at the same time, my paintings were a part of me. If he rejected it, I'd be devastated.

Logan gifted me with several different bottles of wine, each one labeled by him as different grade wines. Having read about such distinctions online when he'd forced me to sit with him to learn more about the business, I knew a bit about what he'd spent on these, and that made me even more reticent about what I'd brought to give him.

In the end, judging by Logan's emotional reaction, I'd made the right decision. I was amazed he recognized it for what it was too. Usually, people guessed wrong when it came to my abstract art, but not Logan, he knew almost immediately.

I held Logan in my arms as he sobbed, then pulling apart, I reached up to wipe the tears from his face. Despite being in a crowded room with family, he didn't seem to mind the intimate gesture because he leaned into my touch. "I'm really happy you like it," I said quietly.

"No, I love it. I just don't have the words."

I kissed his temple as he chuckled through the rest of his tears. "Thank you," he whispered, and kissed me sweetly.

The family took over then and everyone took turns looking at the painting. Logan's father ended up moving a framed print they had sitting on the mantel and placed the painting up there so everyone could enjoy it for the rest of the evening.

Logan got a little emotional each time he looked at it, which, if I was honest, I totally loved. It just confirmed for me that he and I were really working as a team. I poured so much of myself into my artwork, and it felt like he could really see me—the artist and the man—in the painting. That thought made *me* emotional too.

Thirty-Two

Logan

I T TOOK EVERYTHING IN me to get through the rest of the evening without becoming a basket case. I had fallen in love with a kind, gentle, thoughtful, and wickedly talented man who also just happened to be my boss, and I didn't know what to do with that realization. Did Matt feel the same? What would happen if he didn't? Would I still have a job? Should I be looking for another job?

All the questions whirled in my mind as the night wore on. As everyone began gathering up their gifts to take home, I caught sight of the concerned look on Mom's face. When I went to the kitchen to finish up the pots and pans, which was really just an excuse to give myself space, she came in and quietly confronted me.

"You okay?" she whispered as she pretended to help me with the washing and drying.

I nodded. "Yeah, just my emotions running rampant. Matt's got me feeling all wonky inside."

She chuckled. "You know a mom loves seeing her baby with that look on his face."

"Mom," I chastised, and she bumped up against me.

"He seems like a great guy, and based on the gift he gave you, I'd say he's having some wonky feelings of his own too."

"Yeah," I admitted. "But am I jumping the gun here?" I paused and looked around, making sure no one was in the kitchen. "Mom, I think I'm falling in love with him."

She nodded as if I'd stated the obvious rather than blowing my own mind, which was how I felt saying the words out loud. "Well, if you really want to find out how he's feeling, then you'd better tell him."

"No, I can't, it's not that simple. He's my boss and he's already told me that we're basically just friends. I just can't put myself out there for nothing, Mom."

She sighed. "Baby, I'm going to tell you something. If you don't deal with your emotions, they can railroad you in the future." She thought for a moment before setting down the dishtowel she'd been holding, which meant shit was about to get real. "You're more like me than your dad in that regard. We tend to bottle up our emotions, then when they get too big for us to handle, they blow up on us. I'm telling you, be upfront with him, tell him how you feel. Good or bad, at least it won't become a regret down the road."

I leaned into her, and said, "I'll think about it."

True to form, I packed it all down then, determined to stop behaving like the overly dramatic, lovesick gay boy I knew I was being and just enjoy the rest of the time we were together for the holiday. After Mom and I finished cleaning the pots and pans and stacked them to dry, we all gathered around the table for dessert.

I looked over at Matt and smiled. Friends, friends that cuddle and kiss, or whatever we actually were at this point was fine. He'd melted my heart tonight, and that was... fine. I just had to temper my feelings and see how things went. Surely I could do that, right?

THIRTY-THREE

MATT

I KNEW I WAS falling for the man and falling hard. Logan clearly loving the painting as much as I did, and getting emotional about it just made me like him that much more. But even I knew *like* was an understatement.

Was it appropriate for me to be feeling this way about an employee? No, probably not. Several of my artist friends had complained about how men had come onto them, being inappropriate and pushing their own agendas. I didn't want to be a creep like that. So, I pushed my emotions down and was determined to remain professional while at work. The rest of the time, well, I had no plan for that.

At least he didn't mind my kissing him and the occasional cuddle. That helped, at least. It also left me feeling confused about where exactly things stood with us. Was there really even an *us*?

That night when we got back to the farm, Lia excused herself to her bedroom, saying she was so full and tired she didn't think she could stay up any longer. I stared at the fire as Logan positioned the harvest painting on the mantel above the fireplace.

He popped open a bottle of wine we hadn't drunk at dinner and poured us both a glass. Since meeting him, I was beginning to develop a taste for the more dry and complex wines. I was still far from an aficionado, as he called people who loved and understood wines, but at least now, I could appreciate nuances in flavors.

We leaned back on his sofa, Logan's back to my front, and wine glasses in hand, as we watched the dancing flames. The silence was palpable, and I could tell Logan wanted to tell me something. I waited for quite a while, giving him the chance to speak his mind, but in the end, he just said, "I can't believe you gave me that painting. It looks so amazing over the fireplace, but it deserves to be in a fancy gallery or a museum. I feel strange having it here in this little apartment."

I chuckled. "Would you rather I keep in in my trailer?" I asked, and he elbowed me.

"No, you dork. I don't even want to think of this beautiful piece of art in that old rust bucket. I meant I feel like it should be enjoyed by the masses, not squirreled away in my living room."

I smiled. "It means a lot to me that you like it," I said, kissing the top of his head. "I don't care where you put the painting. Just the fact that it moves you, that's what matters to me."

Logan turned his head to the side and cuddled into my chest, and I could feel my shirt becoming damp. "Baby? What's wrong?" I asked, confused by his tears.

"Shh, I'm just an emotional ninny, I'll be okay. You just touched my heart tonight. It'll take me a moment to get myself back under control. But don't worry, I'm happy. Really, really happy."

I slowly ran my hand up and down his back in reassurance. "I'm happy, too, sweetheart. Thank you for a wonderful Christmas."

Thirty-Four

Logan

After the holidays, Lia and Millie went back to college for their final semester. Matt and Lia had multiple arguments about his paying for her tuition and other expenses, until finally, he just said he was doing it and she needed to get over it.

I could tell it was bothering her, though, so I pulled her aside and said, "Matt's a good guy, as you well know, and you're about the only family he has left. Let him do this. It's for him as much as it is for you."

After that, she made no arguments. "He's the only family I have left too," she said quietly.

"Then let him be your family. He can afford it, and he wants to do it. You can tell he does, right?" I asked.

"He's a stubborn old bull about it," she said, but couldn't hide her grin.

"Then you know you aren't gonna get him to change his mind."

"No, but I can plan to pay him back, at least."

I smiled, knowing he'd probably refuse that too, but if it got her to take the help and finish her degree, so be it.

When the cousins were safely back at school, I sat Matt down across from me in the big tasting room, spread my plans out over the counter, and began telling him my ideas.

"If you leave the woodlands, we can landscape this area near the vines enough to place some picnic tables for visitors to have lunch," I said, pointing to the spot in the drone photo. "The tics here are horrible, but I've been doing research, and we can get some Muscovy ducks to help control that. They'll also love the little stream that flows down through there since they are stream ducks."

Matt smirked at my suggestion of getting ducks. "Maybe we need to get some goats, too, to clean out the brush."

"No!" I exclaimed. "Goats and vineyards do *not* go well together. They'd put us completely out of business within an hour if they got out."

Matt chuckled and shook his head. "I didn't think of that, but I was just joking. It seems like you've really thought this through and considered everything."

"That's why you pay me," I said, then cringed inwardly. His paying me was exactly why I'd been ignoring my desire to jump him every chance I got. I quickly shook off the thought, not wanting to derail our conversation about expanding the property.

"I want to develop the upper paddock here to add both red and green grapes. This part of the vineyard isn't quite as ideal for the reds we use for the premier wine," I said, refocusing his attention on the photo. "So, I'd recommend we use these new grapes for the sweeter wines that're more popular for these parts. I mean, I'm not saying I don't want them to be a higher quality, but if we only serve the dry wines, I'm sure we'd be out of business and not attract any local agritourism."

"You're right on that one. What grapes do you have in mind?" he asked.

I tried not to go into much detail, because the bigger ask was yet to come. So, I told Matt about the grape varieties I'd researched and knew did well in this area. The upper paddock was huge, too, so we could produce a lot of the sweet stuff and improve the business side of the vineyard overall.

I also explained how he had a lot of other areas around the property we could expand the vineyard into later as well. If we did that, we'd have to hire people, but until we started drumming up business and selling the wines, it was too much for now.

"Just adding the sweets and the lower vines your grandpa planted will keep us busy, and should at least get the winery on the map," I said.

"Okay, that sounds like a perfect plan," he said. "I say let's do it."

"There's something else." I stared at him for a moment before I took a deep breath. "I know you might not like this next part, so if you don't want to do it, I'll understand. I've spoken with a few wineries that're close to Lebanon, as well as further east, and they all tell me they make most of their money from tourism. That's usually the case for wineries out West too. So, I think we need something more than just the barn and some picnic tables."

"You think I need another building?"

I nodded. "Yeah, a dedicated space for tasting rooms and selling wine that's separate from processing. I think it needs to be a regular store, too, selling merchandise and wine accessories. Getting tour groups in could lead to a lot of sales as well as promote the wine. But, we've got to have something to bring in the traffic."

"What do you suggest?" Matt asked. He looked a bit perplexed, with his brow furrowed, but he was listening closely.

"Two things. One, you yourself are a draw because of your art being part of the museum in Murfreesboro. People will come here to meet Matt Brinks, the artist, regardless of this place being a winery. But I also think the history of the farm will be a draw as well, especially once the homestead buildings are restored."

I reached under the counter, pulled out my rough sketch of the label I'd been tinkering with, and laid it in front of him.

I'd drawn a really rough sketch of the old mill, with the wheel dripping water, and written the name I'd come up with in bold colors: Brinks Mill Winery.

Matt picked up the sketch and a slow smile spread across his face. "I love this, Logan. I hadn't even thought about tying the mill into the winery side of things."

I nodded and waited until he looked back up at me. It was now or never. I cleared my throat nervously, and said, "I think you should turn the mill into the store."

He stared at me a moment, and his furrowed brow returned. "I was going to use it to host an artist in residence. That's why I hired Todd and Amos to renovate it."

I nodded. "Yeah, this would be a huge leap of faith and a change of your plans." I went over to the large printout of his property and pointed at a wooded area above the mill that I'd toured with Matt. "This would be an extra cost, but if you put your artists up here in a new building, they could easily display their art in the mill, without *painting* in the mill. They'd gain more exposure from the winery foot traffic, and create a potential revenue stream for us both if they agreed to sell their work."

Being surrounded by large boulders, the area didn't really have any potential to plant vines. But the location was beautiful, and considerable enough to construct a building to house visiting artists or even host workshops. The idea seemed like an obvious win-win to me, but I still had to convince the man who owned it all that it was the most viable option.

When Matt didn't respond and his eyes remained fixed on the property map between us, I almost chickened out. When I'd seen the initial plans for combining the old log cabin with the old mill, I immediately thought it was a bad idea. The mill itself was a cool old rugged building, but it didn't match the logs of the cabin. The logs had been salvaged and were sitting in a yard in North Georgia, about an hour and a half from here, for the time being.

"This isn't any of my business, Matt, but I've had some time on my hands and have been thinking about how best to utilize the whole property. There's also this area, just under that huge boulder at the top of the hill, where the stream bursts out of the ground," I said, pointing to the spot on the map. "It's so picturesque and it's tucked away, so there'd be all kinds of privacy. I think that'd be the best homesite... for you."

I glanced at him and, seeing he was still listening, I pushed forward. "The way the land moves along the hill, I think you could move the log cabin up there. With the improvements you're doing to the back and the huge porch you're adding to the front, you'd have privacy but still be able to see clear across the vineyard."

My hands were practically shaking, either from excitement or nerves, I wasn't sure. At least I'd finally given voice to the big idea I'd been chewing on for weeks. I took a breath and quickly added, "So, I mean, I don't really have the right to be making these suggestions, and I know it'll add a lot of expense, but if you're already having to spend the money..."

Before I could babble on any further, Matt leaned across the counter, grabbed the front of my shirt, and pulled me into a kiss. I sighed into the kiss and nearly crawled over the counter and into his lap before he pulled back.

"This is incredible, Logan. I hadn't thought it all through but you clearly have, and you're right. That area on the hill would be perfect for the cabin, and the little area above the mill *would* be a great place for the artist in residence. In fact, I'm already picturing one of those old barns with the apartment on one side and the rest of the space be a dedicated art studio. Have you talked to Todd about any of this?"

I shook my head. "No, all these plans hinge on what you want to do. This is your property, after all."

"Todd's been telling me over and over that they can't connect the cabin from behind without digging into the hillside, and since it's so rocky there, they'd probably have to blast, which would put the mill in jeopardy. I don't really want to rebuild the cabin where it was because I want that kept as a meadow. It was looking like we wouldn't have much choice, but now we do. This really does give us everything, doesn't it."

"Well, it'll be a beast to get off that hill in icy or snowy weather, but it'll be like heaven up there the rest of the year."

Matt kissed me again. "Let me run this by Todd and Amos to see what they think. If it's not too cost-prohibitive, it might just solve all our problems."

That caused me to let out the breath I'd been holding. "So, you're not mad at me for sticking my nose where it doesn't belong?"

Matt laughed. "Why doesn't it belong? I'm flying by the seat of my pants here. I knew I wanted to rehab the buildings, I just didn't know exactly how. You've given me a solution I'd never have come up with on my own. Thank you," he said, and kissed me again.

We hadn't been this intimate in a while. Not since I'd come to the realization about how I felt about Matt. As our kiss deepened, to my great reluctance, I forced myself to pull back.

"I'm... Matt, I'm sorry. Are we colleagues right now or boyfriends, or what? I'm having a hard time keeping all this separate."

Matt looked crestfallen and nodded. "No, I'm the one who's sorry. We should probably push things back to the friend zone and keep it there, at least until things are more stable and we get this business off the ground." He quickly gathered up the papers and photos strewn across the counter. "I'll take these with me to show Todd and Amos and get an estimate on the costs."

He hustled out the door before I could say much else.

Fuck. I was fucking this all up, but I couldn't keep kissing Matt like that and keep myself at a distance. It was just too hard, and it was tearing me apart inside.

He liked my ideas, though, not just about the winery, but about the entire property. In my mind, I could see this place becoming a huge tourism pull, considering how close we were to Nashville, Knoxville, and Chattanooga. If I was right, the entire farm could quickly be overrun with tourists. I probably should've shared my thoughts about that with him, but putting the artist in residence and his home up into the hills would offer considerable privacy, even on the busiest tourism days. I knew from watching other families in the wine business, like Gren's, that having your home in the middle of all the chaos could quickly interfere with your private life. Gren and his dad had struggled for years because his dad was never able to separate himself from his work. Gren had suffered as a result, as did their relationship.

I didn't want that for Matt. He was an incredibly private person, and I respected that. If he took my suggestion, he'd always be able to protect his privacy. If only he'd let me in, though.

Thirty-Five

Matt

A FTER LOGAN PULLED AWAY from me on an otherwise amazing day where he'd re-envisioned the entire mill project, I decided I needed to give him adequate space. If we didn't need to discuss the business, then I left him alone. Not chatting with him every day proved difficult at first, and I caught myself several times about to text or call him. I hadn't realized just how in-contact we'd been until the radio silence between us.

With the cabin dismantled, it was time to pull out the old trailer and give it the proper burial it deserved. Since I couldn't exactly take Logan's spare room, and not wanting to burden Ms. Beth by staying at her house, I ended up renting an apartment over an old bakery in Crawford City that'd recently closed down. The woman who'd run it was a friend of Ms. Beth's, and agreed to the rental when she'd heard I was looking for a temporary apartment with studio space until construction was completed on the farm.

The apartment came fully furnished, since the woman had just married a man with a beautiful home in Nashville, and left most of her household belongings behind. It was perfect for me since I traveled light. I hadn't kept my apartment furniture upon moving into the trailer, and Grandpa's old furniture was, for the most part, garbage to be tossed.

The few family heirlooms worth keeping had already been stored away at Ms. Beth's and would remain there until I had somewhere decent to house them. She, like Logan, wasn't a fan of the old trailer.

I moved into the bakery right before February, and was so happy to have enough elbow room to comfortably paint again. I hadn't realized just how much the small trailer had limited me.

I only saw Logan a few times that month, preferring email or text messages to conduct business as needed. Being away from him felt like something heavy sat on my chest, like I'd lost someone important. Goodness knows I knew that feeling well enough, what with having lost my parents and then my grandpa. The only difference being this loss was largely self-imposed, which stung my bruised heart.

For the past three years, and despite having an absentee boyfriend during some of that stretch, I'd spent Valentine's weekend with a group of female friends who were all perpetually single. We'd all decided that Valentine's Day was difficult to manage on our own, so we got together, got massages and mani-pedis, and basically pretended like the holiday didn't exist. The fact that the weekend always included copious amounts of wine just negated the whole forgetting experience for me this year, since it only reminded me of the person most on my mind.

I didn't say anything to the girls about my situation with Logan, though. No use making them feel bad with my sad social life, or the pitiful story of how I'd never be able to have the man I wanted more than I'd ever wanted anyone before. Things had gotten so mixed up between us since Christmas. Had Logan stayed away because I'd kept my distance? Hell if I knew, but it all hurt my heart just the same.

Todd and Amos put a bid together for the new barn and residential building on the hill above the mill, and surprisingly enough, it was very affordable. Putting the log cabin on the top of the hill was a totally different story. Just as with attaching it to the mill, huge boulders posed a problem for the cabin's new location. They stood in the way of building a driveway to the top, and even if we could construct a small one, the trucks wouldn't be able to get up there to deliver the logs or other building equipment to put the cabin together.

The solution came from Logan, once again, who'd shown up while Todd and I were discussing the issue. He showed us that the ridge where we were planting the new vineyard continued on toward where the log cabin could stand. The drive up to it would be long, but the solution was a gravel road, which we'd already decided to use to access the grapes.

When Todd's crew cleared the area where the cabin would go, he called me and asked me to meet him there.

I climbed off the old ATV I'd ridden up there and turned around three hundred and sixty degrees. "Wow, this is even prettier than I thought," I said as Todd came up beside me.

He was smiling. "I wanted you to see how beautiful it was now that we've cleared out the brush and small trees blocking the view. And the best part, even this time of winter, it's protected from the wind by being tucked just below the top of the hill and it's helped by the trees that line the downhill slope. It's truly going to be one of the best house spots in the county. You should take Logan out for a steak dinner for figuring all this out."

If only he'd let me, I thought to myself.

March was all about prepping the new vineyards and planting the new grapes Logan had sourced from the next county over.

The intensity of work helped to keep things cooled off between Logan and me. We were also surrounded by a team of people Todd and Amos had recommended. Usually, they ran a landscape company, but didn't need full crews this early in the year, so we were able to hire them to help us prepare and plant.

I could tell our progress made Logan happy. Other than that, though, he seemed guarded around me. I mourned the easiness between us that had disappeared after the holidays. I couldn't help but think I'd somehow screwed it all up by pumping the brakes. Now, not only did I not have a boyfriend, but it'd be a stretch to even call us friends at this point.

By April, we had established a nice and much easier workflow. I tended to work in my rented studio in town unless I was needed on the farm. Now that we'd planted another huge section of vines, Logan told me we could officially call a vineyard, rather than celebrating that achievement, though, we continued walking on eggshells around each other.

For the most part, Logan's days revolved around managing the grapes, and he'd email me detailed updates each week. He was also busy building fences around the wooded area that would eventually become a place for visitors to hang out and picnic. Despite his fear of goats, with a local goat farmer's prodding, he'd agreed to let her goats come into the grove to clean out the underbrush.

"You should let them come visit," Mrs. Swanson, who owned a dairy goat farm down the road, said to Logan one afternoon when we were both at the barn discussing the landscaping plans. She'd seen the work trucks coming and going from here, and stopped by to check it out.

"No, way! Goats and grapes don't mix!" he said, not unlike he had with me.

"Oh now, my girls mind their manners, Besides, we use electric fencing nowadays, so they aren't as likely to get out."

He studied her for several moments before he relented. "If you are one hundred percent sure..."

She chuckled. "I could use the brush, since they've already cleared off my land. Yours is just chock full of the yummies my girls like, and that'll help boost their milk production by half!"

Still, he supervised as Mrs. Swanson and her son put up the electric fences and made them promise repeatedly that the goats wouldn't get out. Logan's intense dislike of the animals made me chuckle, but I did think the man had a point. Goats would clean us out fast and furiously if we didn't keep them reined in.

Todd and Amos finished the rehab on the mill in mid-May and, for the time being, I moved out of the bakery and into the apartment we'd originally planned for a resident artist. The entire mill was weather-proofed now and had heating and cooling systems, so until we converted the place into a store to sell our wines and merchandise, I could use it as my studio and living space.

The new resident artist building was on the back burner since creating an official place I could call home took priority. The logs from the old cabin were being transported up to my new house site, and Amos and Todd assured me the place would be habitable by November.

I was in the mill, painting and enjoying the huge well-lit room on the second floor, when I heard Logan hollering for me.

"I'm upstairs. Come on up," I called down to him.

When he came up the stairs and saw the studio, he whistled. "This is an amazing space."

"Yeah, it is," I responded with a distracted smile. "Hold on a moment, let me finish this last part, then we can talk."

I was working on my third attempt at painting the mill as part of our official label. I wanted the label to look professional and not seem too country or too cliché. As yet, I'd not been able to make it what I wanted.

Logan stepped closer and looked over my shoulder at the canvas. When he didn't say anything, I knew he could tell it wasn't quite right either. So, I tossed my brushes in the mineral spirits I had sitting on the table and turned my attention to him.

"What's up?" I asked.

"I've got a couple more ideas," he said, and I groaned before I could stop myself.

"Your ideas are awesome, Logan, but I'm storming through my inheritance, and we haven't even sold a bottle of wine yet. I'm getting a bit nervous."

Logan chuckled. "This idea won't cost... well, it won't cost *that* much."

I sighed and gestured for him to follow me to the back, toward the apartment.

"Wow, Todd and Amos have transformed this place. It's gone from a glorified snake pit to being so modern and perfect for what I have in mind."

I turned toward him and cocked an eyebrow before pointing toward the set of recliners I'd found at Goodwill.

He sat down and returned my cocked eyebrow when he tipped slightly to the right.

"Hey," I said with a shrug. "They're temporary. I didn't want to purchase anything too nice since I'm going to have a home to move into soon."

He just shook his head before saying, "As you know, your cousin is graduating this weekend with her business and marketing degree. Lia did her final project on the winery, and I really liked her ideas. I thought maybe we could hire her to run the store and do our marketing. Since you're not going to be living in the mill much longer, and she'll need a place to stay too…"

He made a sweeping gesture with his hand, clearly referring to the apartment, and I smiled. "Logan, that's perfect. Lia showed me her project too, and I think she'd do great working for us. I bet she'd enjoy setting up the store as well."

"So, shall we offer her the job?" he said, looking hopeful.

I wanted so badly to pull Logan into my arms and kiss him silly for his brilliant idea. It almost hurt to keep them by my side, but I managed to smile and nod. "Yeah, I'll let you offer her the job, though. I don't want her to think it's just me being nice 'cause we're related."

"Deal. We'll start by tasking her with deciding what to purchase for the store. I was thinking we could sponsor the products from some of the other East Tennessee wineries. They're our competition, but if we're selling each other's stuff, it seems we can cross-promote ourselves too. I've seen that done in Oregon, and cooperating with competitors can actually increase sales."

The man was so smart, and he seemed to just have a knack for putting together solutions for things before they became actual problems. I hoped Lia would agree to the arrangement. This apartment was large enough for both of us for now, and would give her a chance to live in the space she'd be designing, not to mention, it'd be great having my cousin around. Logan really had thought of everything.

As usual, I had to pack down the emotions that swirled more and more when I was around him these days. How could I feel so at ease being with Logan, eager to earn his sweet smile and yearning for his gentle touch, but a relationship still seemed out of reach?

Thirty-Six

Logan

THE MOMENT I SAW Lia's marketing project, I knew she'd be the perfect next hire for the winery. I didn't think Matt would give me much grief about it, considering Lia was his cousin, unless he had some issue about nepotism. But even if she wasn't related, she'd have been my first choice. We needed a full-time sales and marketing manager anyway, because once the grapes took off, I wouldn't have time to manage anything else. It was almost as if providence was working alongside us.

I knew Matt and my cousin would both enjoy having Lia close by too. Millie planned on attending law school the following year, and I figured it would be hard on her and Lia to separate. Having Lia based here, secure with a job and around family who cared about her, might make Millie's trek back and forth from Knoxville less stressful.

When Matt called me upstairs, my breath caught at the sight of him covered in paint and working in the ray of light that shone through the giant window along the stream side of the building. I'd pushed him away since Christmas, determined to shield my heart from the likely possibility he would reject me and fire my ass if I gave voice to my love for him. Perhaps love was too big a word, but then again, I couldn't deny–at least not to myself–feeling things for Matt that I never had for anyone else before.

He tended to avoid me for the most part, which I honestly preferred. Every time I saw him, my heart broke just a little more with the reminder he wasn't mine. His avoidance helped ease some of that heartache, but times like this, when I just wanted to reach out and touch him for no other reason than to feel his warm skin under my palm, still hurt.

Oddly enough, while he kept a lid on his feelings around me, Matt wasn't shy about sharing his artwork. He allowed me to walk around him to look at his work in progress, and it was stunning. He'd designed a nearly perfect label for our wine. I bit my tongue, so I didn't give him any suggestions. It was enough to plan where he should put his house, his vines, what to do with his mill... God, I was such a busybody. *But thinking ahead is what I'd been hired to do*, I thought as a way to make myself feel better.

However, telling a talented and soon-to-be-renowned artist how to paint? Nope, even I would keep my mouth shut there.

As I had hoped, Matt quickly agreed to hiring Lia. I was so excited that I almost jumped into his arms and kissed him. I turned away instead and quickly walked around the newly renovated building to distract myself. The place had undergone a spectacular transformation. Todd and Amos had pulled away the crap ceiling and exposed the virgin wood beams in what was a vaulted room. The apartment only took up half the upstairs space, and the rest of the room would be great for hosting parties or dinners.

The huge windows looked down over the stream and paddle wheel. If I had any artistic talent, I'd be inspired to capture the serene nature scene on canvas. "Matt, this space is amazing. I can see now why you thought it'd make a perfect artist studio."

"It'll be better for what you proposed, though. But, yeah, I've really enjoyed the last couple of days being able to paint in here."

We walked down to the first floor, and I could see in my mind's eye the general layout of the new store and tasting room. The grindstone had been left in its original place and surrounded by glass. Todd and Amos had preserved the original wood, keeping it intact to show visitors what the mill looked like back when it was built. I couldn't be prouder of the renovation or the nod to the building's history.

I began pointing out where I thought things could go. "I'd put the wine tasting to the rear of the wheel to keep people from trying to go out the door, but as people are tasting the wine, they can also see out the windows to get a bird's-eye view of how the gristmill used to work," I said, lost in the vision of it all.

When I turned back toward Matt, his expression seemed sad. I almost asked him why when I realized it was about us and everything we weren't. For what I'd pulled away from him, and me for that matter. At the risk of either saying more than I should or kissing the frown off his face, I decided it was best to take my leave.

"So, Mom and Dad said we could ride with them up to see Lia and Millie graduate. You still up for going together?" I asked.

Matt nodded. "Yeah, just text me when and I'll be ready."

"Perfect," I said, and disappeared as quickly as possible out the mill's giant and fully restored antique door.

As I rushed back to my own apartment, I thought about my own stupidity. If Matt liked me, shouldn't I be giving him a chance? Then I remembered just how much I had to lose, not only my job, but having an affair with my boss could tarnish my professional reputation as well, and for what? A quick roll in the hay? That was probably all it'd be for Matt, and if that's how it ended, I'd be heartbroken for the rest of my life.

THIRTY-SEVEN

MATT

As proud as I was to see Lia and Millie graduate, the ceremony itself was boring as hell. I'd suffer through it all again, though, just to see how happy it made my cousin having at least one family member in the audience for what should've been a big celebration for her immediate family. *Oh well, screw them.* I was Lia's family now, and had always been despite her parents' efforts to erase me from the family tree. If they were so backward and ignorant they'd let some vague Bible verses separate them from their child, all the while ignoring a host of other passages that they freely broke without concern, they didn't deserve to be in her life. They didn't deserve to be in either of our lives.

Between me, Logan, and his parents and aunt, Lia and Millie had a good-sized cheering section when they each received their diploma. We all helped the girls pack, and moved them back to Mayville and Crawford City. When Logan pulled Lia aside to offer her the job, I assumed she accepted when we heard squealing coming from his apartment.

Lia rushed into the tasting room of the barn and straight into my arms a few moments later. "For real, you're willing to hire me and let me help you open the store? Wait... you aren't doing this because you feel obligated, are you?" she asked as her face fell.

"I didn't do anything. I'm assuming you were just hired by my winery manager?" I said with a smile.

She batted my arm and through freshly shed tears, said, "Yeah, and I am so gonna knock your socks off. I can't believe you want me to work here. I don't have any experience running anything."

"Logan was very clear he wanted you for the job. I have no doubt you'll make us a major tourist attraction, and when we actually have wine to sell, you'll be the one to sell it."

Millie and Lia, of course, had to see the space then, and so we all went over to the newly renovated mill and took a tour.

Lia began talking a mile a minute with Logan about where to put things while Millie walked around the glass enclosure where the millstone moved in time with the paddle wheel. I wandered over to where she stood spellbound, staring out over the stream.

"You okay?" I discreetly asked.

"Oh, yeah," Millie said, and when she noticed we were out of earshot of everyone else, she sighed. "It's just hit me that we aren't going to be together anymore, I mean physically together. I'm gonna be in law school and Lia's gonna be here turning this into a ridiculously successful business."

"That may be true, but you know you're always welcome here too. Or if you'd rather have your own space, I could probably arrange to have Matt's old trailer hauled out of the dump and you could move into it."

"Um, no. I'm several generations removed from the hillbillyness of our family."

That made me laugh out loud, and momentarily drew everyone else's attention. "Oh, not true. You know, when we were kids, I remember being forced to go to church where your grandpa, Bob, served as a deacon. He'd stand in the back and rattle his keys to remind us of when it was time for the service to be over. I also remember all the chickens he used to have running around his yard. I'd say the hillbilly is right below the surface, Miss Millie."

"Sometimes it doesn't pay to stick around where your people are from," she said on a sigh, then chuckled. "I'm fine, Matt, it's just I love Lia so much, and I don't know how I'm going to handle missing her."

I glanced over at Logan, who was as caught up in envisioning our new store as Lia, and smiled. "When your heart wants something, it's hard to look away."

Millie nodded, luckily not seeming to notice that I was talking as much about Logan as giving her advice.

THIRTY-EIGHT

LOGAN

BETWEEN EXPANDING THE VINEYARD and redesigning the old mill's interior for the store, summer flew by, and before I knew it, we were preparing for harvest again. The vines on the hill had taken off nicely, and I was confident they would produce viable grapes by year three.

Lia had been doing copious amounts of research about how best to break into the market and came up with entering the Southeastern Wine Competition.

I'd learned from Gren's winery manager to pull a barrel of wine aside for tasting. Doing so would help ensure we didn't accidentally contaminate our main barrels. I tested the flavors once every month to monitor that it was aging correctly and was very pleased with its progress.

I thought the wine was good, great even, and believed it could be an award-winner. Even if we didn't place, competing guaranteed exposure, and exposure could only benefit our new brand. Well, provided our wine was competition-worthy at this point.

I sent Gren a text knowing he had a barrel of our wine, asking him what he thought. Could we compete with the other wineries in the region and not be embarrassed by our wine?

He immediately wrote back, saying he thought it was some of the best of that variety he'd tasted.

So, feeling confident, I submitted the competition paperwork. Luckily, I didn't have to send the wine for another couple of months, giving it just a little more time to rest. Secretly, I felt like this could be my chance. I'd wanted a gold medal behind my name as a vintner since I'd begun taking classes. This wine could very well be my ticket to that major accolade.

I kept that to myself, however, and plowed ahead with the work that needed to be done. I was depriving the grapes of water again, hoping to get the same results I'd gotten from stressing them last year. My efforts had already been undone by pouring rain in both July and August. I never thought I'd miss the droughts of California, but I damn sure did this summer.

Gren called me the last week of August and asked if he could visit over Labor Day. When I ran it by Matt, he momentarily tensed, but agreed.

Gren convinced me I should also plan to bottle at least one barrel of wine during his visit so he could help me distinguish which barrel was best for the competition. He was arrogant about his abilities, but I couldn't deny he was the best around. So, I readily agreed.

The day Gren arrived, he greeted me with his typical hug. When he saw Matt, though, I could feel his body stiffen before he apparently forced himself to relax. What was going on between these two? When Matt left us that evening, I found out.

"I want you to come work for me," Gren said out of the blue.

"What? In case you haven't noticed, I've already got a job. Besides, your manager isn't going to let me come back anytime soon."

"He's retired, along with my father. I'm running the vineyard now, or at least I will be come January."

The news came as a shock, and all I could do was stare at him. "You're taking over your family vineyard? But you're an attorney. Are you going to quit your practice?"

He smiled and shook his head. "No, of course not, but Dad had a health scare with his heart this summer, and he and Mom want to spend more time together. You know my dad. He can't be on the vineyard and not work. So, he's handing me the reins."

"And Mr. Pepperwood is leaving too?"

"Yeah, he said he didn't have the energy to break in another green owner."

"Pfft, like you're green. You've been knee-deep in grapes practically since birth. Hell, you're named after a grape, *Grenache*," I said, emphasizing his given name.

"Didn't we agree to keep that between us?" he asked, scowling at me, and I chuckled. He'd always been embarrassed by his name. I'd always thought it was cool, but I'd sworn when we'd been dating to never use it in public.

"So, I need a manager, someone who can run the operation while I'm off being an attorney. You're as capable as they come, Logan, and I already trust you."

It'd been my dream for years to run a large, renowned vineyard. At one time, I'd even dreamed that one day I'd take Mr. Pepperwood's place as manager. Gren knew all that, and here he was serving me his family's vineyard on a silver platter.

"I'm already running a vineyard," I said, shrugging and trying to mask the simultaneous surges of excitement and apprehension his job offer had me feeling.

"You're swinging in a batting cage here," Gren said. "I mean, what you've done here so far is impressive, but it's a long way from being what our winery is, Logan."

He wasn't saying anything I didn't already know, but hearing it out loud had me questioning the limits of what I'd be able to achieve here long-term. When I didn't respond, he said, "Okay, I don't need your answer right this moment, but I'll need to know one way or the other by the end of October. I've got a couple other ideas, in case you say no, but Logan, don't say no!"

I nodded to let him know I'd consider his offer, then decided to go for a walk to really think about it and seriously weigh my options.

The heat was still holding on and the humidity was just as intense as it was during the summer. I knew to avoid the rocks along the streams since snakes seemed to have been tucked in there all summer long. I'd already begun the process of trying to rid the place of them, and as yet, the best solution was replacing the goats that had eaten up the grove with pigs. I hadn't suggested going that route to Matt yet, though, since I wasn't quite ready for that kind of commitment.

Since I needed to inspect the upper vines anyway, I decided to hike up that direction. As I walked among them, I couldn't help but feel proud of how quickly they were growing. The sandy loam naturally provided well-drained soil combined with just the right amount of nutrients for the fruit to take off.

When I came to the end of the long row of green grapes, I looked down the hillside at the perfectly aligned rows of reds that'd made such amazing wine last year and caught a glimpse of the picturesque barn where I lived.

Yes, this winery was small. Even with the added vines, we were just a tenth the size of Gren's place. But the rugged little winery had inspired me. It'd gotten under my skin, just as the winery owner had. "That's one plus," I said out loud. "I'm never going to be in love with Gren."

The words fell flat even to my ears. Was being in love with Matt really a plus at this point? We remained practically on eggshells around each other, and who knew when or if that would change. Meanwhile, Gren's offer was an incredible opportunity, one that wouldn't come around again. On paper, it was an easy decision, but the prospect of abandoning all I'd helped create here—and abandoning Matt—left me feeling conflicted and a touch heartsick.

A gentle breeze blew past me through the vines, causing the leaves to gently bend in the wind. "I need a sign. What should I do?" I asked the universe. "Stay here or go back to Oregon?"

Another breeze, stronger than the last, blew my hair around, and I chuckled. "It'll need it to be a bit clearer than that," I said. "But thank you anyway."

I finished inspecting the vines and walked back down the hill toward the barn, still no closer to a decision. Regardless of my staying or going, I couldn't discount the fortunate position in which I found myself. Whereas I'd been facing joblessness last year, now I was weighing up two incredible career opportunities. If only my personal life wasn't so tangled up in all of it.

Thirty-Nine

Matt

I STOOD LEANING AGAINST the doorframe of the tasting room, watching Gren and Logan sample wine from the different barrels. I enjoyed seeing their reactions to the varying flavors, all part of their process in selecting our best offering for the competition, and I thought we all felt some excitement in discovering what a year of rest had done for the wine.

Gren told Logan his barrel was magnificent, and that he thought it had a good chance of placing first. The comment caused Logan to break into a huge grin, and I'd be damned if the pleased look on his handsome face didn't make my heart flutter. I knew what it felt like to make Logan light up like that, and I longed to do it again. But that wasn't why we were here, and I needed to keep my emotions in check for all our sakes.

When they used some strange-looking device to pull wine out of the top of the next barrel, I knew something was wrong by the way both of them turned their noses up at the smell.

"Vinegar," Logan said with distaste.

Gren frowned and nodded in agreement.

They went around to the rest of the barrels and each one was the same. The entire batch was screwed up.

"Why?" Logan asked Gren in what looked like pure panic. I fought the urge to wrap him in a reassuring hug, even if I had no answers either.

Gren shrugged. "I'm guessing fruit flies, or maybe you didn't put it in barrels quick enough?"

"But yours is fine, right?" he asked, and Gren nodded.

"The one you sent to me in Oregon is delicious."

"So is the small barrel I kept out for myself," Logan said, sounding even more frustrated. "This doesn't make sense."

"It's almost like sabotage," Gren said, more off the cuff than anything.

Logan's face bloomed bright red. He rushed into his apartment with Gren and me hot on his heels, and dug through a box until he came to a flash drive. He went to his computer, plugged it in, and began watching intently. We crowded in behind him, looking at the screen over both his shoulders.

"I saved the surveillance footage from the party we had last winter," Logan said, eyes fixed on his laptop as the video began playing. "I found some kid wandering out of the barn after everyone else had gone, saying he had to use the restroom. I'd saved this just in case we discovered something was missing later, but that didn't happen, and I forgot about it. To my knowledge, there hasn't been any other chance for sabotage."

Logan fast-forwarded until he got to the point where he locked up the barn and left. The barn's interior remained dark for a few moments until a flashlight appeared. When the lights flicked back on in the room, sure enough, a young man could easily be seen walking toward the barrels. He seemed nervous, continually looking from side to side as if he expected to get caught, and held a large jug of what appeared to be Bragg vinegar.

He opened the tops of the barrels and poured some of the vinegar into each one before quickly stashing the jug into his backpack, turning the lights off, and heading for the barn's main door. Less than a minute later, Logan opened the barn door and appeared to confront the kid before Lia and Millie came into view outside.

"Well, fuck me!" Logan said, stopping the video. "That little shit destroyed the wine, but why?"

"Pastor Atwell," I said matter-of-factly.

"What?" Logan asked.

"The kid attends my grandpa's church. I don't know him personally, but I recognize him from the times Grandpa demanded I watch the service on TV. The kid sometimes sings in the church choir with Millie."

"So, you think that son of a bitch pastor put him up to this?"

"I do, and I think our party gave him the perfect opportunity."

"Fuck me," Logan said again and fell back into his office chair. "Well, that's that then. No competition, no last year's vintage. After all that time... I'm so sorry, Matt, I failed you."

"Hey, you did *not* fail me," I said, squatting down so I was eye level with him. "None of us could've guessed that lowdown scum would stoop to this, and he's been quiet since the church ousted him. Seriously, Logan, don't blame yourself for his dirty tricks."

Gren had been watching us as we talked it out, and said, "You aren't without wine for this vintage either."

"What do you mean, Gren?" Logan asked, almost impatiently.

"There's a barrel of your own wine in Oregon."

"That's yours, Gren. I couldn't ask you to return it now."

When he opened his mouth to disagree, I subtly shook my head, and he stopped talking. I wasn't sure why, but it felt like the wrong time to tell Logan that I'd manipulated that situation to win his affection. I was determined to enter his wine, under the Logan's First label, with a bottle from the barrel Gren had kept for me, but Logan had made it clear since Christmas he didn't want me. It put me in an awkward position, and I didn't want to overstep and come across as unable to accept his rejection.

We three spent the rest of the evening showing the video to the sheriff and then showing her how the kid's actions had contaminated all the barrels of wine and wasted tens of thousands of dollars as a result. Of course, when we accused Atwell of being the mastermind, she cautioned us to not be so fast in casting blame. Just as she planned to do in her investigation, we needed to follow the trail of evidence and see where it led.

FORTY

LOGAN

T HE AIR WENT OUT of the room when that first sample we drew out tasted like vinegar. As we went through barrel after barrel, each one the same as the last, it felt like the life was pouring out of me, too, as if I were the ruined wine. All that work, all those months of keeping the temperatures perfectly normal. Babying the barrels to ensure each was cared for properly. Before that, tending to the grapes, stressing the vines and begging the sky not to rain. The excruciating weeks I'd kept the juice on the peels, all the time terrified I was going to ruin it.

And in the end, it had been ruined, by a snot-nosed kid who'd snuck in here despite our security efforts and poured vinegar into my precious barrels. To think, he'd destroyed all of that potential more than nine months ago. Yet here I was thinking I was sitting on a gold mine—a gold-medal winner—when, in fact, I was sitting on slop not fit for the pigs I'd been reluctant to let roam free here.

I felt like a fool. Poor Gren had come all this way to help us bottle our potentially award-winning wine and all I had to offer now was surveillance footage and my own disappointment.

The minute I saw the boy in the video, traipsing through the barn that I'd so carefully guarded, I knew I was capable of violence. The kid needed to be held accountable, and I'd see to that, but I didn't doubt for a second that he was just a pawn in this. All of my anger was directed toward one man, the real culprit—that low-life son of a bitch Atwell.

I was relieved when the sheriff showed up, watched the video, and began the process of arresting the brat and chasing down the evidence. It wouldn't be in anyone's best interest if I took the law into my own hands, but I wanted Atwell to suffer. I knew he was the man responsible, all I needed was proof.

I went to bed after the sheriff left. It was still early, but I'd lost all energy and needed to be alone. Gren and Matt stayed up and I could occasionally hear their voices carry from the wine-tasting bar back into the apartment.

My future was wrapped up in the hands of one of those men, but after the loss I'd suffered today, I didn't know if I had it in me to try again. I cared about Matt, probably too much at this point, but I also owed it to him to bring in the harvest. Not that I had it in me to do this job anymore. It just seemed like everything was conspiring against me to prevent me from ever being successful. Maybe this was the sign I'd needed to make my fork-in-the-road choice clear.

Word of the sabotage must've traveled fast, because the next morning, a Sunday, I found the tasting room full of my family. They took turns comforting me, though Millie and Lia appeared just as upset after learning what'd happened, while Gren remained quiet and distant. Matt didn't show up, not that I would've expected him to be there.

He was too nice a guy to blame me for all this, and he'd already said as much, although I did blame myself. Throughout last night, I blamed him and my parents for throwing the stupid party in the first place, but in the end, what did or didn't happen came down to me. I'd known there was a good chance of sabotage, and I hadn't gone through the building to double-check it was empty before I'd left. And I'd had my suspicions about the kid after finding him in the barn, but gave him the benefit of all my doubts. That's what I got for not trusting my gut.

After my family had gone, I told Gren no to his offer. "I don't think I'm qualified for that level of responsibility," I confessed, and when he tried to argue, I gave him a brief hug before walking away.

Depression coursed through me like the venom of a poisonous snake. I didn't even try to stop it. With the wine ruined, and nothing to show for all I'd labored so hard on and basically sacrificed a real relationship with Matt for, I felt hopeless.

On Monday afternoon, Gren left for home, and I wrote my letter of resignation and emailed it to Matt. I couldn't face him, couldn't stomach the look of disappointment and probably abandonment I'd see in his beautiful green eyes, but I knew my career in the wine business was done. Clearly, this wasn't the calling I thought it had been. Between the Napa fire and these ruined barrels, it felt more like my curse.

Forty-One

Matt

S HOCK AND CONCERN COURSED through me when I opened my email to find a resignation letter from Logan. *I don't accept*, I typed as my reply back to him.

Gren had given me his number before he returned to Oregon so we could communicate and set up Logan's First wine to be delivered. I texted him a couple times, informing him Logan had resigned and seemed depressed, and asked for advice on what I could do to help, but Gren wasn't much help either.

Logan didn't respond to my email, which told me the resignation wasn't negotiable. In the letter, he'd told me he would stay on until spring to get us through the current harvest and help find another manager to replace him, but he'd be leaving after that.

Just the thought of not having Logan close by, of not seeing his handsome face or being able to talk to him—even if our conversations were basically all business these days—made my heart hurt. I mean, it already hurt before this. Not only had he rejected me as a lover, now he was rejecting the winery, and for what? Because some idiotic, hate-filled pastor with an over-inflated ego had decided to mess with us?

No, that didn't feel right either. Logan throwing in the towel now, just as we were getting the winery off the ground, felt like an outright rejection of me personally. I couldn't really blame Atwell for him leaving. I had to take responsibility for that myself. I'd let my desire for Logan get in the way. By trying to keep a respectful distance and giving into temptation at the same time, I'd given him mixed signals and obliterated the professional relationship we'd only begun developing. It was no wonder the man wanted to go.

The submission for the wine competition was due in mid-October. Logan was busy harvesting the grapes and managing the crew we'd hired to help. Doc, Todd and Amos came out again to pitch in, and for a moment, it felt like Logan was back to his happy self, but when everyone left, he avoided me by retreating to his apartment. I couldn't deny that it stung, but I had to keep my eye on the bigger prize of helping him find his joy in wine-making again.

The bottles of Logan's First arrived the week before the submission deadline, and I inwardly cursed Gren for waiting until the last moment to send them. Regardless, I drove to the competition site, handed over the three bottles as required, and stored the rest in the cellar below the first floor of the mill for safekeeping.

I'd learned a lot about wine in working with Logan over the past year, including that fluctuating temperature and light were both no-nos. So, the cellar seemed the ideal place to keep those precious bottles.

Lia remained hard at work putting the store together and, before discovering we had vinegar instead of wine, we'd proudly announced the grand opening would be on the anniversary of the ribbon-cutting. Logan had been excited then, but since he had tendered his resignation, we hardly saw him outside his duties.

When Lia came to me worried about Logan, I could only shrug. "He's shut us all out, Lia. I'm not sure what to do either. It pains me to see him just going through the motions here."

"He's done the same to the family," she confirmed, "but he needs someone to talk to, Matt."

I nodded. "I'll go over to his place tomorrow and talk to him," I promised her. "Or I'll try, at least."

With that, she seemed mollified. "Oh, can I get a sample of the vinegar?" Lia asked. "Just a mason jar is fine." When I pressed her for more information, she shook her head. "It's nothing, or might be, but I had an idea of what we can do with it. If it's not too farfetched, I'll let you know."

The next day, I went to the barn and knocked on Logan's apartment door. When he didn't answer, I went into the processing room and, using the same method I'd seen Gren and Logan use, I withdrew the vinegar and poured it into a mason jar as Lia had requested. I was just coming out of the room when Logan met me at the door. His mouth was set in a grimace, unlike anything I'd ever seen on his face before.

"Oh, it's only you," he said when our eyes locked, then he turned and started walking back toward the apartment.

"Logan, wait," I said, and for a moment, I thought he would ignore me.

Without a word, he stopped and turned around to face me. The anger I'd seen before was gone. In its place was sheer agony.

The pain in his beautiful eyes lanced through me. I didn't think. Instead, I walked up to him until we were toe to toe and pulled him into an embrace. He quickly stiffened and I cursed inwardly at what must feel like me pushing myself on him again. When he softened against me, though, I sighed in relief.

"Logan," I spoke into his hair. "We're all so worried about you. Why have you shut us all out?"

He shook his head, but didn't speak. Instead, he let me hold him and I thought he might be crying, given how his body trembled against mine.

When he pulled back, he didn't meet my eyes. He just mumbled a thank you, then disappeared back into his apartment.

It was all very confusing. I knew Logan was upset about what had happened, depressed even, but this seemed a bit over the top to only be about that. Besides, there was another batch of wine currently in the pipeline. I knew he was working on it, because all the same equipment he'd used last year was out just like it had been then.

When I'd come out of the processing room, I thought he'd assumed I was the same saboteur back to do more damage. Not possible, though, since the kid was currently being held in the county jail. He'd refused to talk about why he'd done it or if anyone had prompted him to, although we were sure it all led back to Atwell. The boy's family had refused to post bail. So, the kid sat in jail, remaining tight-lipped and bringing the investigation to a standstill. At least, that's how it looked to me. I only hoped he'd eventually crack under pressure.

I was helping Lia with the final preparations for the store's grand opening when Logan showed up at the mill. I came down the stairs when Lia called for me and smiled when I saw Logan.

"How?" he asked the moment he saw me. "How did you do it?"

"How did I do what?" I asked, confused.

"The competition, they said you entered us. Where did you get the bottles?"

I studied Logan's face, expecting to see appreciation. Instead, I saw accusation. "Logan, come in and sit down."

"No, not until I find out how you did it. Did you use someone else's wine?" he asked, his face getting red.

"No, of course not. What a thing to ask. I used the wine we'd sent to Gren."

"That's not ours to enter," he accused. "That was his, Matt. You can't compete using what you've already distributed to other people."

"That wasn't his. That was ours," I said. "Gren never owned it, Logan. I sent it to him to have it bottled so I could surprise you with it."

I felt frustrated. The man had ignored me for months and now he was angry because I'd submitted my own fucking wine, because it *was* technically still mine, to a competition. How the hell did that make a lick of sense?

I practically stormed down into the cellar, grabbed a bottle from one of the boxes of wine with his label on it, and brought it up the stairs. I handed the bottle of Logan's First without a word, then went back up to the second floor. He could figure the rest out on his own.

I plopped down on the ratty recliner and opened my computer to respond to some of the emails I'd received from fans who'd seen my artwork at the new museum in Murfreesboro. Before I could hit reply, however, Logan came into the room and sat across from me.

"You had this made for me?" he asked, holding up a bottle.

I nodded but didn't say anything. I was tired of doing everything wrong. It seemed to me I couldn't win no matter what I tried, not even gifting the man with his own namesake label.

Logan stared at me while I tried ignoring him until he finally broke the silence. "I've felt so lost these past few weeks, Matt. I mean, I poured everything I had into that wine, and it failed. Gren had asked me just the day before to take over his vineyard in Oregon, and you have depended on me..."

"Wait, what?" I asked, cutting him short.

"What?" he asked.

"Gren asked you to take over the vineyard in Oregon. That's why you resigned?" I asked, feeling my own anger kicking up. "You've ignored me for most of the summer, making me feel like I've done something wrong, like I've caused you to hate me. But all this time, you were really just planning to go work for Gren? If you'd respected me at all, Logan, you would've been straight with me about why you're leaving."

I got up to leave when he tried to stop me. "Matt, listen..."

"No, Logan. I thought you were better than this. Congratulations on the new job! You can go now, go be with your new boyfriend, or old boyfriend, or whatever the hell you and Gren are to each other now. Don't feel like you've got to stick around here for my sake."

I was about to haul ass down the stairs when I remembered the wine. "The rest of your wine is in the cellar. Lia can show you where. Please, take it when you go."

"Wait, Matt," he said, but I ignored him. My entire body vibrated with a torturous blend of betrayal, frustration, and just plain fucking hurt. I wanted to get away, had to get away, before the man who caused it had a chance to see my tears fall.

FORTY-TWO

LOGAN

I FOLLOWED MATT DOWN the stairs and out the door, pleading with him to stop, to let me explain, but he was too upset. He jumped into his car, slammed the door, and sped away.

"Fuck," I said a little too loudly as Lia came up behind me.

"What was that all about?" she asked.

"He thinks I resigned to go work for Gren."

"Did you?" she asked, not exactly sounding accusatory but I could hear disappointment in her voice.

"No, I resigned because I think I'm cursed and shouldn't be doing this."

"That's bull, Logan, and you know it. Why didn't you just tell Matt you didn't quit to go work for Gren?"

"'Cause he wouldn't let me. You saw how he dashed out of here."

She sighed. "Logan, in case you haven't noticed, Matt is in love with you. Millie and I have talked about it for a while. Your mom and mine thinks so too. When you resigned, it shook him. He's been moping around for weeks, same as you have, and he's not even painted since then. The only thing that's cheered him up was getting the wine from Gren and entering it in the competition." She hesitated for a moment, glancing at the bottle of said wine that I still held in my hand and looking puzzled. "Why were you upset about the competition? Did you lose, or was it vinegar too?"

"No," I said, embarrassed now about how I'd acted. "The contest organizers contacted the winery. They called to inform us that we won the gold medal."

Lia's face lit up. "Really? Oh my God, Logan, that's so awesome! I'm going to have a field day promoting this," she said excitedly before her confused look returned. "But you were angry when you came in to talk to Matt. This is good news, isn't it? What am I missing?"

"I thought Matt had cheated."

She stared at me like I'd grown a horn on top of my head. "You don't know Matt at all, do you?" she asked.

I shrugged. "I've been in such a dark place..."

"Logan, you and I both know Matt would never cheat, professionally or personally. He's the very embodiment of all things good and you're fooling yourself thinking otherwise." I could tell she was trying to figure out what more to say. Instead, she turned and walked back into the mill. I followed her in, knowing I deserved whatever else she had to dish out.

"Lia, I need to make this up to him."

"I think he just fired you, didn't he? If that's even possible, considering you already quit."

"Yeah, but he can't manage tending to the wine by himself. It's still got two more weeks on the peels and every day requires me to adjust the temperature. He hasn't learned all that. There's no way I'm going to leave and let that go to waste, especially after losing all of last year's barrels."

"You haven't lost a damn thing, other than drinkable wine," she said matter-of-factly, and it was my turn to be confused. "I sent a sample of it to the university's food department. What you've got in those ruined barrels is a very high-grade red wine vinegar. You don't have wine, but you've got another product. One that very well could outsell your wine. I've put some feelers out and am already receiving requests from restaurants in Nashville that want to order it."

I stared at her, completely dumbstruck. "Why didn't you say something?"

"Because you're an ass. You've been holed up feeling sorry for your damned self when this thing happened to all of us. How were we supposed to tell you anything? You know you aren't the only person who got hurt here. The difference is Matt and I have been trying to carry on and come up with a solution to the problem. Now, you've gone and hurt one of the best people I've ever known."

"I'm not sure what you want me to do with all this information you've dropped on me," I said, still feeling as if I were playing catch-up.

Lia turned then and slammed her fist on the counter. "Matt saved your ass, and all our asses, really, by sending a barrel of wine to your friend to have it bottled as a gift for you. He also custom made you a freaking label and named the damned wine after you so you would feel special. Then, after all his wine—and it is *his* wine—was destroyed, you accuse him of cheating. You're a jerk, Logan. I didn't know that about you until just now."

She walked away from me then and headed up the stairs, clearly dismissing me.

She was right, though. I had been a jerk. I'd let my own hurt feelings get in the way of my relationships with everyone else. The person most affected by that, of course, was Matt. A man who'd only been kind, understanding, and caring toward me.

I immediately texted Matt. He didn't respond by the time I'd driven the ATV back to the barn, and I understood why. But I kept trying to reach him, firing off text after text, trying to explain myself.

Matt, I'm sorry. I've been an ass.

I don't work for Gren. I told him no.

I wasn't leaving you for him. I was leaving the business altogether.

Please text me back. Or call me? We need to talk.

I waited, staring at my phone, hoping to see those three dots pop up indicating he was responding. When no dots appeared, I collapsed on the living room sofa.

My eyes drifted to the mantel and Matt's harvest painting, now the perfect illustration of all I stood to lose here. I'd probably destroyed everything with my stupid temper and bruised ego. My thoughts drifted to last Christmas, when my mom had told me not to bottle up my emotions and to be straight with Matt about being in love with him. I'd ignored her and now it'd blown up in my face.

Naturally, Mom was who I called.

"Hey, baby, you feeling better?" she answered immediately.

"No, Mom. I've never been so miserable and it's all my fault."

"I'm so sorry, honey, but you're making a new batch of wine now. Who knows, it might even be better."

That made me smile. Classic Mom, always trying to see the bright side of any situation. "Seriously doubt that. We just placed first in a regional competition with that wine. I've finally got a gold medal to my name."

"Really?" she nearly shouted into the phone. "That is amazing. I'm so proud of you!" She paused then, and I could practically hear her mind working double time to explain my sullen tone. "Logan, why don't you sound as thrilled as I am for you? Wasn't that one of your big goals?"

"Yeah, it was. But Mom, I've screwed things up so bad. I basically accused Matt of cheating in the competition, which, of course, he didn't do, and now he's so angry with me, and rightfully so. He even fired me, but I'd already resigned, so I don't even know if I should even be here right now."

She listened patiently as I sniveled my way through the laundry list of ways I'd pushed everyone away. The distrust, the accusation, the wallowing in self-pity, Lia's reaming me, and ultimately, how I'd hurt Matt in so many ways that I hadn't even realized until now.

"Mom, he thought I was avoiding him, ignoring him, because he did something wrong. But *that's* what he's got all wrong. I'm the one who kept blurring the lines of what we were to each other, and when he tried to straighten them out, I just shut down."

She remained silent on the other end, and the truth lay between us. She'd warned me this would happen, and I'd ignored her.

I finally broke the silence by saying, "I've tried to ignore my feelings for him, to pack them down so far that I could carry on doing my job, but I love him now more than ever. He's one of the best people I've ever known, and my stupidity has crushed him. How can I possibly fix this, Mom?"

"Honey, I don't have any easy answers. You're gonna have to grovel, and not just about your job. You resigned, and he had the right to fire you, but I think you're right to stay until the wine is in the barrels, at least. I think when he calms down, he won't interfere with that. But then you might have to let the job go. You can't really expect him to keep you on after... well, after all you've put him through. I'm sorry to talk so harshly, son, but you know I've always put things out there for you."

She paused, giving me time to digest her hard truths, and although tears were streaming down my face, I knew she was right. After a moment, she began speaking again. "What I *don't* think you should do is give up on your feelings for him. If you love him, tell him. Better yet, show him. He created a beautiful painting for you, bottled wine for you, entered a competition for you... it's clear to me that Matt's love language is through his actions rather than words. And I have no doubt that man loves you, Logan. Seems to me he's been trying to tell you that every which way he knows how this whole time."

"I get it, Mom. You're right, and I can see it now too. I need to show him how I feel. I think I'll email him, letting him know I'm going to stay on until the wine is in the barrels, then I'll move into town since I can't be living at the vineyard if I'm no longer an employee. But I'm not giving up on a relationship with Matt. I just hope it isn't too late."

I knew my chances of successfully rekindling our relationship were slim. After all, why would Matt give me another chance after all this? I didn't know, but if he truly cared about me even a fraction of how much I cared about him, I owed it to both of us to try.

FORTY-THREE

MATT

I HAD FRIENDS IN Atlanta who'd been trying to get me to come down for a long time. Cristina and Larry had moved there a few years back and opened a gallery in one of the old Victorian parts of town. I'd only visited a couple times, but after the blowup with Logan, I knew I needed a change of scenery. I'd need to be back to help Lia with the grand opening, but I could afford to take a few days off in the meantime.

I received Logan's texts, but ignored them. I wasn't ready to talk to him yet anyway. I figured he'd leave now that I'd basically fired him, but I couldn't bring myself to care. Or maybe I cared too much, but I wasn't in the mood to try sorting out my jumbled feelings. That'd caused me enough heartache already. I texted Lia to let her know I'd be gone for a while, then spent the night in Chattanooga.

When Logan's email landed in my inbox, I decided to read it for professional reasons, if nothing else. He informed me he would stay until we'd barreled the wine. Shit, I'd forgotten all about that during my tirade. Thank God he'd thought that through. Not that I was ready to thank him, but I couldn't imagine the mess I'd have come back to if we'd all deserted the wine at this stage.

I really was a crappy winery owner. I should think about selling up. I knew the land had been in my family for generations, but I doubted I'd ever have kids anyway, so it wasn't like it was going to pass down the line any further.

I didn't respond to Logan's email, choosing instead to shut my computer down and go to bed early. The next morning, I traveled down to Atlanta and spent the weekend just enjoying being away from the farm. Truth be told, I sort of missed the freedom to do this kind of thing. I'd never had much money to spend, despite Grandpa paying for my apartment for several years, but now that my paintings had been purchased by the museum, I didn't feel like I needed to nickel and dime myself. I was also developing quite a following.

I still didn't like the idea of selling my paintings to the highest bidder, but then again, having them displayed in a museum meant my work could be seen and enjoyed by the masses. Plus, even if I hadn't inherited Grandpa's money, I would be able to live comfortably for some time on what the museum had paid me, to say nothing of future commissions.

By the time I started the drive back home, I'd decided I would sell off the vineyard and the mill. I'd keep the new resident artist building and the log cabin, because, damn, Todd and Amos had nearly completed the cabin renovation and done a masterful job. The views, the huge studio… it really was a place I could spend the rest of my life. That Logan had envisioned it all for me and helped make it happen wasn't something I wanted to dwell on at the moment, though.

When I pulled into the parking area around the mill, I spotted Logan talking to Lia near the front door. They looked my way, but I stayed put, taking a few moments to figure out how best to deal with the situation. If I was half as mature as someone my age should be, I would've read his texts, but I was clearly not, because I'd left them all unopened.

I took several deep breaths, got out of my car, and walked toward them.

"Hi, Matt," Lia said.

Logan stared at the ground, clearly not wanting to hash things out. If that was how he wanted to play it, fine. We didn't really need to talk to one another at this point anyway. He could go to Oregon and be the big-shot manager of a well-known winery, and I'd get back to living the quiet life of a Podunk Southern artist living in the hills of Tennessee.

After another quick glance at Logan, I quickly said, "I'm gonna head up, Lia. Let me know if you need any-thing."

"Before you go, I've got some news," Lia said. "We've got a buyer for the vinegar. They want it all."

"What? Why?" I asked.

"Because it's delicious and perfect for high-end restaurants, and that's who wants it."

"Really?" I asked. "How much are they willing to pay?"

When she told me, I almost fell down. "That's a lot of money for ruined wine."

"It's probably more than we would've gotten for the wine, even though it was a gold-medal winner."

I looked at Logan. "We won?" I asked.

He nodded, finally meeting my eyes. "Yeah, we did, thanks to you."

I sighed. "Well, that's something. Lia, unless there's a reason I'm not aware of, please let the buyer know that hell yes, they can collect our vinegar wine–or whatever we're calling it–as soon as possible."

"There's a catch," she added.

"Of course, there is. What's the catch?"

"They want the same amount next year."

I laughed. "So, they want us to sabotage our own wine this time so we can sell them the vinegar?"

"Except it wouldn't be sabotage, would it?" she said. "It'd be intentional."

"What do you think, Logan?" I asked.

"It's an amazing offer. We can use the mother, that's what the stuff that causes the wine to turn to vinegar is called, in our existing barrels."

"And you're okay with that?" I asked, surprised he'd be willing to sacrifice drinkable wine for it.

"It's not up to me," he said quietly, eyes downcast again.

"It's not going to be up to me for much longer either. I'm selling up," I said, and walked into the mill before either one had a chance to respond. I was done with the conversation.

"Matt, what should I tell the buyer?" Lia called behind me.

"Tell them we can do one more year, then they'll have to make arrangements with a new owner."

FORTY-FOUR

LOGAN

W HEN THE MILL'S FRONT door closed behind Matt, Lia turned to me. "You aren't okay with turning your precious wine to vinegar, are you? You were lying... again."

I'd told her and Millie about my talk with Mom and how I realized now that I'd fucked up when I pushed Matt away instead of talking to him.

Lia crossed her arms, and I knew I was in for another dose of hard truth. "He doesn't want to sell the vineyard any more than you want to make vinegar, Logan. Get your ass up to his apartment and work this out. Seriously, do I need to be a mom to you two idiots?" she asked, frustration rolling off her.

"If I remember right, I'm still your boss," I countered, albeit weakly.

"Um, no, you aren't. Matt fired you, and you basically fired yourself beforehand anyway. But if you wanna be my boss again, you know what you need to do."

I sighed. She was right about it all. It was time to face the music.

I slowly ascended the stairs and stood outside the apartment door for several moments while I built up my nerve. My knock went unanswered. It wasn't like I could blame him for ignoring me. I'd done the same fucking thing to him just a few weeks before.

I opened the door, praying he didn't end up shooting me or calling the sheriff. I hollered, "Matt, I need to talk to you."

"Logan, we don't have anything left to say. You're gonna finish your job turning that juice into wine and then fuck it all 'cause I'm gonna sell everything and get back to my normal life. It was a farce thinking I could run a winery anyway."

I walked into the apartment and stood in front of him while he finished speaking.

"I'm in love with you," I blurted, finally putting it right out there.

"What?" he asked, genuine shock in his expression.

"I'm in love with you, Matt. I have been for a long time. I didn't know how to deal with it, with us working together too, so I pushed it down and pushed you away. I'm sorry. You have every right to kick me out of your life forever, and I'll go because..."

"Stop rambling," Matt said sternly. "You've treated me like cold dog crap for months and now you're telling me it's 'cause you love me?"

I nodded. "I figured it out last Christmas."

Matt stared at me. "Logan, you've ripped my heart to shreds and I thought all this time it was because I was coming on too strong, making you feel uncomfortable. That you didn't really like me, but put up with it 'cause I'm your boss, and you didn't know how to tell me to back off, but now you tell me that for almost an entire year, you've been in love with me? What the hell am I supposed to do with that information?"

"I don't know, Matt. I should've told you back then, but we were still trying to figure everything out. Then, we had a really nice working relationship, and I got to see you almost daily and we were able to have fun together. We have common friends with Doc, Todd, Amos and Ash. It just felt like things were nearly perfect. I didn't want to screw it up with my emotions."

"What about Gren? If you were so happy here, why are you leaving to go work for him?"

"You didn't get my texts?" I asked, and Matt cringed.

"I didn't read them."

"I didn't take the job with Gren, Matt. I wasn't just leaving the winery. I intended on getting out of the business altogether. I felt sorry for myself. I just didn't know how to handle everything falling apart with the sabotaged wine and my on-and-off relationship with you, and then being offered what I'd always thought was the job of my dreams."

"What were you gonna do by running away? Go work at McDonald's? Logan, making wine is what inspires you. You don't have to work for me. If you want to work for Gren, do that. Just don't quit this business because of some bigoted jackass who claims to be a man of God."

"I know, I've already figured that out. But, Matt, I don't want to work for Gren. I love it here. I love our friends, our family we're building together. I love the way the vineyard is growing and expanding, and I love you most of all. That probably makes me an idiot, and may be the part that prevents this from working, but it's the honest truth."

My voice cracked at that, and I was about to turn to leave when Matt stepped in front of me.

"I must be an idiot then, too, because I'm just as in love with you. It's been torture not being able to touch you, to hold you. I decided to sell up 'cause, frankly, I don't want to do this without you. This was never my dream, it wasn't even my grandpa's, at least not when I knew him. But you've turned this into something amazing. Apparently, even our crappy vinegar is worth the same as freaking gold, and that's because of you. I won't ask you to stay if your dream is to go run a huge operation like the one in Oregon, but if what you said is true, and you want to be here, do it as my partner."

"What? Like fifty-fifty?"

"No," Matt said. "Like as my husband."

My eyes must've grown twice their size. "Marry you?"

"Yes, Logan. I love you more than I even thought possible, and that's while you've been keeping me at arm's length. If you want to stay and will let me in, really let me into your heart, I'll love you with everything I have. Will you marry me?"

I leaped into his arms then, wrapped my legs around him, and kissed him like my life depended on it. "Yes, yes, yes!" I said when I pulled back. "Oh my God, yes, in every way possible." The tears slid down my cheeks and I didn't think I'd ever felt happier than I did at that moment. Even if he changed his mind, I would hold onto this moment when the only man I'd ever loved had gone from pissed-off beyond words to asking me to be his husband.

FORTY-FIVE

MATT

How I went from thinking I was about to lose Logan and sell the farm to asking him to marry me was a total blur, but damn, I'd always remember the feeling of hearing him say yes.

Holding Logan in my arms as he peppered me with kisses and yesses felt like heaven.

We were both weeping when we finally came back down to earth. After kissing until we were both out of breath, Logan rushed downstairs to tell Lia the news, while I followed behind in a daze. Someday soon, I'd be married to this amazing, handsome, and talented man. I was really gonna get the guy in the end.

Time started moving fast then. I moved into the barn apartment with Logan, giving Lia the apartment in the mill. The plan had been for her to move into it once the cabin was done anyway.

The store grand opening happened just a week after I proposed, and we announced our engagement to the cheers of the entire community. Of course, Logan's mom and aunt came down on us like an asteroid on the dinosaurs.

When they began pulling out wedding magazines from Lord only knows where, I started hiding whenever they showed up. God help me, I wanted to be Logan's husband with everything I had in me, but damn, I wasn't prepared to plan a wedding with those two. Logan and I would laugh every time they left, him saying he wished he could escape their wedding planning madness too.

Lia told the buyer no to a second year of vinegar. Logan wanted to be a winemaker, not a vinegar maker, and I wanted to do whatever would make Logan happiest, personally and professionally. Although, we did decide to reserve one barrel each year to build the vinegar from the original batch, because that was a good business option for the future, if we chose to pursue it.

By the time Christmas came around, everything was beginning to buzz around us. Todd handed me the keys to the log cabin the week after the store's grand opening, which was also the week before Christmas. I wrapped the keys in a box to give to Logan as a Christmas present. He'd oohed and aahed enough over the build that I knew he would love living there.

There was something magical about the rebuilt old cabin. Of course, it didn't really look much like the original structure I remembered growing up. It'd already half fallen down by the time I was born. Now, it stood proudly as a huge two-story dogtrot house. A large wrap-around porch surrounded the first floor and two extensions had been added on the sides. One side was my studio and Logan's office, and the other was our living quarters.

The upstairs held all the bedrooms and extended out over the same extensions, making the home larger. Although we didn't really need that much space, when I saw the drawings from the architect, I knew the old cabin needed the space to give it the regal yet down-home look it deserved.

Our bedroom looked out over the headwaters of the stream that flowed down past the old mill. The landscape crew had already begun telling me how they thought we should accent that area with flowers and native plants from Tennessee to make it a special place to sit and enjoy the scenery.

My studio looked out over the vista, inspiring me already to paint not just the beauty of the vineyard and old homestead site down below, but other nature scenes as well. It was the perfect space for an artist.

We joined Logan's entire family for Christmas at his parents' house in Nashville. When Logan opened his present and saw the keys, he looked at me confused. When I then handed over the small, wrapped canvas I'd painted of the cabin, his eyes filled with tears. "I didn't even think about living there. I guess I'd be moving in there once we got married, though, wouldn't I? I doubt you'd want to live with me in the barn forever," he said, causing everyone in the room to chuckle.

"I sure hope so. The cabin is too big for just me."

"It's too big for just two of us," he said. When Lia and Millie both drew in a breath to make a comment, Logan pointed at them, and added, "No!"

We all laughed at that. We knew when Millie finished law school, she'd probably end up living in the mill apartment with Lia. But I wasn't sure Ms. Polly was ready to be thinking about such things, so I held back from teasing them about it.

Earlier that evening, before we sat down to open presents, I helped finish cleaning up when Ms. Jennie followed me into the kitchen. I knew she had something on her mind, so I kept cleaning until she was ready to have her say.

"Logan and I are a lot alike, Matt. When it comes to emotions, we're more likely to bottle them up than talk about them. Over the years, my Raymond has had to learn to coax them out of me. Even now, it's hard for me to share how I'm feeling sometimes."

I stopped rinsing the dishes and met her eyes. "You're telling me not to get too upset when Logan doesn't tell me how he's feeling. Like how he didn't tell me he was in love with me for almost an entire year."

She chuckled, but it sounded a little pained. "Yeah, that's what I'm saying. We feel things so strongly, Matt, it's hard to explain how scary it is when you feel that way toward someone. Right now, he's still scared to death you're gonna change your mind. I assure you, he's probably on the verge of another meltdown. Unfortunately, I'm his mom, so telling him that does no good whatsoever. You, however, are *the one*. If you remember to reassure him, and be patient with him, it'll go a long way toward keeping your relationship healthy and happy."

I laughed. "I'm pretty good about sharing my emotions. This whole thing fell apart the first time because I was his boss, not because I didn't feel just as strongly about him. I couldn't really cross that boundary unless he was okay with it, and I was never certain how he felt. Now, though, I'll do a better job at helping him express his emotions—good, bad, or otherwise."

She smiled and was about to leave, when I added, "I'll need your help, though, Ms. Jennie. If you ever notice I'm missing something with Logan or just plain missing the boat on how he's feeling, don't just let it fester until he explodes. Call me, or come by the winery. I mean, I don't want you to ever jeopardize his confidence, but if you think he's at risk of falling apart again..."

"I'll let you know. Eventually, like my Raymond, you'll just pick up on the signs. But, for now, you've got us. Believe me, we want your relationship with Logan to work as much as you both do." She patted my shoulder and turned to leave, then added, "We both like you, Matt. You're a good person, and good for Logan, and we'd like it if you could stick around."

I couldn't help the nervous laugh that escaped me. "I like y'all, too, even if you're gonna be my in-laws."

"And you're lucky for that too," she teased, then pushed me out of the kitchen. "Now, let's go open presents. That's an order, future son-in-law."

Forty-Six

Epilogue: Logan

W E GOT MARRIED IN late February, just as the growing season was about to begin. Not only was it perfect timing for the wedding, but we knew that looking ahead, even as the winery grew, we'd be able to escape at this same time each year to celebrate our anniversary.

We'd hoped to have the wedding ceremony in the new chapel I'd envisioned for the property, but it was still in the planning stages, and we weren't willing to wait. So, we were married in the old mill, after moving all the store merchandise up to the second floor, and Logan's mom and aunt led the family in decorating the entire room.

Hundreds of people, seemingly the whole of Mayville and Crawford City, asked to come but there just wasn't that much room in the mill. So, for the reception, we rented Ms. Beth's church's fellowship hall and planned to join the townsfolk gathered there to celebrate after the ceremony.

As Matt and I stood at the altar, facing Ms. Beth's minister who was officiating the ceremony, we held each other's hands and soaked in this momentous occasion surrounded by our closest friends and family.

We both decided we were too emotional to read our own vows in front of a crowd, so the night before, as we'd held each other, I told him, "Matt, I will always be yours. I promise to be here for you even when things are scary or when I'm afraid. I'll try not to ignore my feelings, although I'll probably screw that up."

When Matt tried to interrupt, I shook my head. "No, let me get all this out," I said as I was becoming emotional. "I promise to be your best friend, to tell you the things I love about you, and to remind myself you have given me everything I ever wanted in this life. Even though I'm not saying this in front of everyone tomorrow, it's my solemn vow to you, now and always."

When I looked up into Matt's eyes, tears were running down his cheeks.

"I love you so much, Logan," he said. He took a long breath before beginning his own vows.

"I only make one promise, and that is to love you like you deserve to be loved. I'm yours and yours alone, have been since I first laid eyes on you." He wiped the tears from his face and chuckled. "I've never been this emotional with anyone else before. I'm not sure if that's a good or bad thing," he said. "You complete me, Logan. I always thought that was just a silly line from a movie, but it's true. It's like meeting you put all of my puzzle pieces into place."

Matt squeezed me tighter and kissed the top of my head. "I will continue to do everything I can to make you happy."

When I looked up, he leaned down and captured my lips in a passionate kiss.

"I'm yours, Logan. Always."

Forty-Seven

Matt

THE ARREST OF LEON Atwell came just weeks after the wedding. The family of the kid who'd sabotaged the wine finally intervened when the sheriff informed him he'd face felony charges alone unless he fessed up.

Atwell was a bizarre man. Somehow, he'd gotten it into his head that he was the illegitimate son of my great-grandpa. Something to do with them both being men of the cloth, or some such nonsense. He also decided that made him the rightful heir to Brinks property.

I listened to the sheriff as she explained all this to me, and while I didn't believe it for a second, it still gave me pause. "Is what he's saying actually possible? Could he be my...what? Great-uncle?" I asked.

"Anything's possible, but I wouldn't put much credibility in it. He wasn't even born in this area. He was born in Lexington, Tennessee, a long way from here, and we've got his birth certificate to prove it. His family moved into these parts when he was ten."

"It's confusing, why he'd be pulling this stunt now," I said, and the sheriff shook her head.

"Listen, Matt, the longer he sits in my jail, the more disconnected from reality he seems to become. I honestly think he's got something going on that hasn't been diagnosed yet. That don't mean you should feel bad about him being held accountable, but it's something we need to take a deeper look at before we begin the prosecution."

"I agree. I really dislike him. He made my life miserable growing up and what he did with Logan's wine was horrible. But, I agree, if there's something more going on medically, I'd like to know before we go to trial."

With that, the sheriff left, and I heard a few weeks later that Atwell's psych eval revealed he had a previously undiagnosed mental illness. After discussing it, Logan and I decided to drop the charges against him, provided he agreed to get the psychiatric help he needed. That, and he was never to set foot on our property again for any reason.

As for the kid, well, Logan got creative there. Logan spoke to the prosecutor and the kid's parents, although he'd turned eighteen already. The prosecutor agreed to drop the case on our condition that the kid, Leland, spend the summer working in the vineyard alongside Logan as a way to make amends for what he'd done.

After working to pay us back for the wine he'd destroyed, Logan offered Leland a full-time job that fall, provided he enrolled in college and kept his grades up.

His parents were ecstatic with that, and even though they had also been brainwashed by Atwell to hate gay people, they quickly warmed to us when they saw we wanted to do right by their kid.

Leland ended up being a good apple. Atwell had just led him astray like so many other people in our area. He also seemed to blossom under Logan's strict but caring instruction. Of course, Lia and Millie took him to task as well, and to be honest, both the cousins could be intimidating even to us.

We met his girlfriend that fall and liked her immediately. He'd almost ruined things with her when he got in trouble, but because he now had a good job and had paid back his debt to us and society, she'd forgiven him. Lia ended up hiring her the following summer as an assistant in the store. It was funny how things worked out in the end. Like someone was there watching out for us all. Of course, I couldn't help but think it was my grandpa.

The chapel built in his honor was more than I'd expected it to be. The place stood tall and regal in the little clearing I'd chosen near my special spot. Because it rose up out of the forest, you could see the top of it from our cabin, and I never failed to look down at it and think of my grandpa. The chapel represented his spirituality and faith, and his commitment to the people–our people–in this corner of the world.

The new pastor at Grandpa's old church had blessed the place, and probably because he was young and from Nashville, he didn't seem to harbor the hatred his predecessor had. Not that he seemed totally accepting either, but at least we didn't think he'd ever try to intentionally disparage us.

Families began coming to the chapel, and I recognized most of them from the church in Mayville. It warmed my heart that this had become an extension of the church my grandpa had loved so much. In the end, I thought the chapel became a haven for the spiritual side of that congregation. The place where people could come and pray, or meditate, and reconnect with God in their own, personal ways.

That in and of itself touched me more than I could say.

Lia and Millie had plans to move in together that first summer, but Aunt Polly put her foot down. "You'll not be living together in sin, especially when it's perfectly legal for you to get married."

I think the two were shocked that Aunt Polly—after the wedding, she insisted I call her that as well—would push those kinds of boundaries with a lesbian couple. When we challenged her, she said, "What's good for the goose is good for the gander." Translated, that meant she didn't care what orientation they were. What's right was right, and for Aunt Polly, that entailed seeing her daughter married.

Since the two weren't even remotely ready for marriage, Lia opted to stay in the mill apartment and Millie unofficially lived in the winery barn apartment Logan had vacated. Of course, that didn't mean Millie and Lia didn't spend all their time together, but even Aunt Polly couldn't control that.

Crawford City, and to a lesser extent Mayville, had become our home. Our friendships became as deep as our commitment to the land. When Todd and Ash ended up with three very opinionated infants, we'd go over and help with babysitting, because triplets were a lot to handle, and it was fun to have the little ones around.

Todd immediately began calling us Uncle Matt and Uncle Logan, which sat right with us. Logan and I had talked about it and neither of us really wanted to have kids of our own, but we'd both decided we'd love to be the eccentric wine-making uncles to our friends' and family's kids.

For Millie and Lia's sake, I sure hoped they planned on having kids someday, because when we announced over Thanksgiving the following year that we'd decided to play uncles, both Logan's parents and Aunt Polly immediately looked at them and the message was clear. Bless their hearts.

Sure, family could be annoying and meddlesome at times, but I felt damn lucky to have them. I missed Grandpa and always would, but the love I felt from our friends and being welcomed into the fold by Logan's relatives eased my sadness. I'd found my people and the place where I belonged. I'd finally discovered home.

If you enjoyed Discovering Home, please consider leaving a review at:

https://blakeallwood.com/booklink/3204273

In the small town of Crawford City, two men from different worlds collide as their lives spiral into turmoil. Will they follow their hearts, or succumb to the pressures of career and family?
Continue the Coming Home Series with *Finding Home*

Available at your favorite bookseller!

Join Blake's email list to get advance notice of new books and receive his occasional newsletter:

www.blakeallwood.com

MM Romance
By Blake Allwood

Transitions Series
Aiden Inspired
Suzie Empowered (MF Romance)
Bobby Transformed

Chance Series
Love By Chance
Another Chance With Love
Taking A Chance For Love

Romantic Series
Romantic Renovations (1)
Romantic Rescue (2)
Romantic Recon (3)

Melody Series
Melody of the Heart
Melody of the Snow

Road to Rocktoberfest Anthology
Changing His Tune - 2022

Coming Home Series (2023)
A Long Way Home
Family Home
Discovering Home
Finding Home
Bound For Home
…and many more

Novellas
Tenacious
Moon's Place

Romantic Fantasy
By Adam J. Ridley

Big Bend Series
Love's Legacy (1)
Love's Heirloom (2)
Love's Bequest (3)

The Witch Brothers Series
Emerald Earth (1)
Diamond Air (2)
Ruby Fire (3)
Sapphire Water (4)

Blake Allwood was born in west Tennessee, then moved to Kansas City MO after earning a degree in Early Childhood Education from Graceland College in Lamoni, Iowa. He met his husband Shaun in 1995 and they officially married in 2015, once gay marriage was legalized; although they still consider Valentines Day 1995 as their true "anniversary date". Twenty-two years later (2017), after fostering 12 children together, he and his husband sold their home, purchased an RV and began traveling the country with their two dogs.

Typically, Blake can be found relaxing in the RV or by the fire with his laptop and their Jack Russell Terrier, Buddy, curled up between his legs demanding attention. Denver, their Siberian Husky mix is often asleep at his feet or playing tug of war with Blake's husband.

Most of Blake's stories are inspired by the places they have visited in their ongoing travels. His first book, **_Aiden Inspired_**, was released in 2019 and he has now written over 20 books. In 2023 he is releasing the *Coming Home* series which is comprised of ten-plus sweet contemporary romance novels that are based on a fictional town in his home state of Tennessee.

Blake also writes under the pen name of Adam J. Ridley for his urban fantasy fans looking for stories revolving around gay characters. His first series is The Witch Brothers Saga, starting with *Emerald Earth*.

BIBLIOPRIDE.COM

BOOKS BY LGBTQ+ AUTHORS